MW01327861

The Blind Earthworm in the Labyrinth

A novel by

Veeraporn Nitiprapha

Translated by Kong Rithdee

First published and distributed in 2018 by
River Books
396 Maharaj Road, Tatien, Bangkok 10200
Tel. 66 2 622-1900, 224-6686
Fax. 66 2 225-3861
E-mail: order@riverbooksbk.com
www.riverbooksbk.com

Design: Ruetairat Nanta
Cover and Interior Illustrations: Nakrob Moonmanas

ISBN 978 616 451 013 5

Printed and bound in Thailand
by Bangkok Printing Co., Ltd.

To those lost in conflict

Contents

Translator's Note

There are several Thai texts that pose great challenges to translators, and Veeraporn Nitiprapha's *The Blind Earthworm in the Labyrinth* is certainly one of them. Partly – and this is from my non-academic understanding – the difficulty is rooted in the fundamental structure and extreme pliability of the Thai language, which loom over any translator's attempt to transform a work into the more rigid, grammar-governed English. And partly, in this specific effort, it's because Veeraporn is a prose stylist who entertains her readers (and there are a huge number of them here in Thailand) with free-flowing lyricism and lexical ornamentations. She disassembles words and clauses and then reconstructs them – a near-inimitable trick in the English language – and she deploys a range of devices from irony to digression, symbolism to fabulism, rhapsodic dramatisation to cinematic scene-sketching.

The translation required some untangling of phrasal and idiomatic constructions; those elegant, luscious and addictive passages in punctuation-free Thai that had to be ironed out. In general, I accompanied Veeraporn and her characters as they galloped to their acidic sunset by listening to their voices, their heartbeats, and by being fully aware of the author's aesthetic choices and preoccupations (my excellent editor, Sarah Rooney, made sure of that too). We also have the writer's – and her character Chareeya's – horticultural obsession, which results in a teeming catalogue of plant names, mundane or exotic, tropical or temperate. While it's simple enough to find the common names of these species, I was constantly aware of textural nuances. Hence, names of local plants have been transliterated from the Thai language unless they have English names in common usage; their less common English names can be found in the Botanical List on page 206.

This is a book suffused with colours, sounds and smells, and while we can interpret words, it's harder to capture those sensory signals deeply inspired by geography and culture. Likewise, the setting of the house by the river in Nakhon Chai Si, a short drive from Bangkok, immediately conjures up a scene of tranquility, fruit orchards and vintage charm. Such cultural familiarity – which appears in other details of the book – is sometimes a gap that can't be easily bridged despite the linguistic fidelity of this translator.

The hardest part, however, was to detect the subterranean quivers that course through this sad and beautiful book. *The Blind Earthworm in the Labyrinth*, in the author's own words, is a melodrama of shipwrecked romance. To this translator, it's a razor blade dripping with honey, or a sugar-coated poison pill – dangerous and irresistible. Set loosely over the 1980s and '90s, with mention of a political incident in 2010 as a temporal marker – in fact, time is slippery and indeterminate here – the story can be read either as a nod to old-fashioned Thai romance novels, or as a sophisticated, literary upgrade of the soap opera genre that most Thais grew up reading or watching on television, or as a bitter commentary on the myths, smokescreens and delusions that seem to have disoriented Thailand and brought heartache over the past many years. In Veeraporn's preface to the Thai publication, she made an allusion to the political malaise, historical and contemporary, as one of the motives for her writing.

The Blind Earthworm in the Labyrinth won the S.E.A. Write Award, Southeast Asia's most prestigious literary prize, in 2015. Before and especially after that, it has grown in popularity among literature fans and younger readers alike, an unusual feat in a country where fiction is hardly ever on the bestseller list. So it's a pleasure for me and the publisher to introduce this translation to wider, non-Thai audiences.

I would like to thank those who have made this translation possible: M.R. Narisa Chakrabongse, Phrae Chittiphalangsri, Pornpisuth Osathanond, Kaona Pongpipat, Chris Baker, Pasuk Phongpaichit, Sarah Rooney and Veeraporn Nitiprapha. I'm grateful for your help, patience and trust.

Kong Rithdee
Bangkok, Thailand
September 2018

I

The Girl in the Fish Tank

Chalika, who was old enough to have a shadow of memory, could recall the time when the house was filled with sounds. Shards of sound, barely audible, humming ceaselessly from the nooks and crannies: murmurs, lamentations, garbled whispers, sighing, bawling, howling, weeping. The sobbing in the dark. Footsteps echoing through the night. The whistling of wind spiralling out of water. It's hard to tell if those sounds were really sounds or if they were merely signals, imprisoned and ricocheting around the house for years from the day Chareeya was born and Mother caught Father having an affair.

A bright ray of sunlight blasted down from a moody sky as Mother's friend arrived at the house and the voyage of tears began. *Well*, she started, trailing off to a near-whisper. *People are talking*. A nod. *The teacher goes there every afternoon*. She had buck teeth and large round eyes that darted left and right, giving her the look of a panicked mouse. *She's a dancer, they say, a traditional dancer, she teaches at the school*. Mother pictured slender arms sweeping languidly through the air: *Are you sure it's Teacher Tos? / My brother Tim saw him, too – he wouldn't get that wrong. His friend lives around there and said they've been seeing each other for nearly a year*. The slender arms kept moving inside Mother's head. *It's not wise to leave such a thing unattended for too long*.

With one hand on her swollen belly and the other resting on the door, Mother found herself standing awkwardly in front of that house. *It's the blueish house*, the panicked mouse had gestured. *Domestic dispute, leave me out of it.* Tilting chin, rolling eyes, the mouse had slipped away. Mother prayed it was all a misunderstanding but, before she could knock, the door swung open and Mother closed her eyes as a gust of wind struck her face without warning; when she opened them, she saw her husband.

He didn't look in the least surprised. It was as if he had been waiting for her, as if he had expected the eventuality of the day his wife would arrive at this very door. The faint aroma of distant rain was mixed with something else, a floral fragrance maybe, though she couldn't place which kind of flower. Over his shoulder she saw a woman inside the room. Mother didn't cry or scream; rather, she couldn't take her eyes off the woman's arm, the part just above her hand, which rested on a table. The woman wasn't as attractive as Mother had imagined but she looked modern – unlike what a traditional dancer was supposed to look like – in jeans and a blue-and-orange striped top, hair falling down her back, eyes tinged with sadness. A wind-chime jingled somewhere. It wasn't yet raining when Father stepped outside, closed the door without looking behind him, and took Mother home.

Only when they reached the house did the downpour commence. Only when they reached the house did Mother acknowledge the incontrovertible existence of that woman. She recalled the small pockets of time when her husband hadn't been there; those mornings when he had looked at himself in the mirror with forlorn eyes, and those evenings when he had gone out walking and stopped to gaze at the river with an air of melancholy.

Only when they reached the house did Mother begin to cry. She wept and shielded her eyes with both hands and cursed the stars that had conspired with the lovers' union. She cursed the swollen belly that had driven him to seek new love. But above all she cursed Chareeya, asleep in her womb, and, using all her willpower, Mother denounced the tyranny of fate: with one massive contraction Chareeya was born in the middle of the night, born while still asleep with her thumb stuck in her mouth.

She had spent scarcely seven months in her mother's womb and the doctor fought hard to keep her alive in this drab and dry world, storing her in a rectangular glass box – an astonishing invention that mimicked the womb and shielded her from death and motherly embrace. For months the baby girl lay there watching the room spin, the girl in the fish tank kept alive by canisters of air brought in from another world, fed by tubes and narrowly escaping death induced by those lonely moments. She grew up to be a healthy girl and no one ever suspected she had contracted the malady of loneliness – undetectable by any hypermodern medical equipment, an incurable disease that would condemn her to solitude for the rest of her life.

Not only that, Chareeya also ached for the presence of the fish tank. Its power to isolate notwithstanding, it had protected her from a death that had pursued her from her Mother's heart. The desire to find herself a new tank was persistent.

As a little girl, Chareeya collected all sorts of creatures she found on the road and surrounded herself with them, like someone in a bunker: dogs, cats, ants, birds, squirrels, lizards, turtles. There was the tree frog that leapt from the pocket of her school uniform and disappeared forever into the garden, the soft jelly that transformed into a blue butterfly and fluttered away when she opened its box one morning, and the cicadas that rubbed their wings to produce annoying shrieks that went on all night long.

Chareeya didn't just take good care of her pets, she counted them as family and addressed them with respectable honorifics: Brother Yuyee, Auntie Meow, Uncle Foon, Aunt Tarn and Sister Tawarn, another tree frog that fled the fish bowl and returned to the banana grove near the house. Once, when she went with Chalika to pick butterfly-pea flowers for making sweet purple sticky rice, Chareeya was so overcome by her desire to collect stray creatures that she wanted to bring home a boy who was sitting by himself under the flame tree outside her school. She wanted to keep him, too, as her brother.

Can we take him home, Lika? / No / Why not…? / Because his mother would miss him and she would cry. Basked in an indigo twilight that concealed all other heavenly colours except for the orange burst of the flame tree flowers falling like a swarm of jellyfish Chareeya had once seen in a documentary, that boy, who was about her age, sat with his head bowed and glanced sideways at the two girls with shrill hostility. *His mother won't come, Lika, it's already dark / She'll come, Charee / But I want a brother / No / His mother won't cry / No, let's go, Charee.* Chalika half-dragged her younger sister away but after a few steps Chareeya turned back to look at the flame tree. Amidst the shimmering orange dots of that ephemeral evening, she thought the boy was being swallowed by the indigo light as he smiled at her, the most tender smile she had ever seen. Chareeya smiled back. *His mother won't cry, Lika. The sky is already dark.* And, then, in an instant, she forgot all about the boy.

As Chareeya grew up she found it harder to stand the pain of seeing her zoological family succumb to their short lifespans. To remedy that, she established a new family with the trees in the garden because they lived longer. She gave her chlorophyllous clan euphonic names: Majestic Auntie *Saiyut*; Dreamy Sister *Lamduan*; All-Embracing Auntie *Huu-Kwang*. Pushing it further, she bestowed them with honorifics: Miss *Pu-Rahong* or Dame *Kannikar*. She honoured them with names inspired by heroines in radio dramas. Or, in the case of the Mon rose, she liked to call it by its vintage name *Yeesoon* like Grandma Jerd from next door did, so it became *Yeesoonsri*, which was in turn inspired by those verses from Khun Chang Khun Phaen* – "Oh *Lamduan*, I lament having to hurry away. *Kaet*, *Kaew*, *Pikul* and *Yeesoonsri*, I'll miss the scent of your falling flowers. Dear *Jampi*, till I see you, how many years?"

How odd then that Chareeya called her sister Chalika "Lika", a bastardised pronunciation of Rita, an American TV character. Just Lika, with neither title nor honorific; no "Sister Lika" or any respectful suffixes. Chalika, meanwhile, called her younger sister "Charee", a bastardised form of the TV series *Charlie's Angels*, and that name spawned a catalogue of oddball puns: Taree's Angels, Roti Angels, Charitable Angels. There were other nonsensical angels but, in the end, she settled on Charee – Charee who was no longer an angel to her elder sister.

* Khun Chang Khun Phaen is an epic Thai poem that evolved from oral story-telling traditions and has become a literary touchstone often referenced in modern-day cultural contexts.

And so silence conquered the house without anyone noticing. There was a fine mist on that banal morning as Father was having breakfast and Chalika was trying to tie her shoelaces for the first time, a task that seemed to puzzle her. Chareeya, too young for school, squatted next to her sister, her face tipped back slightly, elbows out, fists on her chest, imagining herself as a sparrow. This was when Mother calmly told Father that she was going to kill herself. *And the two kids are coming with me.*

Sunlight bounced off water in the glass that Nual the nanny was handing to Chalika and the sharp gleam pierced Father's eyes so suddenly that he ducked. For a while, he remained still with his head down and, when he looked up again, the blaze that had blurred his vision was gone. He squinted against the sun to look at the house; seeing past his wife who had got up to go to the kitchen, past the furniture sulking in the dim light, past his own tears as he blinked away the shadows in the corners of the room, and past the dissolving mist…

There, Chalika was pulling her sister up from being a sparrow. They were silhouetted against the hazy background of a pomelo tree. Chareeya was upset, stomping her feet, craning her neck and crowing like a rooster while wiping away tears with the back of her balled-up hand. But everything was silent. There was no sound of Chareeya crying or of Chalika running away. No sound of the large crow that usually cawed at that hour. No sound of leaves rustling. Not even the sound of the ceaseless breeze off the river.

In that moment, Father recalled the sobbing that had disappeared from the night. He remembered all the other sounds that had left the house and blanketed it in total silence, and he suddenly realised the certitude hidden in Mother's threat; it came at him like a smooth round stone from the riverbed and he unconditionally cut all ties with the other woman. Yet, long after that, silence continued to rule the house.

Father quit his teaching job. He stayed indoors and never left the house, as if he'd also quit the entire world. Once in a while he would go down to the orchards, just to make a show of his existence. Father knew nothing about farming. That didn't matter because the labourers had been working there since Mother's parents were still alive, and they knew how to take care of the soil on the banks of the Nakhon Chai Si River. In any case, Father had no interest in doing anything anymore. His heart kept beating pangs of hurt that he could hardly bear.

Mother, in turn, started taking care of the man she loved with the same force she had used to win him back. Slowly the gloom lifted and the light shone, so brightly that no one would have noticed the house had once borne the wet scars of tears. Mother would wake up while everyone was still dreaming, write down a daily to-do list, and delegate it to Aunt Phong the cook, Nual the nanny and Niang the maidservant. During the day, she would patrol the house to check on progress. She managed Father's business, telling him which phone calls to answer, which letters to read and who had written them, what he should and shouldn't do.

When she had time, she rummaged through old photographs, picking out the ones with Father and herself, and framing them to hang on the wall. Once she had exhausted the stock of old pictures, she asked Uncle Poj, son of Grandma Jerd next door, to take some more. She changed into her Sunday best, even though it wasn't Sunday, and she smiled and posed next to Father by the door, the stairs, the car, or the riverbank with the backdrop of the big *lampu* tree. She accepted every party invitation so that she could hurriedly make new dresses and rush out to a hair salon. Sometimes, in the mornings, she would call a hairdresser to the house to fix her up, just so that she could take more pictures to frame and hang on the wall.

In the house where the windows had been closed since the time when it was full of sounds Mother hadn't wanted her neighbours to hear, Mother followed Father everywhere, like a shadow, to ensure that he would not experience even a second of loneliness that could drive him back into that hurtful trap of desire. Father, meanwhile, became anxious, getting up and sitting down and moving himself from one chair to another in order to elude the thumping sound of his wife's heartbeat, which infiltrated his chest interminably. He ended up wandering around the house, a nomad in his own home, his tour coming to an end only in the late afternoons when Mother, busying herself in the kitchen with dinner preparations, would allow him to doze off in the wicker chair under the *pikul* tree. Only the children knew that Father wasn't really sleeping.

To the girls, Father's existence was a mystifying phenomenon: he was a transparent entity they could almost see through. He would show up silently at random corners of the house and disappear without a trace when no one was looking. He was a man whose inability to have contact with other human beings was absolute. His only means of communicating with his daughters was to stare at their faces for long stretches of time, one after the other, back and forth, until the girls became frustrated from anticipating what he was about to say. But he never said anything. He would close his eyes and frown as if concentrating on his brain waves and transmitting thoughts he had retrieved from the girls' heads to a faraway galaxy.

And Mother? She was a familiar stranger, the woman who wearily wandered the labyrinth of furniture within the house. The woman who seemed to know happiness only when she sat down, arms crossed, slowly rubbing her arms while looking at the framed photographs crowding the walls. She was the woman who had never embraced Chareeya: not on the day the girl had come out of the fish tank, not on the day she had stood up from a crawling position and started walking on her own, and not on the day she had uttered her first word and become a living, thinking girl.

Mother was the woman who kept her distance, even though she never failed to take care of her children. She maintained that distance until she died without ever realising that she had deprived them of her embrace, not just the embrace she never gave to Chareeya, the daughter she had never loved, but also to Chalika, the one whom she loved more than everything in the world combined, though she would never know it. *My precious Chalika*, she used to call the girl when she was asleep in her arms in an embrace that would vanish forever the second the world became as empty as if it had never existed – that minute on that day when Chareeya was born.

And when the voyage of tears began.

II

Valley of the Fuchsia Storks

While Mother devoted herself to consoling her heartbroken husband, Nual the nanny, who had three lovers and exhausted all her energy in a tangle of desire, cared for Chalika and Chareeya, and despite everything the girls grew up happily.

It's the nature of children. War, flash floods, landslides or the fall of empires can't diminish the simple happiness that can only be felt by someone who doesn't understand she's just a child. The girls leapt out of the charred ruins of their parents' marriage with only a few scars on their hearts. They rolled about in the orchards all day like animal cubs, scooping laughter and joy out of thin air as if by magic.

The games they played: rolling around trying to dodge wet drops dripping from foliage ablaze in sunshine; exchanging ghost stories smuggled from adults while sitting in shade damp with aromatic green moss; improvising a song for a flower – *talaybaytalaytay talaytaytalatalay flower*, and quickly forgetting it the next minute… *Goodbye, tabaytalatala lala flower.*

In the glare of sunbeams that felt like so many ants crawling across their backs, they hid behind a thicket of reeds, cupping each other's mouths to muffle laughter as the increasingly hopeless calls of Nual the nanny approached and then faded. In the fine drizzle, they slunk into puddles, mouths open to catch raindrops sweetened by a rainbow. Their gleeful laughter was splintered by early wintry breezes into a hundred tiny giggles that wafted down the river.

Like children growing up in a war zone, they did everything together. They ate together, slept on the same bed, coiled up in the same chair, laughed in unison, cried in tandem, got sick at the same time, dreamt the same dream – a dream in which they held hands and ran all night through a valley full of fuchsia storks, a dream they had completely forgotten by the time they woke up. They tied their hands together with a handkerchief before going to bed to make sure neither of them would slip alone across the fuzzy borders between wakefulness and sleep.

Sometimes, the two sisters roamed about wrapped in a single sarong, arms entwined like Siamese twins. They proclaimed themselves Madame Eng and Madame Chan, and came up with a language to communicate within the Eng-Chan tribe, which consisted of exactly two members in the whole world. They tapped secret codes on each other's arms under the table: once "Yes", twice "No", three times "Maybe", and in that way reached a consensus before negotiating with the adults. They even took each other's strands of hair and braided them together so they could transmit their thoughts in secret. Whatever they did, their heads leaned towards each other all day long. The house already conquered by silence was also deprived of the sisters' chattering since they had trained themselves to laugh and sob quietly, on the inside.

Madame Eng / Hmm? / I want to drink rainbow-sweetened syrup / We have to wait for the magical day / When is that? / When it rains while the sun shines / And when will it rain while the sun shines? / On the magical day, I told you / But… / Sleep, Madame Chan / Madame Eng… / Sleep, little Miss Chan / Madame Eng… / Go to sleep, Charee, I'm sleepy.

No one knew when Madame Eng and Madame Chan stopped tying their hands together before going to bed, or when they overcame the fear of losing each other in the gap that separated sleep and wakefulness. In their minds, they remained Siamese twins who followed each other everywhere but when Chalika was ten years old she started spending most of her time lost in the world of novels; a fantastical world in which an aristocratic lady could fall in love with a lowborn man, a world preoccupied by the need to find proof of love through complicated and unscientific processes, a mysterious world in which the miracle of love inspired bliss and tragedy, a world strewn with traps, thorns, jealousy, and black comedy written by fate. A world in which the quest for true love existed only in the imagination.

Chareeya, three years younger, spent her days hunting strange creatures with strange cries in the santol orchard, or putting a kitten in a ditch to teach her to swim, or kidnapping baby snakehead fish to provoke their mother's wrath, or digging up clumps of earth in various colours from the riverbank to sculpt frogs. The Red Frog came alive in the sun, the Yellow Frog under the moon, and the Blue Frog by the year's first storm; only the Lightning Frog could come back from the dead because after it was washed away by the rain it returned at night with its incessant croaking and left poor Sun Frog and Moon Frog sitting there caked in dust.

As soon as the rains let up, Chareeya would start tracking a blind earthworm lost in a labyrinth it had dug itself. She never found any clues but once accidentally uncovered a string of ancient Dvaravati beads that looked like they had been buried just days before, though they crumbled to dust at the touch of her breath. In the same manner in which Chareeya tracked the blind earthworm, Chalika would shadow her wherever she went. The elder sister, seated on Father's wicker chair reading love stories about men and women with poetic names, would move around after her, from under the santol tree with its faint aroma to the riverside gazebo, to the reed grove, to the branch of a tree, to anywhere and everywhere.

Lika, why does an earthworm have no eyes? / I don't know / How do we know if it's awake or asleep? / Well, I don't know / And does it know? / Know what? / Does it know if it's awake or asleep when it's digging? / It should know / But I used to sleepwalk… Chareeya looked at an eyeless earthworm wriggling in her palm. *When I was sleepwalking, Lika, I saw everything so clearly, not like when I'm dreaming / So you've told me several times / I have, and I didn't know I was asleep when I was sleepwalking / Sleepwalkers don't know / And does the earthworm know? / Know what? / That it's asleep when it's digging / God, Charee! How would I know? / Grandpa Earthworm eats earth, shits earth, eats earth, shits earth...* So the girl sang a song about Grandpa Earthworm she made up in that moment and ran back into the orchard.

Chalika was twelve; Chareeya nine. Six years after wandering hopelessly confined in his own house amidst all the framed photographs, Father fell ill. He was hospitalised, then came home and spent all his time in bed. One morning, he disappeared. Mother searched for him all over the neighbourhood, like a madwoman.

That night, the girls were woken by an endless screaming fit. They found Mother weeping and writhing around on the floor, having yanked her hair so violently that there were only a few tufts left on her scalp. Before her lay Father, his body serene amidst four thousand two hundred and twenty-two letters, each bearing an address written in his own handwriting. He lay in an engraved wooden coffin that had been sent from a woman – *that* woman.

Before dawn broke, Mother burned the letters, circling the bonfire and spitting into it. She refused to call a monk to perform funeral rites. Instead, she ordered workmen to dig a hole. *As deep as possible.* Mother buried Father under the old *pikul* tree. *You'll stay here forever. You will never be reborn.*

Every day until she died one year later, Mother sat from dawn to dusk above the grave of the only man she had ever loved. With a strip of sad-looking purple cloth wound around her head where the hair never grew back, she sat on the wicker chair, its surface gnawed by her husband's implacable longing for that woman. She sat, just like that, in a cocoon of agony, amid the bittersweet perfume of *pikul* flowers, in the eternal river breeze, sitting on guard to be certain that Father's spirit would never slip out to see that woman, or any other woman.

To be certain he would never rest in peace.

III

The Goldfish that Sang

In the same way as Chalika and Chareeya grew up among plants, animals and gaggles of people who wandered out of the pages of novels, Pran had a warm childhood growing up amidst a huge family made up of dozens of uncles, aunts and grandparents.

The day Pran's father came home and saw his wife in the arms of a stranger, he stood there for hours watching the lovers sleep in the coil of their embrace. All he did was go into the next room and pick up his baby, then he left the house and never went back. From that time on, he let Pran sleep and dream, crawl and grow up to the swaying motion of a train.

By the time Pran was old enough to know what was what, he was able to take care of himself, to be left alone for long periods while his father, who was employed by the state railway, was on duty or getting drunk in the rear carriage. He was told not to get close to strangers, regardless of their rank or status, and this made Pran a boy of few words; he hardly even talked to himself. He would sit quietly, staring out of the window, watching the world go by and contemplating the universe by night so that he wouldn't have to experience the boredom of a return trip along the train's narrow, gloomy corridors where he overheard the strange breathing of passengers asleep in all sorts of positions; their throaty wheezing, the murmurings that escaped from their dreams, the whispered moans finding their way back from some forgotten past.

One night while Pran was fumbling in the dark, a man sat up from his seat and called out, *What are you selling? / Boiled eggs*, Pran blurted without thinking. At that moment the boy realised that the man was talking with his eyes closed. *How much? / Six salueng*[*] */ Give me two.* Pran handed him two imaginary boiled eggs and watched the man fiddle emptiness from his shirt pocket and put it in the boy's hand. Tenderly, he peeled the nothing-egg, bit half of it off and chewed steadily, his eyes still closed, looking satisfied. He peeled another and smiled. Then he leant back against his seat and snored.

It wasn't clear why Pran's father was preoccupied by an unusual urge: he wanted to keep moving and refused to stay any place longer than a year at most. No sooner had he settled down in a house than he would find an excuse to request a route change, asking to be transferred from the northern to the southern line, from one province to another, from one railway junction to another, from one railway-worker community to another, from one grey house to another one that looked exactly the same.

When he was young, Pran roamed the latitudes of the country, wherever his father's schedule took them. When he started school and when his father had to take an overnight shift, the boy was entrusted with neighbours who fed him, and took him to bed at night and to school in the morning. Though father and son never lived anywhere long enough to get close to anyone, it wasn't a problem. The railway workers considered themselves an exclusive tribe cut off from the general population, and they were prepared to take care of each other like members of a large family. It helped that Pran was an uncomplicated, undemanding and unfussy kid who hardly spoke and caused no trouble.

In order not to put too heavy a burden on any one household, Pran was sent to a different family each time his father was away. In the late afternoon, he'd sit at the school gate with a mattress and

* A *salueng* is obsolete Thai currency equivalent to 25 *satang* (the Thai baht is made up of 100 *satang*); today's 25-*satang* coin is still commonly referred to as a *salueng*.

pillow sewn together in a bundle and an envelope with some cash for food in his shirt pocket. He would wait for someone whose face he'd never seen before to pick him up and take him to a house he'd never been to, to become a transient family member for one night, two at the most. The families treated him as if he were one of their own, and then they let the boy go in the morning without ever asking about him again.

Pran's status as a one-night family member meant that he grew up having hundreds of siblings, though none of them really thought of him as a real sibling. Moving schools once, or sometimes as many as three times, a year, Pran also made friends with thousands of kids around the country, though hardly any of them remembered him. Counting the transitory family tree of all the various uncles and aunties who showed up at various train platforms, Pran's early life enjoyed a warmth generated by sheer number; it was a heavily populated childhood that comfortably made up for the loss of his mother.

Only on some weekends and summer breaks did Pran rejoin his father in his railway nomadism. On the train, he sat staring at the world flashing by in a quiet blur: at verdant fields laid out in a checkerboard pattern that resembled fluffy *salee*[*] in their trays; at scarecrows with arms outstretched in the blinding heat, wiggling their fingers as if to tease him; at a forest of shadows on a lonely platform in the dead of night, stirred into bustling motion when the train approached and resuming motionlessness once it had passed; at a crescent moon dangling in the sky like the dismembered claw of a giant. The boy stared at thousands of light bulbs big and small, all competing to illuminate morning markets in the distance, and tempting his heart with the vision of a future that lay ahead.

Never once was Pran aware that somewhere in the world that passed by the window, Chalika and Chareeya were running and playing, crying and laughing, sleeping with their hands tied together with a handkerchief for fear of losing each other in their dreams, and that one day the three of them would become the best of friends.

* *Salee* is a steamed pudding made of cassava and tapioca flour, topped with shredded coconut.

Not only did Pran grow up in a family like Chalika's and Chareeya's, but his home, which came in many shades of grey, was also conquered by silence. When his father wanted the boy to eat, he would glance at a plate of rice. If he wanted Pran to take a shower, he would hand him a towel. He would point at objects he wanted his son to pick up for him. To get Pran to carry something, he would hold it at the boy's eye level. His cough was a warning and he stroked his hair to indicate he was in a good mood. At bedtime, he would turn off the light and the television, and let the boy drift into sleep.

After work, his father would take Pran along to his drinking sessions at cafes near the station, or at cheap saloons frequented by low-wage earners, invariably there was an open-air shack with twinkling coloured lights festooning the front door and an old jukebox with peeled-off paint chained to a post like an old, angry dog. Once in a while his father would take Pran along to a Pink House, which was either an actual house, or a rowhouse painted pink, or a place decked with neon bulbs wrapped in cellophane that gave off a halo of pinkish light. The houses customarily boasted pink-coloured decor and knick-knacks – flowers, curtains, cushions, plant pots, lamps – and there was something that made them all identical, besides the platoon of heavily powdered women who smiled with listless eyes.

During such visits his father would disappear with one of the women, leaving Pran to watch television with the rest of them. He might play with his superhero dolls in the corner or fall asleep on a sofa so densely laden with the stench of cigarettes that it was damp in the middle. Pran came to believe that these Pink Houses were a network of secret organisations: the pink motif was a symbol of sorority, the women were espionage operatives hiding their real faces beneath their powdered masks as they embarked on missions to save the world from destructive villains, and the men who visited them were field agents who came to retrieve information and left furtively and in haste.

One night, the women were in a playful mood and dressed Pran up as a girl. His father seethed with rage, baring his fangs like a she-dog protecting her newborn puppies, when he came into the room and saw his son smiling sheepishly in a loose lace blouse that fell to his feet, a plastic flower and bows crowning his head, and cosmetics smeared on his face. He ripped the blouse from Pran's body, clenched his teeth and blasted expletives: *Bitches, my son isn't your toy*, as he tore the flower from his head. *My son isn't anybody's toy*, as he pulled out his handkerchief and violently wiped the boy's face. *Stupid whores*, as he dragged the boy out of the room. But the women weren't angry; they just giggled in delight and waved goodbye. *Come back when you're a man, Pran.*

That night, Pran almost cried when he went to bed. He thought back to his involvement in a secret mission during which he had to disguise himself as a girl, working alongside five brave, saving-the-world female spies who briefed and admired him with high-pitched voices, like those he heard in commercials. *My dear Pran, my dear Pran*, they kept saying and rewarded him by taking turns to kiss his cheek. But his father had used a dirty handkerchief to erase those marks of honour until there was nothing left.

And the urge to cry was overwhelming when Pran thought about the woman whose lips were glistening orange. When she sang, her moving lips reminded the boy of a gold fish swimming. In a shrill voice she had belted out, *My man's gone, it's over... All that's left is his lighter...* Interspersed with throaty clucking that resembled sobs, she sang while gently applying powder to his face in a circular motion from his hairline to his chin. She used something that looked like a pair of scissors to squeeze his eyelashes and glossed his eyelids with pieces of glitter so minuscule that, for years, Pran would continue to believe they were the scales of a Siamese fighting fish. She smoothed his brows with a doll's toothbrush and daubed shocking-pink powder onto his cheeks with a soft blush brush fragrant as bubble gum.

And Pran's urge to cry eventually became unbearable when he thought back to the ephemeral tenderness of a single moment: a magical moment when the particles of cosmetic powder swirled in the air and the woman said something to him in a silky whisper. A speck of glitter shimmered at the tip of his eyelash, and then time stopped.

Pran never returned to that Pink House, as he had mentally promised the women he would. And his father didn't take him to any other Pink Houses until his death, just a few months after that last visit when he miscalculated a jump onto a speeding train by one-eighth of a second. Pran met his grandmother for the first time when she came to take him to stay with her. Grandmother was small and beautiful, both when she was young and when she grew old. Her eyes were penetrating. The old woman rarely smiled or spoke, just like Pran, his father and Uncle Chit. Everyone in the family had inherited from her the legacy of silence.

Pran's grandfather had been a civil servant, heavy drinker, womaniser and hot-tempered husband who beat his wife out of jealousy even though he kept mistresses everywhere. When he was drunk, he spoke in rough and vulgar language, capping it off with imaginary accusations to justify beating up Grandmother. Consumed by paranoia that his wife's beauty would attract men, he shaved her head on more than one occasion, and Grandmother had to run away to her friends or relatives with bruises on her body and stubby tufts of hair on her head. When his senses returned, Grandfather would track her down and make up with her. When he drank, the same chain of events happened again, round and round in an endless cycle of domestic melodrama.

Once, Grandfather locked her up in a closet for three days and got too drunk to remember where he had put the key. Her screams prompted a neighbour to come to the rescue and break down the closet with an axe. Instead of feeling remorse, Grandfather accused her of having an affair with her saviour and lunged at her again. He also demanded compensation from the neighbour for wrecking a piece of his furniture. The entire neighbourhood became fed up with him and left Grandmother to her fate. After a few years, she decided she had had enough, too. She gathered her two sons and ran away to Nakhon Chai Si to live with her aunt.

But, again, Grandfather found her. She was in the kitchen when he walked in and tried to drag her away. She picked up a butcher knife and threatened to cut off her own finger if he refused to leave but he didn't budge and kept moving forward. Just as he was about to touch her, Grandmother pushed the blade on her little finger without a gasp. Still holding the knife in one hand, she threw the severed finger at her husband. *If you don't leave me alone, next time it won't be my finger. It'll be your goddamn dick.*

The sprinkles of blood on his face had the desired effect. Taken aback, Grandfather left and never bothered her again except for one time, when a boy of Pran's age came to the house, called her "Mother", and told her his father was dying and wanted to see her for the last time. *Go back and tell your father, "Hurry up and die, don't stick around – there's no need to ask for my permission." And don't call me "mother". I'm not your mother.*

To Grandmother, men were selfish creatures and the begetters of all suffering. That many decent men had since approached her did not change her mind; she remained single and supported her children by tending a chilli plantation on a small plot of land with her aunt, whose husband had died years ago from smallpox. She also rented another plot by the river to grow lotuses and morning glory. She did odd jobs for people in the neighbourhood, like altering clothes, and earned enough to get by without her children going hungry. When her son, Pran's father, found a wife and moved with her to Ayutthaya when he was eighteen, she didn't object. It had been preordained, she said, since it was impossible to keep a man in the house forever. And when she learned of his death, there was no drama; she just got on a train and picked up Pran, who was seven, and raised him without prejudice and without making him feel unwanted. They lived a simple, quiet life.

By the time Pran arrived at the house, Grandmother's aunt had died many years ago. The only other person living there was Uncle Chit, his father's younger brother, whose presence came to represent the only period – however brief – in the boy's life during which he felt that someone was there for him. Uncle Chit was a cheerful, exuberant man with an unreserved pool of energy that meant he was occupied with one activity or another at all times. He took Pran with him wherever he went and they did what male buddies do together – speared frogs, trapped birds, fished, rowed, played football, tinkered with stuff and fixed functional equipment only to make it malfunction. But the following year Uncle Chit fell in love with the daughter of the owner of a Chinese pharmacy in the market, and a year later went to work as a construction foreman in the Middle East with the hope of earning money to come back and ask for her hand. Then he disappeared.

Pran never understood how a person could disappear as if they had never existed, just like that. It distressed him and a childish impulse almost spurred him into stealing money from Grandmother so he could get to Bangkok, hide in the cargo hole of a plane and go to look for Uncle Chit in the vast desert. Sometimes, the boy consoled himself with a fantasy that one day Uncle Chit, without prior notice, would return as a wealthy man and adopt him as his son. But that dream, that hope, and everything else, slowly lost its clarity.

The last rumour they heard was of a woman whose face was covered with intricate tattoos, hidden behind a black shawl, who had spiked Uncle Chit's drink with a love potion so powerful that he lost his mind. The last time someone ran into him, so the story went, he could neither understand the Thai language nor remember anyone. Grandmother didn't try to look for him. To her, it had been preordained.

Damn, no need to slip him a love potion – men will always find an excuse to leave.

IV

The Cocoon of Misery

Uncle Thanit arrived at the house by the river at dawn one day before Mother died, as if she had been waiting for him without even knowing whether he would be coming at all. Or perhaps it was his arrival that made her decide it was time to go. For a long time, no one had known what Mother thought, felt, or if she was still capable of thinking or feeling anything at all.

Don't ever think you can slip through my fingers, even in death. Mother had persisted in cursing the spirit of her husband since the day he died, mumbling, sobbing, and once frantically clawing the mound of his grave like a desperate dog searching for a bone it had buried. But she stopped all that after a few months and, from then on, never spoke to anybody ever again, as if she had let everything out and there was nothing left inside her. More than that, she stopped acknowledging anyone who was speaking to her and anything that was going on around her.

Every morning Mother proceeded to the wicker chair under the *pikul* tree and sat there mutely. During the early days, Aunt Phong would bring her food and water, but Mother wouldn't touch it. Chalika had to spoon-feed her and, from that day on, the girl, who was then twelve, became her mother's sole caretaker. She bathed her, dressed her, fed her, clipped her toenails, wrapped the piece of cloth around her head still dotted with clumps of hair, took her to bed, looked for help to put up a tarpaulin cover when an afternoon storm broke and Mother refused to budge from her seat.

In time Chalika took over the running of the household. She looked after basic chores such as preparing food, taking Chareeya to the doctor, forging Mother's signature on her sister's report card and assuming the role of her guardian, as well as more serious transactions like managing the daily expenses, utility payments, school fees. She paid salaries to Aunt Phong and Nual the nanny – who was then pregnant with her first child and had three men prepared to share joint fatherhood – but didn't have to worry about Niang, who had quit right after Father died because she was afraid of his ghost. Chalika managed all of this quite simply, with income from the rented plots of land that her mother had allotted to people in the neighbourhood; the only plot the family had left was the one that circled the house and stretched from the road to the river. It was Chalika, too, who had written to Uncle Thanit and asked him to come to Mother's deathbed.

In her last few months Mother hardly touched any food. She shrank and became so small that Uncle Thanit couldn't help but be confused as to whether the woman he saw was actually his ten-year-old sister as she had been decades ago. As soon as he arrived that morning, he sat down beside his sister and watched the golden sunlight in wonder and disbelief while talking to her in a gentle voice under the *pikul* tree they had planted together when they were children.

The childhood stories Uncle Thanit recalled: the time he removed the head of her new doll to work out how it could open and close its eyes but was then unable to reattach it, sending his sister into a crying fit that had lasted for days; the time he dug a hole, filled it with sand and covered it with sheets of newspaper in order to trap a monitor lizard that often snuck in to eat their bantam chickens, only for his sister to fall into the trap herself; the time their mother took them on a boat, letting them rest their heads on her lap as she rowed out into the twilight with the sun looking like a giant salted egg, when they had watched the silhouettes of tree branches gliding past them on both sides, the birds flying home and the moon making its amorphous entrance to the sky.

He then confessed the secrets he had kept from her: the time he got up in the middle of the night to assemble model planes he had hidden for fear she would wreck them and toss the tiny pieces around; the time he stole a puppy from a store and lied to her that he had bought it for her as a birthday present; the time he had a crush on her friend and wrote her anonymous love letters for two years.

When the sun was about to set, Uncle Thanit told his sister under the *pikul* tree how much he had missed her. He told her how he wore two watches – one showing Thai time so he could picture what she was doing – and how he checked his postbox twice a day because he never stopped waiting for her letters. He told her he had always wanted to come home so that he could grow old with her.

After the reminiscing he sat quietly with his sister, looking serene – even when the *pikul* flowers fell around them like rain, even when he saw the last dewdrops of her life evaporate before his eyes, even when darkness enveloped them like ink. And he still looked serene when Mother didn't wake up the following morning. Uncle Thanit told the workers to dig up Father's body so they could arrange religious rites for both of them. To everyone's surprise, the buried coffin had sunk deeper into the earth, so deep they had to spend an entire day excavating, four metres down, before they found it.

As she set out on a boat to scatter her parents' ashes, out into the dark grey realm where the sea and sky merge, Chalika wondered where the irrepressible weight of Mother's tears and the misery that had pushed Father's coffin into the ground had gone. She couldn't fathom how it was possible that the lives of two people could be reduced to dust wrapped in the two little cloth bundles before her.

My friend Sukanya told me she can't remember her mother's voice and she only died two years ago / We can't remember everything, Charee / My memory of our childhood is beginning to fade / So is mine / When we forget something, sometimes it comes back in a flash that quickly vanishes, but as time passes we forget that we ever knew it / Yeah / Lika… / What? / Do you think one day we'll forget Father and Mother and they'll be lost forever? / No, Charee, I don't know… There are many things I can't remember about Father anymore.

Like someone dead and non-existent stranded in the middle of the sea with no land visible, three orphans steadied themselves in the bobbing uncertainty of life as they watched the infinitesimal dust that was once the lives of two people combine into one long, transparent strip, rippling, fading, spiralling on the surface of the water, like the Milky Way, as it floated further and further away, into a final farewell.

Uncle Thanit arrived with one small bag, inside which were some clothes, a few personal belongings, and an orange Japanese cat doll wearing a kimono for Chalika, a blue one for Chareeya. Three weeks after the funeral, sixty-three boxes followed, fifty-five of them filled with vinyl records, eight packed with books, plus a leather violin case.

Their uncle was in his late-thirties, tall, skinny, bespectacled, hair grazing his shoulders. He was a no-fuss man with a faint smile permanently painted on his face, and polite to a fault. When someone spoke to him, he'd listen wide-eyed like a child, as if it was the most interesting subject and he was hearing about it for the first time in his life. When the person had finished, he would nod once, and he punctuated his own sentences with the same gesture.

During the first few weeks, Uncle Thanit went around the orchards introducing himself to the neighbours and tenants. Some of them had met him at the funeral. Others remembered him from the time he had lived there as a child, even though he had been a quiet boy who kept to himself and he had been away for such a long time. At fifteen, he left home to study in Krungthep*, or "Bang Gawk" as people used to call it then. After he finished university, he won a scholarship to study in Fukuoka where he fell in love and had a brief marriage before falling in love again and having another brief marriage. After that, he quit his teaching job to open a record store on the outskirts of Kyoto. He had only come home once, for his sister's wedding.

* In the Thai language, the capital city of Bangkok is referred to by its Thai name, Krungthep.

When he was done doing the rounds with the neighbours, Uncle Thanit summoned the family lawyer to the house to verify all the rent contracts and sort out the shambolic accounting Chalika had done. He divided his sister's savings in two and placed one half each into the bank accounts of his nieces. Then he went through the income earned from the rentals and split it into three parts for school fees, household expenses, and a remainder further divided into another three portions for himself and the two girls, which would be paid into their accounts every month.

His next mission took him an entire week. Uncle Thanit went through the framed photographs adorning every vertical surface of the house. One by one he looked at them. There were photos of various scenes, each seemingly showing Father glancing at himself in the adjacent photo, always with Mother standing next to him, her eyes lonely and her smile too broad. In some they stood, in others they sat; photographs large and small, some vertically aligned, others horizontal.

The thousand photographs that bedecked the walls to declare a glorious victory over the "other woman" became, in the end, a monument to Mother's hopeless attempts to validate a marriage that had already been shattered to pieces. It was a marriage, the depths of which she had never really been able to see, and, not only had she been desperate to see it, she had spent much of her life force trying to do so. Yet, in the end, she found herself ambushed by countless other eyes prying into her life. Worst of all, she had messed up the walls; all those faces peering back at her like lifeless images from the repositories of dead people's ashes at temples.

Uncle Thanit removed all the photographs and put them in boxes. Then he fixed up the house. He painted the rooms a pale shade of green that bled into white, threw away the wicker chair ruined by Father's desire and Mother's wrath, and changed the furniture. He opened windows that had stayed shut since the days when silence took over the house and let in a breeze to blow away the remnants of crystallised tears still shimmering in its nooks and crannies. He put up shelves on three walls of the living room that had once been colonised by the photographs and arranged his vinyls in orderly rows.

Of the thousands of photos he packed away, Uncle Thanit picked out just one. It was a black-and-white picture taken in a studio around the time Father and Mother had just got married. Father stood in a finely tailored cream-coloured suit, Mother sitting before him in white, with his hand on her shoulder in a touch of reassurance. They were both young with faint smiles on their faces and sparkling eyes, sweet and serene in the halo of studio lights that gave the impression of a swirling mist. The frame was white, run through with gold threads like those pictures of Catholic saints in churches. And the couple looked immaculate, pure, happy, uncorrupted – like saints, too.

Uncle Thanit hung the photograph on the wall next to the dining table so the girls would remember their parents that way and could be reassured, without any moments of doubt in the long years ahead of them, that they had been conceived out of nothing but love.

V

Fighting Fish in a Bottle of Glue

Pran, Pran. She waved at him. *It's Charee, Pran, remember?* The cheery smile, the twinkling eyes. Strangers before him, strangers behind him. Strangers all around him. But he remembered. Pran returned the greeting with a smile, an indistinct one. A scene from years ago came rushing back: when he opened the palms of his cupped hands and the firefly he had caught from the *lampu* tree flew away into the blue twilight, and she broke into that cheery smile, her eyes twinkling like they did now. It was a long time ago. Such a long time ago…

The Cure's "Pictures of You" boomed and shuddered. *There was nothing in the world / That I ever wanted more / Than to feel you deep in my heart.* Pran put his guitar down on the stage and picked his way through the grey cigarette smoke and flashing lights. *Hey, Charee,* he said, looking sheepish as he approached the corner table littered with tequila shot glasses, squeezed lemon slices, and spilt salt like stardust. *Pran,* she replied softly. *Your hair is long.* He smiled. Her hair was long too, tied back, with a velvet red rose tucked behind her ear. She was a grown woman, wearing a black sleeveless blouse, a deep-purple tiered gypsy skirt and something like one hundred necklaces.

I never thought… / You're doing fine? She shouted above the din. *Yeah, you? / Good, good. Witches, this is Pran – Pran, Witches.* The three Witches laughed, blood throbbing under their cheeks, gloriously drunk. *Witch Thanya / Witch Urai / Witch Rawee.* They introduced themselves. *You're a musician? Been playing here long? / Two years at this bar / I'm so happy, I thought I'd never see you again.* Chareeya used the childish pronoun *nu* when speaking to Chalika and to him, but she never addressed them using a respectful prefix like Elder Sister or Elder Brother.

You're into rock music? Pran teased. *Hmm. My friends are / Have you seen Lika?* He asked, realising he didn't want to hear her answer. *Once in a while. I haven't been home in a few months. And you?* From her answer, he knew she already knew his answer. *No, I work every night. Is Uncle Thanit fine?*

Is Uncle Thanit fine? Is Chalika fine? Is the river fine? The glare of sunshine bouncing off those calm waters from many years ago suddenly returned, so bright he had to close his eyes. When he opened them again, it was just the bright lights in the bar, heralding the hour of the shipwrecked heart – the time when the bar was closing and the night was over. *My house isn't far - walk me back, I want to catch up with you.* The Witches giggled. Chareeya smiled and gestured them to stop. *Pran is my best friend / Best friend...* The Witches retorted in unison, as if casting a spell.

The streets were deserted and the city was fast asleep. Chareeya led Pran to an intersection and they watched the traffic light changing colours over the vast desolation of the nocturnal cityscape. They cut into small lanes, past shophouses dating back various decades, deep into a residential quarter hidden in a tranquil spot behind rows of shops that had been busy just a few hours earlier. Turning left and right a dozen times, they reached a house with a front gate covered in overgrown trees, so dense he thought it must be an abandoned lot. *Come in,* she said softly and tip-toed through the tiny space between slender *pheep* flowers that carpeted the ground. *It's a mess – you know I love plants.* I know, I know. Pran smiled in the dark but didn't say a word. They were enveloped in a cloud of floral perfume.

Crisscrossing the unlit garden and going through a door, they entered a room painted yellow that seemed to be filled with everything in the world. There were earrings and necklaces hung all over the walls, a postcard of the woman with bangs and a black dress painted by Modigliani, concert and movie tickets, scattered note papers, receipts for water and electricity bills. In the centre of it all was a poster of Frida Kahlo's final work, showing a juicy slice of watermelon emblazoned with her famous line: *Viva la vida.*

Books were stacked in piles on the floor, climbing up the walls. A silky pink peony stood in a green vase next to Uncle Thanit's violin case. There were towers of CDs on the shelves, a floral-print scarf in sad purple on the back of a chair, and a ginger tabby cat snug against a shocking pink cushion printed with a peony pattern. *Pran, Uncle Yellow. Uncle Yellow, Pran.* She introduced the cat the same way as she had done the Witches. But Chareeya's uncle was uninterested; he stretched wearily, cast a glance at Pran through half-closed eyes, then sat down, and looked away, gazing not at Pran but somewhere just beyond his eyes. There was no eye contact, no feline courtesy.

There was a vintage floor lamp with a beaded fringe, and next to it a study desk with piles of papers, a wooden statuette of an African woman with sagging breasts, her face glum like that of a fish, a cat doll in a blue kimono, a couple of white river stones. And there was a photograph of her and Chalika, arms around each other's waists like Eng and Chan, the Siamese twins, both looking at the camera with the same melancholy eyes, smiling the same lonely smile, a dark-green sea and sky behind them.

Under the window was a peony-patterned cushion like Uncle Cat's cushion, but bigger. Next to it was a Burmese make-up case, carved, vibrantly painted, and fashionably worn out; the mirror was missing, probably broken at some point in its life. *I've always wanted you to listen to something.* The bitter aroma of ylang-ylang, melded with that of the *mok* flowers, Mon rose, and the faint misty scent of the *pheep* tree. *Schumann's Opus 47, third movement.* Chareeya smiled, a lonely smile almost identical to the one in the photograph, and the air trembled. *The first time I heard it, I thought of you.* She pressed the Play button and lay down in a half-reclining position beside him on the peony-print pillow. *Close your eyes, Pran.*

And the raspy cello laid tender chords upon the violin as it chased the viola in the background. Pran closed his eyes and leant back against the wall. He'd never heard this piece before. It was sweet and imploring, but with something painful and nervous coursing through its melody; beautiful yet faintly atonal, it conjured up such soulful warmth and yet it was detached and indifferent. Then the piano rolled out its soft notes like a succession of slow dewdrops above her whisper. *I miss you, Pran.*

Pran suddenly felt deprived of the ability to protest when the loneliness that had long been burnt into oblivion surged inside him, in a heart that had once been empty. Had she never missed him over those many years since she had left everyone just like that? Have you ever, Charee, even once, missed me? The old buried feelings resurfaced like waves, flooding his insides, as a longing so profound he never knew he had it in him came barrelling down.

Like fingertips holding a diaphanous silk thread that flutters in the wind and slips away without a warning to be blown away forever, the beautiful melody gradually came to a sweet silence. Pran swallowed the bitter feeling and a million other emotions in his chest, and opened his eyes. Through the bruised mists of ylang-ylang he saw that the gypsy woman before him had fallen asleep. The light-purple drop-shaped earrings shone next to her eyes so that she looked like someone crying in her sleep. Uncle, the ginger cat, had moved next to his mistress and was also sleeping.

This was it. This was the picture of her he wanted to etch into his mind forever. He wanted to remember her like this: a wandering waif, asleep whilst crying amethyst tears, her faintly glowing hand placed over her heart, in a room filled with everything in the world, in the middle of a city ruined by dreams.

I miss you too, Charee.

She was still sleeping with her right hand on her heart when he left in the morning, a morning unlike any other morning he had ever known. No sooner had he flung the door open than the invisible garden from the previous night burst forth in the splendid sunshine. Before him was a profusion of flowers in bloom against a background of every shade of green that existed in the world. A large *pu-jormpol* tree stood aloft in the middle of the garden, spreading an opulence of pink flowers like festival fireworks. The twisted body of the *jik-nam* rained down star-shaped flowers. The garden was filled with trees: *faikham*, *lamduan*, *tabaek*, *asoke sapun*, *kalapruek*, *bunnag*, *intanin*, flame and Indian rubber sprouting new leaves, red and glossy. There was also *kankrao* and, further in, *mok* with a few other plants whose names he didn't know.

Closer to the ground were the bush plants: *puttarn*, *montha*, *nang yaem*, *kannikar,* dahlia, chrysanthemum, gardenias and Mon roses boasting their lush pink flowers here and there. And "Madame *Yeesoonsri*", as she had named her first Mon rose with that old-fashioned moniker and an honorific. An undergrowth of unnamed small flowers in violet, orange, pink and blue, clustered against vegetables and herbs. Various families of ferns huddled in the shadows, so dense they covered the stone pathway snaking along the alcoves before disappearing in a jungle of oddly shaped wild orchids and *krachao sidaa* with their dangling, beard-like roots grazing their neighbours.

Dizzied by the horticultural riches, as if he was progressing through the dream of a stranger, Pran stepped cautiously into the smothering fragrance of innumerable flowers condensed through morning dew. He proceeded slowly along the shapeless stone path in rays of dappled sunlight, which occasionally shot through the overhanging leaves like burning stars. Through a light breeze, past birds, butterflies, and insects buzzing, it took Pran several minutes to realise he was lost. It took him another long while of aimless wandering in that labyrinth of aromas before he found the front gate. The intoxicating feeling remained with him as he made his way back through the narrow lanes along which he had come with Chareeya the previous night.

Pran failed to notice that he had missed a turn, or maybe a few turns, or even more, and soon he found himself retracing his steps in an alleyway he remembered having just passed moments before. As he was about to ask for directions from an old man standing in front of a corner shophouse, he saw a "For Rent" sign behind him. Instead of asking the way out, he asked the old man about the rental. Trudging up a dimly lit four-storey building choked with the smell of the past and discarded objects, Pran emerged at a rooftop lodging, not too small but not especially big. The rent was cheap and the open space triggered his old penchant for the clay works he had been obsessed with at school. What appealed to him most, however, was that there was no one else in the building except Uncle Jang, the old landlord.

Maybe, he thought… Maybe. Not so far from the window through which he was looking, the enchanted garden basked in the jubilation of morning sunshine. The thought of those red star-shaped flowers suddenly provoked self-pity: he thought about the tiny flat in a rundown apartment block where he was staying, his room sandwiched between that of a couple who hurled insults at each other by day and made noisy love, like cats, by night, and that of a bald, obese salesman who went around promoting a wonderful invention that was an iron, an oven, a kettle, a hair dryer, a rat-repellant laser, a radio, as well as an alarm clock – all rolled into one. The salesman looked for even the slightest excuse to knock on Pran's door so he could brag about his sexual adventures, his irresistible charm, his opulent manhood and the prowess in carnal athleticism with which he tormented every woman and whore in the country.

And there was the woman in the flat across the hall who kept asking Pran to fix her television, though it was never broken, and who took every opportunity to gossip about their neighbours in the first flat to the last, up to the floor above and including many he didn't even know existed, before concluding with an homage to the fossils of her lost romance. *I was so in love with him, Pran*, the woman stressed the word "love" in every scene of every chapter of the romantic epic she narrated. Pran was certain he had listened to her story no fewer than one hundred times.

Then there were others who slammed doors, started commotions, spewed curses. There was the simultaneous screaming of the same soap opera blasted out from every television set in every flat, creating a surround-sound system of extravagant theatricality that spread its dominance endlessly. There was spoiled food left to rot on plates and in rubbish bags oozing sludge outside the doors. And there was the cold loneliness that wrapped around him like a spiderweb when he woke up each day.

Unlike Chalika who became a sworn reader of romance novels when she was barely ten, and unlike Chareeya who wanted to be something new every day – an explorer of ancient ruins along the Nakhon Chai Si River or the High Priestess of a newly invented feline cult, forgetting that the previous day she had committed herself to becoming a tap dancer after seeing one in an American film – unlike the two sisters, Pran had never really known what he wanted to be.

When he looked at himself again, he saw a long-haired guy in a crummy T-shirt and torn jeans who played bass in a four-piece indie band, usually to a small group of loyal fans that took turns watching them perform at a small rock bar called the Bleeding Heart. Yet that half-cooked adolescent dream had given him nothing but the unbearable weariness of having to repeat the same rock numbers over and over again and of watching his own bleeding heart crash, through melancholic cigarette smoke, into the depths of sticky sex – awkward, slow and soundless, like two Siamese fighting fish grappling each other in a bottle of glue.

It usually took nothing more than a casual acquaintance, some unreal coincidences, and the pale smiles of women who often hid half their faces in shadow. That was enough for Pran to surrender his heart at the end of a night. Some nights, he would let strangers he had never seen before lead him into bedrooms he had never been to before where he would perform the part of casual lover for one night, two at the most. Through the bodies of so many women he now realised, at the age of twenty-six, that the entwining of naked bodies and the coupling of hollow desire could only take him as far as not having to wake up alone on his own taut, unslept-in bed.

Many times one of those women would return the following night, and the following. Then, sooner or later: *Do you love me?* Pran would find himself at his wit's end trying to explain how desirable she was, how he felt privileged to have spent the night with her, and how he would never feel sad if he woke up seeing her face every morning for the rest of his life. But no, sorry, love was an entirely different story.

And the woman would chase him out of the room, so she could cry a little before going off to work. Pran would set out on some dark and narrow backstreet, picking up random sounds that escaped from shuttered doors: bad news from a television, someone sighing, an alarm clock screeching, wind whooshing along the alley, someone thrashing about in a dream. Sometimes he would hear the sound of another woman, in another room, crying a little before she went to work.

Until one day he woke up and decided not to let himself drift into another hopelessly sweet and thorny embrace ever again. He chose a regime of loneliness. Those women had a lot to cry about, and Pran gave up trying to explain the inexplicable. Everyone he loved had disappeared, all the family he had now lay in ruins. He didn't want to become attached to anyone that he would have to lose again. Let loneliness wrap around him like a shroud until the last days of his life. After all, it was just a bitter aftertaste in the mouth, just a stab of cold wind through the heart, just a *feeling*.

But at that moment and without warning, the sea of flowers swelled and wafted its gentle perfume. The ginger cat that had followed him out now took up a position in front of the house, and the woman was still asleep in the room that was filled with everything in the world, the room that was just a few steps away, the room that he could see from where he was.

That afternoon, Pran moved all his belongings and settled into the rooftop rental. He slept for a while, without dreaming, amid a faint aroma of Mon roses carried on the breeze from Chareeya's garden.

VI

The Emerald Spider

It must have been the year Mother died, or sometime later, not long after Chareeya decided to pursue the career of a great explorer and patrol the orchards – which by then belonged to the neighbours – to collect samples of rocks, minerals, archaeological relics, fossilised monsters and unclassifiable insects of the Nakhon Chai Si River, putting them in an empty jam jar slung around her neck with a plastic magnifying glass borrowed from Grandma Jerd next door, her expeditions beginning at dawn when the garden was still wet with dew… It must have been around that time that Chareeya found the spider in the pomelo tree.

The spider was the size of a match head, deep green like a jewel beetle. Its legs were an inch-and-a-half long, and its bum was lemon-yellow and flashed a strange sparkle. Chareeya tried to trap it in the jam jar but it bamboozled her by leaping from one pomelo tree to another, on and on, traversing the garden all morning, before plopping into the house in the late afternoon.

In Chareeya's mind she could see the National Explorer Award, so confident was the girl of the momentous entomological contribution she would be making through the discovery of this emerald arachnid with its diamond bum. For the very first time, the kingdom of insects would reveal its secrets in a spider with a jewel organ, and her finding would probably draw scholars from a thousand other disciplines to come and unearth the ancient city buried beneath the riverbanks, which might or might not be connected to the existence of this unusual species.

Confused by the tangle of her own imagination, Chareeya set out in hot pursuit of the spider. She leapt up the stairs two steps at a time, convinced that the insect would lead her to its mysterious lair, the secret entrance to which must be somewhere inside her own house. The girl ran, holding the jam jar, arm arched at a sixty-degree angle according to instructions she had read in a textbook. Once upstairs, her target sensed imminent danger and altered its course by suddenly making a big leap into the bathroom and bolting into a corner.

It was then that Chareeya caught sight of something unusual through the magnifying glass. The innermost wooden plank of the bathroom floor jutted out a quarter of a centimetre higher than the rest. She pried it open without much effort and found a narrow recess that didn't seem big enough to store anything. Yet there was something there: a blue tin box with pictures of a heart tied with a red ribbon and luscious-looking chocolates on its lid. She opened it. The box was packed with blank papers. Rummaging through them she found handwritten notes at the bottom, as well as a pen and a couple of envelopes.

Rosarin, Rosarin, Rosarin, I will keep calling your name in my heart. When I wake up in the morning I wonder if you're still asleep or if you're awake, if you're alone or if you're in someone's embrace. I wonder what you're doing, what you're eating, how you're sleeping.

My dear Rosarin, the worst thing about being so far from you is that I don't have any news about you (crossed out). *But the greater the distance between us, the clearer your image is in my head. In my mind you're even more beautiful, and the reality of my life becomes uglier by the day.*

I have no idea how I could have endured the passage of time had I not had the hope of returning to see you. I (crossed out)... *I miss you with every breath I take. The torment of not seeing you burns me like I am burning in hell. How long can we bear this? We* (crossed out)... *I will come and see you, dear Rosarin, no matter what happens. I will come to you, if not in life then in death.*

Chareeya flicked through a couple more letters addressed to this person called Rosarin without paying much attention and then put them back in the tin box. Next, she stuck her head into the recess, magnifying glass in hand, in a last-ditch effort to look for the Olympian-like vaulting spider. But she saw only darkness. She put the box back in its place, fitted the plank into the slot, and for the rest of her life never told a soul what she had found.

Lika, do you think there's an ancient city under the riverbanks? / What? / And strange insects living there too… / Strange? In what way strange? Chalika looked up from her book. *Strange like having a diamond bum / A diamond bum is too strange, I think / Right,* Chareeya pursed her lips: *But I saw it, Lika, I really saw it, just now, a spider with a sparkling diamond bum / Maybe, but how do you know if the diamond isn't actually the bug's eggs? / Diamond eggs? / Yes / Then there must be others like it and they're looking for a place to lay eggs in our garden, tens of thousands of diamond eggs, Lika!*

Nervously, greedily, and leaving her ten-year-old sister on the fuzzy threshold between reality and the dream of a novel she was reading, Chareeya got up and dashed into the garden to hunt for a clutch of tiny eggs that glittered in the dark. But the vaulting emerald spider had slipped through her hands and was never seen again.

That was one of Chareeya's final expeditions in her career as an entomologist though, for another year or so, she still abducted fireflies and tried to invent a bio-lamp, and she still collected wet garbage to feed her colony of baby shrimps. Months later, she channelled all her energy into tap dancing, utterly committed to following the example of a foreign woman she had seen on television, having decided that her true calling was to be a Broadway star. This sudden change of heart took place just days after her fateful dive into the riverbed in search of a lost city.

It was the hottest day in five hundred years. The crickets had been shrieking since noon and the blaze heated the river into a fine vapour that hung low like wintry mist. The heat tormented Chalika until she became fed up with the irredeemable naivety of a foreign-educated hero in the romance novel she was reading, making her wonder what kind of education they provided overseas and why those who went to all the trouble of going abroad returned even more gullible than when they had left.

But, all of a sudden, the insects closed their wings and went quiet. Chalika looked up at the *lampu* tree, its leaves had shrunk from the heat even though it was standing in water. Beads of sweat slowly trickled down her back. The soft breeze that had touched her skin a moment ago was also gone, leaving only the unruffled surface of the river, its sheen resembling a giant mirror that reflected a mass of black clouds overshadowing the blue patches of sky. Just like that, Chalika stood up and screamed. She screamed when she could no longer see her sister who had been swimming right there just a moment ago. She screamed when she saw the black clouds race across the sky, when the strangers from god-knows-where crowded along the bank, when the boy who had been fishing nearby ran to the river. She screamed and screamed a cacophony of unknown words until that boy plunged into the unruffled water.

To escape the heat that scalded the tip of her nose, Chareeya had lowered herself into the water in a leisurely manner. She had looked up and seen large and small bubbles racing out of her nostrils like silver constellations rising towards the sun and melting at the surface. At that moment, she had realised that the submerged ancient city must have been somewhere around there, storm-tossed and lying in ruins like Atlantis, which Uncle Thanit had told her about the other day. She spun around, squinted through the murky water, but couldn't see much except the shimmering, shapeless haze of sunlight filtered through the surface and illuminating a dead tree.

Two jellyfish bobbed past in slow motion. Chareeya thought they were like Chalika and herself, swept upstream from the ocean. She tried to signal to them: not that way, Charee-Lika, the ocean is the other way. But the jellyfish paid no heed and kept moving their transparent figures further up river. A bird was cawing from the shore, repeating a nebulous note. Four or five carp fish twisted and turned, their silver scales flashing rhythmically like Morse code.

Chareeya spun around again and scanned the aquatic surroundings for signs of the lost city, or a cluster of emerald spiders with diamond bums – maybe they were an amphibious species after all. She heard the humming of underwater currents, the strange bubbly sound of air escaping from her body, the pounding of her own heartbeat echoing in the water, and she saw something moving in the corner of her eye. It was a big manta ray. Chareeya stayed still, hoping it would swim closer so she could take a good look at it. But it went gliding in the other direction. A little further on she saw a boy waving his hands frantically and looking around in search of something. Please don't see me, Chareeya prayed. Closing her eyes, she held her breath and drifted weightlessly, disguising herself as a river weed.

Water engulfed Pran and shielded him from the earsplitting screams of the girl on the shore. Her yelling became vague, distant, as if it had been yanked back to the other end of the horizon. He waved his arms around and peered into the cloudiness, but he saw nothing except the shimmering, shapeless haze of sunlight filtered through the surface and illuminating a dead tree.

And then he saw something moving in the corner of his eye. It was a manta ray, and only when it glided past him did he see the river weed, floating at a peculiar angle between the sludgy riverbed and the surface. Pran fixed his eyes on it and realised it was a girl, her eyes closed, her limbs weightless, her skin emitting a strange halo, and her long wavy hair billowing upward like black flames. The boy swam towards her and for a moment he thought she had opened her eyes. It was in that instant that Pran remembered the only person in the world who had ever thought of adopting him as her brother. But when he approached, the girl's eyes remained shut. She was unconscious.

In her state as a river weed, Chareeya didn't see the boy approach. Only when he grabbed her from the back did she suddenly become so alarmed that, oblivious to the fact she was underwater, she shouted, *Leave me alo...* The rush of water shoved her voice back into her body. Chareeya choked, thrashed about, struggled, and Pran was so focused on bringing her to the surface that he didn't understand she was resisting him. Dazed and in a rage, Chareeya shouted again, *Leave me a...* And, again, the bubbles of words were silenced by water. She saw the two jellyfish, wriggling together in the shadows, further and further away. They were the last things she saw.

She was heavier than he had imagined. Pran felt as if it took him forever to heave her, with what little muscles and strength he had, up from the water and towards the gazebo. With his last drop of energy, he hauled her on his shoulder and started walking back and forth. He didn't know that he, too, was choking, didn't know that one of his legs was gripped by cramp, didn't know whether the water streaming down his face was river water or his own tears. And he didn't know why he was trembling in such heat, or where the fear that gripped his heart had come from.

But the world became calm when he heard her cough. Her body stirred lightly on his shoulder. Pran was gently putting her down when he saw that the elder sister had stopped screaming and was now sobbing nearby. The girl opened her eyes, trying to blink away the circles of rainbows that glistened on her eyelashes. Chareeya now stared at Pran's angular face, which was on the verge of leaving childhood, at his moving but soundless lips, at his penetrating eyes that betrayed a hint of melancholy.

She remembered and didn't remember that time she had wanted to bring home a boy she had met and adopt him as her brother. She remembered and didn't remember that Pran was that boy in the blue twilight who had appeared amidst the ruined petals of the flame tree flowers. She remembered and didn't remember that she had met him before, if not here in this life then somewhere else, in some other life.

The sky hung so low that it seemed as if an outstretched hand could touch it. Falling leaves, like yellow dots, left marks on the eddying black clouds above. The last rays of sunlight idly shone on part of Pran's face, and those penetrating eyes softened into the kind gaze of a father looking at his newborn for the first time.

It was like something she had planned a long time ago, and she made it sound as if it was the most natural thing to say: *It's about to rain, would you like to come to my house?* Chareeya whispered to him as a bright smile lit up her face.

And the little girl finally took the boy home.

VII

Four Orphans and the Tree of Dreams

All kinds of sounds found their way back into the house again. To begin with, Uncle Thanit played Satie's *Gymnopédies*, one number after another, basking the house in a soundscape so ethereal that the girls hardly perceived there was anything in the air. Once everyone, including Pran, developed the habit of sitting around in the living room to read or do their homework, Uncle Thanit decided it was time to guide the children into the world of music.

He switched to more accessible compositions such as Beethoven's Spring Sonata and Borodin's String Quartet No.2, in which a few instruments created a sound so sweet that the gardenias suddenly blossomed and Chalika, who still couldn't understand why a tornado was generated around her every time she saw the military cadet who lived three doors down, was compelled to bite her lips and stifle a cry.

Then came a lesson in the music of overwhelming passion: the tremors that shook the heart in Brahms's Symphony No.4, a piece that drove Chareeya to dig manically for the Dvaravati beads again only to find a lost earthworm in the dark pit; or those desolate Nocturnes by Chopin; or the funereal dirge for the heart that dies whilst looking for love in the second movement of Beethoven's Symphony No.7, which infected the children with inexplicable gloom; or the brokenhearted melody of Rachmaninoff's Piano Concerto No.2, which from its first movement left a bittersweet aftertaste in the mouth, like raw tamarind, that took days to disappear.

For years, the house was held together by the tender anguish of Romantic music. They slowly inched their way to the fanciful imagery of Debussy's "Clair de Lune", which forever changed the way they perceived the magic of moonlight. And there was the post-First World War desolation of Elgar's Cello Concerto, a melodic portrait of death that was more beautiful than life itself. A year later they arrived in the early 20th century with Janáček's *In the Mists*, which bemoans the grief of a father who lost his daughter with the outpouring of a million emotions, to Dutilleux's *The Tree of Dreams* through which complex layers of sorrow became mixed up with objects in the house and compelled the children to wander restlessly and forget their homework.

Along the way they also heard the passionate lamentations of countless operas with a succession of heroines who kept killing themselves in screaming fits at the end of every final act. They also heard the hot breath of Piazzolla's tango, and occasionally the acidic jazz of Miles Davis.

Not only was Uncle Thanit a connoisseur of classical music with deep insights in the art, he was also an animated, soulful and well-rounded storyteller with a large repertoire of stories that he shared with the children in his smooth and engaging voice. Sometimes the story itself wasn't interesting, but the way he told it made the children beg him to repeat it again and again. Some stories they heard only once, and yet they were etched into them well into adulthood.

He told them factoids about certain movements of certain compositions, stories from operas; tragedies with climaxes triggered by banal fate, triangulated romance, misunderstanding or images derived from divination. He told them how great music was conceived not out of the imagination but out of the composer's despair and decrepitude: of Beethoven's secret love, documented in the single letter he wrote to a woman whose identity remains a secret, though his desire was revealed in all its nakedness in hundreds and thousands of melodies fraught with agony and disquiet, or of the solitude that devoured Chopin's soul until there was nothing left of him except his two hands, which had to be severed from his body after he died so that his sister could smuggle them back to his mother. He told them about Mozart's Requiem, a paean for the soul written with such unwavering belief that it could prove the existence of God, and how it was performed at the funerals of kings and dignitaries but not at the composer's own because he had died a pauper and was buried without even a gravestone.

There were fantastic stories unrelated to music: a library so enormous that it contained all knowledge of the past, present and even the future, and how it had been burned to ashes by a drunkard, leaving humanity in a pit of stupidity forever after; a desert made of fine diamond dust that rippled like waves in the wind; a man whose body was covered in warts, who looked like an ancient tree, and who had to keep walking through all eternity because if he stopped, his feet would grow roots and he really would become a tree.

And the great white snake that made its way alone through the galaxy and was often spotted by astronauts; the twin stars that roved aimlessly around the universe before their trajectories brought them together for a day every year, so they could flicker pale light at each other before drifting apart again; the savagery of the Crusades; the Vedas; dark matter; the Rosetta Stone and its missing piece; solar storms; invisible particles; the balance of the imbalance of power; Zoroastrianism; black holes; and civilisations reduced to legends.

And other stories: an old lady that went around collecting the shadows of dead people who didn't know who they were or what to do next and cast them in a play so they could have half of their lives back; the story of a tomcat who never cried but every time it died, each of its owners wept and sobbed, until one day the cat fell in love with a she-cat and when she died the cat cried for the first time and then died for the last time, without ever being reborn again; and, finally, the story of a bizarre tribe of humans who fed on a preternaturally sweet lotus that made them forget the bitterness of life and refuse to return home to their loved ones. Many years later, when Pran had grown up, that last tale was still the one he could never forget.

A magical world slowly took shape, its translucent outline becoming clearer and clearer, between the intervals of each song. When the music resumed, Chareeya's real world and imaginary world vanished, leaving her motionless, eyes shut, as she took in every note with every atom of her body, and it was impossible to tell if it was she that was rapaciously consuming the melodies or if it was the music that was eating her alive. Meanwhile, Chalika read her novels and did her chores, and Pran stared blankly into space, just letting the sounds enter him and leave as they wished.

Since that afternoon when Chareeya had brought him home to avoid the rain, Pran had become a regular guest at the house. Later, when Uncle Thanit started his pesticide-free vegetable garden by the river and asked the boy to help so he could earn some money, Pran dropped by every day after school and even on the weekends. He rode his bicycle to pick up the sisters from school, with Chareeya riding pillion while Chalika was next to them on her own bike, and he became their personal bodyguard against the menace of stray dogs and boys from the other side of town who were drawn by the reputation of Chalika's beauty and who hid in the shade stealing dreamy looks at her. Along the way, Pran picked flowers for the girls to put in a vase on the dining table.

As soon as they arrived, Pran would start working in the garden: pruning, watering, weeding, mixing manure, spraying biopesticides, and wrapping sheets of newspaper around young shoots to protect them from worms. When he finished he would come inside the house to listen to music he'd never heard before, do his homework, repair broken household appliances, and help Chareeya with her art projects or even her embroidery. He would stay until dinner, which was cooked by Nual the nanny after Aunt Phong quit to become a lottery vendor in Bangkok – Nual, who by then was the mother of two children and still had three men sharing fatherhood, each taking turns to visit and contribute to child support.

VIII

The Universe on the Wall

Once a month the four orphans squeezed into Uncle Thanit's beaten up pickup truck and headed to Bangkok. They shopped for books and records, watched a movie if the programme caught their interest, or, on rare occasions when they got lucky, attended a concert or ballet performed by visiting foreign artists. Or else they would drop in at the few galleries in town, or wander around admiring the splendour of the temples that dotted the streets of Bangkok.

Chareeya's favourite attraction was the giant mural at Suthat temple. She would pester Uncle Thanit to take her there when the group had run out of ideas as to what to do next. In the afternoon, when the prayer hall was empty, Chareeya would lie down, her feet pointing towards the wall, a position that allowed her to take in the entire mural at a wide angle without getting a stiff neck. Sometimes, in a moment of strange premonition, Pran would lie down next to her, in silence, and together the two children set out on a voyage into an exhilarating universe that no one else knew existed or had ever heard its sound; an alternate universe that rolled out in swift succession across the temple's wall, through eternity.

As if in endless replay before their eyes, a giant blue-coloured whale launched itself from the water's surface and crashed down on a European junk next to a flock of *kinnarii* swimming languorously amidst an effulgent sea of stars. Above a window, Jatayu – half-

garuda, half-eagle – woke from his slumber, flapped his wings twice in preparation then stretched them, magnificently, full span, and fluttered across the prayer hall to the Himaphan Forest.* Sometimes, if they were lucky, the children would spot the golden deer Marica ambling about in the bushes. And, once, they bore witness to a sacred manifestation when Lord Buddha opened his eyes under the Great Bodhi Tree as he attained enlightenment.

Basking in the jingling of the brass bells hung from the eaves, Chareeya and Pran would sometimes hear the whispers of little novice monks trying to placate the howling of ravenous ghouls, stuck in hell for centuries, or be terrified by the hissing of the *naga*, breathing fire as it swam atop the roaring waves of the Great Ocean, or hear the growling of the great lion Singhakunchorn. Sometimes, if they listened carefully, they could hear the harp song of the celestial *ghandarva* serenading the *apsara* in heaven.

Sore from sitting too long, Uncle Thanit and Chalika would lie down with Chareeya and Pran. One time, a pale Norwegian tourist walked in on the four orphans lying in the middle of the prayer hall and snapped their picture, to be taken home and shown to his family. Years later, when she was an adult, Chareeya would imagine the image of her family lying next to each other at the edge of the Himaphan Forest in the album of a stranger who lived somewhere distant and cold.

The excursions to the capital concluded with dinner: a European, Thai, Chinese, Japanese, Indian or Middle-Eastern restaurant; or a sampling of neighbouring Burmese, Lao or Cambodian cuisines; a vegetarian meal during the Vegetarian Festival; turkey and stollen bread at Christmas; as well as the occasional spiritual meal in accordance with macrobiotic principles.

Food is mindfulness and spirituality. It tells stories that aren't just about human life. When you encounter a new kind of food, try it.

* In Buddhist cosmology the Himaphan Forest exists on the slopes of Mount Meru, the axis of the universe, and is home to mythical creatures that include the *kinnarii* (half-bird, half-human), the *garuda* (king of birds and mount of the Hindu god, Vishnu), the deer Marica (a powerful ogre who disguises himself as a golden deer), and the *naga* (giant serpent). The *apsara* (female celestial beings) and the *ghandarva* (their companions and heavenly musicians) reside in the heavens above.

If you like it, have more. If not, give it a rest. But when you have a chance, try it again, and soon you'll learn to enjoy it, Uncle Thanit told the children as they experimented with snails, jellyfish, sashimi, fermented shrimps, sea urchins, silkworms, stinky *natto* beans, live oysters, stringy seaweed. To Chareeya, Uncle Thanit had the most curious mind when it came to exotic culinary culture, unrivalled by anyone she would meet later in her life, except herself, since she had caught the epicurean bug from him.

Chareeya slowly cut back on her adventures in the neighbourhood wilderness. Instead, she spent more and more time listening to music, which took up hours every day. She beseeched Pran to take her to buy a miniature fountain with a frowning swan as the centrepiece. She grew pygmy roses in a rainbow of colours in a pocket garden in front of the house. She learned to play the violin with Uncle Thanit and assisted Nual in the kitchen, where she discovered her unique talent: Chareeya could instinctively identify the ingredients of any dish in their exact measures and was able to emulate its flavour after just one taste.

Chalika, meanwhile, grew more silent as her beauty grew more intriguing and this was the cause of Pran's constant scuffles with unruly teenagers from the other side of town. The second-hand bookstore she found during one of the Bangkok trips was a treasure trove of old novels and she kept to herself even more, spending hours reading into the night. Still, she had time to emerge from her solitude to bake cakes made from local fruits (santol, zalacca, pomelo, mango, bael, or even mouse-shit chilli), using just a small, basic oven. And, like Chareeya, she had a knack for it. She knew the right moment to take the cake out of the oven without having to time it, and it would be just perfect; not one second too soon or too late. Also, she still had a secret crush on the military cadet who lived down the street.

Pran, who was the same age as Chalika, had by that time started painting, teaching himself by copying pictures from imported books he found at second-hand stalls. He didn't know if it was his calling, but at least images gave him a substitute for his verbal indigence. Not only did he hardly speak, but Pran's footsteps were also soundless, and so mute was his presence that Chareeya thought of hanging a cat's bell around his neck to signal his approach so they wouldn't have to endure mutual shocks when he appeared suddenly behind her. But, in actuality, Chareeya always knew when Pran was within a ten-metre radius; in the same way that laundry hung on a line to dry outside retains that halo of balmy sunlight, she could sense an ethereal, tender aura, invisible but perceptible, almost like a fragrance pasteurised in the air.

Slowly, Pran transformed from a boy into a man. It happened without anyone in the living room and the vegetable garden by the river even noticing. Lanky, awkward, his face all ridges and squares, his mouth curved. The only feature that remained unchanged was the harsh, penetrating gaze he had inherited from his great-great-great-great-grandfather, a rebel who had been executed and whose name was erased from the family tree. No one ever told him about that great-great-great-great-grandfather. In fact, no one ever told Pran anything about his ancestors or anything about his genealogical past.

Then, there was the day when Uncle Thanit walked past a crummy antique shop and didn't realise that his fate was sealed from the moment he turned and saw the shop owner unfurl a roll of ancient silk on a table. As soon as the light from a corner lamp illuminated its hem and the gold damask lit up as if in a dance of flames, Uncle Thanit had no faculty to shield himself from the irresistible seduction of the ancient fabric; it was a temptation that he barely understood and that would lead him on countless more journeys. But that would come much later.

Until the last day of his life, under the glow of the moon on the other side of the earth, Uncle Thanit would still remember these happy days at the house by the river, days of bliss that would have lasted forever had a certain man not arrived.

Her palms didn't become clammy, her heartbeat didn't quicken, and there was no tornado whirling around her as had happened with Chalika. There was just a conviction, profound and silent; the conviction that no matter what happened, regardless of where he went, she would follow him. It was as simple as that when love found Chareeya.

Thana was from Bangkok, a cousin of Earn, Chareeya's close friend. He was one of the democracy activists who had survived the violent crackdown, fled into the jungle and later returned. She overheard him speak to a neighbour with a vigour that she'd never heard in anyone before, about subjects she'd never heard from anyone before; social oppression, injustice, feudal capitalists who trampled on the poor, and the struggle for rights and freedom.

The massacre of 6 October* was twelve years past and its memory had begun to fade. People were no longer even sure if it had actually happened. Besides, Nakhon Chai Si was a rich town that had known no hardship so the issues Thana raised were misunderstood or completely ignored. But his lonesome eyes, hair grazing his shoulders, the Che Guevara beret, and his passion for justice attracted her.

The third time they met, Thana talked to her about youth power, the dream of a land where everyone was equal, about the high mountains and his noontime treks through the clouds. The next time, he sang her the anthem of the Left, "Starlight of Faith": *The sparkling tiny stars lit up the skies as far as the eyes could see...* His head coyly lowered, his voice croaky, and still Chareeya thought it was the most beautiful song in the world. And it was. That night, the memory of her skin glowing in the late afternoon deprived him of the calm of sleep and almost drove him into a fit of tears over an unfathomable longing he had never felt before.

For no obvious reason, Chareeya began waking up when the sky was still dark. Everything was peaceful, except for the fluttering in her stomach when she saw Thana's face without opening her eyes. While everyone else in the house was still asleep, Chareeya would lie down on the sofa, her right hand on her heart, and put Brahms's Symphony No.4 on repeat, before getting dressed for school. On their eleventh date, when Thana told her he was moving back to Bangkok, Chareeya, with the same fierce conviction her mother had, got up and ran away with him.

* On 6 October 1976, government forces and a right-wing mob attacked student protestors at Thammasat University in Bangkok; though the official death toll was 46, survivors believe it was much higher.

Her mind is set, what's the use? He wasn't the expressive type, but everyone knew how distraught Uncle Thanit was, and how much strength he had to muster in letting Chareeya go her own way. Chalika wailed and sobbed and blamed herself for spending all her time reading novels and failing to notice her sister's furtive romance. Meanwhile, Pran said not a word. The tumult in his young blood told him that the day he ran into that man would be the day he committed murder.

Three months later, Chareeya called and then she kept calling every couple of weeks to tell everyone she was fine. But she never said where she was or showed any sign of wanting to see anyone. Not long after that, she got a job at a CD shop on Silom Road. She was just sixteen years old but her knowledge of classical music impressed the shop owner. Working there also guaranteed her an endless supply of music.

Go on, enjoy the feudal music, climb the ladder and pretend you really enjoy it. You don't realise, do you, that the toffs look at you and see a country bumpkin! Thana shouted at her. *What toffs? What's that got to do with anything? Music is music and I like this kind of music / Don't play it around here, it riles me.*

The couple didn't listen to music together. Neither did they go to the cinema and nor did they eat together. They didn't even have conversations with each other. Each morning, Chareeya got up and went to work, and later she came back to her boxy flat and listened to music written centuries ago to soothe the *haute bourgeoisie*. For his part, Thana spent time with his friends at labour union meetings, unable not to feel embarrassed by his unintellectual girlfriend. The only activity they still shared was sleeping together and Chareeya continued to long for the carnal epiphany she had once read about in books even though what she actually experienced was mild pain, a suffocating clasp, being pushed around the bed, and the heavy panting of a locomotive hurtling into the dark.

After watching a French film at the store where she worked, Chareeya thought the opening song was the most beautiful song in the world. It also contained another piece of music, an aria from *La*

Wally, from the scene in which a woman sang a mournful farewell to her sleeping father and eloped with her star-crossed lover into the snowy mountains where no one had ever ventured or returned from so that they could spend the brief remaining moments of their lives together. The film told the story of a young postman who fell in love with an opera singer and the characters spoke in singsong melodies like musical instruments, so captivating that Chareeya decided to take a French language class after work to cure her loneliness and compensate for her lack of education.

What nerve, to learn that imperialist language / It's the language of the first revolutionaries / What do you know about revolutions? You're so dense, your mind has been enslaved by white feudalists – you know nothing about anything.

It was true. Chareeya knew nothing more about the French Revolution than what she had heard from Uncle Thanit's synopsis of the musical *Les Misérables*, which was truncated from a novel based on slices of a real account. She knew nothing about mental enslavement, or about white feudalists. She had never read Marx or Gorky or studied the critical theory of materialism. She had no understanding of those convoluted terms printed on the covers of the books Thana was always reading. In fact, she understood nothing except that she loved a man. Less than a year later, Thana broke up with her and left behind a scribbled letter with only a few words: *You stood between me and the people.*

For the rest of his life – either when he had a great mass of people beside him as they dodged bullets on the streets four years later in the Black May democracy uprising*, during which he was shot in the leg and left lurching ever since, or ten years later when he abandoned his people to become a right-wing politician and eventually threw his weight behind another violent crackdown against democracy protestors who had taken to the streets – Thana would never meet anyone who loved him with such purity, untarnished by any ideology,

* The large-scale protest in May 1992 triggered by the appointment of a military general as Prime Minister is remembered as "Black May" after a government crackdown resulted in an official death toll of 52; as was the case in 1976, many more were reported missing.

IX

Starlight River

The following Friday, and every Friday after that, Chareeya and her friends returned to the Bleeding Heart to clink tequila glasses, laugh for no reason, sometimes whisper into each other's ears in the dim light and stroke a girlfriend's shoulders and back as she cried – the same melodrama that played out on repeat at any bar anywhere in the world. Then the girls would implore Pran to play the same corny, schmaltzy songs – *Without You, I Will Survive*, or anything else along those lines – so whoever's turn it was to cry could cry even harder and infect the rest of the gang with blotchy eyed sentimentalism. But, whether they were laughing or crying, her friends always left Chareeya at the door so that Pran could walk her home every time.

On the drizzly second Friday of that year, Chareeya didn't let Pran return to his room in the rain, and brought out a blanket and pillows for him to sleep with the cat in the room that was filled with everything in the world. But before the clock struck three, she got up and made him sangria as sublime as the kind served at temple fairs. She served apple slices and chilled cheese as snacks, and when they got pleasantly groggy they saluted life by shouting above the rain, Frida's last phrase emblazoned on the wall – *Viva la vida! Long live life!* – whilst playing music that had journeyed across time from the house by the river. They ended up talking until dawn.

Stories, old stories of days gone by: about the fountain with the moody swan statue that Pran had spent months looking for because he couldn't find one in a colour she liked so had ended up buying one in bare concrete, which turned out to be much more attractive; about the *Loy Krathong* ceremony* in which Chareeya put *lampu* seeds in a floating basket in the hopes that the Goddess Ganga would bear them across the oceans to the faraway Pacific islands, but it barely made it past the gazebo before capsizing and Chareeya entreated Pran to make her another one. He succumbed to her pleas and defied the darkness of the banana grove to cut a fresh shoot when Chareeya promised to place only her bad karma in the vessel, even though she ended up smuggling a few *lampu* seeds in anyway.

The never-ending stories of the Himaphan Forest on the wall and the extra ring around Saturn at the Planetarium, which no one else saw except them. And there was the time when Chareeya became obsessed with assassinating Pran using ripe ivy gourds as bullets so that she could later transform from sniper to field nurse and rush to bandage his wounds. Or the time when she hid in a corner and ambushed him from behind before rolling on the ground, eyes gleaming and laughing uncontrollably as if it was the funniest thing on earth.

Stories about what happened during the time that had gone missing between them: Chareeya going so far as to shear off most of her hair so she would get the role of a Vietnamese boy in a foreign movie being filmed in Kanchanaburi, only to appear for a fraction of a second on the screen; Pran getting high on weed, alternately breaking down in fits of laughter and tears, and slamming his fists against the floor until dawn; the sad story of Uncle Yellow the cat; the three Witches and their complicated love sagas; and Pran's friend, Paradorn.

Stories about how Uncle Thanit liked to put on a wedding ring though no one was sure which of his marriages it had come from,

* *Loy Krathong* is an annual Thai festival in which people float baskets constructed on a base cut from the stalks of banana trees (or, in the modern era, styrofoam) to pay respects to the river goddess, Ganga, and to float away any sins or transgessions of the past year.

and how he would fall silent for days after receiving a postcard with a short note in Japanese; Chalika and the military cadet to whom she never uttered a word and who only came home once in a long while; and Chalika's secret habit of rereading Rose Laren's novel *Shadow*, and how she still cried in anticipation before one of the characters died on the page.

Stories about Grandpa Nong who lived around a bend in the river and was so madly in love with his own daughter that he tied his hands and feet together and plunged to his death in the river on the day his daughter ran away with an outdoor cinema projectionist; how Grandpa Nong returned at midnight, his feet and hands still tied, dripping wet, his body transparent in the beam of a flashlight, to sit crying beneath the sugar palm tree behind his house; and how Chareeya had been compelled to drag Pran out not once but twice to verify the mystery of Grandpa Nong's spectral presence, though they didn't find anything but a grey dust, like ash, covering everything inside his house, untouched since the day he died.

Stories about Uncle Poj, the son of Grandma Jerd from next door, who had never shown any feminine proclivities until the day his mother died when he suddenly turned into a drag queen, and yet the longing to see his dead mother was so strong that he put on the clothes she had worn when she was a young woman and cried his heart out at her funeral until his eyeliner melted into rivulets of tears, alarming the neighbours who couldn't wrap their heads around Uncle Poj's transformation and assumed that he was possessed by the ghost of his own mother – a perfect opportunity for them to ask for lucky lottery numbers.

They talked until it was light and Pran asked Chareeya to play Opus 47, and fell asleep listening to Schumann's longing. When he woke up, Chareeya had made him hot chicken soup, which he ate in the midst of bright sunlight and blossoming flowers. Then Chareeya took him to see the garden still dripping with last night's rain. *Aunt Srimala*, she pointed at a strange fiery red flower. *In Spanish its name means desire – Carmen called it her lucky flower / Which Carmen?* Pran didn't follow. *Carmen of the opera*. Pran smiled, lifting the red flower to sniff. *It doesn't have a scent, Pran.* She ran inside and returned with a box, into which she proceeded to stuff Madame *Yeesoonsri* and Miss *Pheep*, telling him to take it back to his room so he could smell their lingering fragrance when he woke up again that evening. Pran had told her he'd rented a room not far from where she lived, but he didn't have the courage to tell her that it was actually so close he could already smell her flowers.

He didn't have the courage to tell her that every night after he went back to the small room, which she could glimpse from afar, he would read, listen to music, tinker with a jigsaw puzzle of the Andromeda Galaxy, or do nothing but stare at the ceiling in silence until the first light crept into the room and illuminated the faint outline of everything. Then he would get up and sit by the window to look at her garden slowly emerging in the morning light, the garden surrounded by dusty old buildings, like an oasis in the desert.

And every day, in moments that could barely be differentiated, he would watch as she came out of the house, tousled, half-awake, cup of coffee in hand, to sit on the wrought-iron chair, the cat having scurried ahead through her legs to wait for his mistress. Then he would smile at her, *Hi Charee...* Sometimes he heard her reply in his head – *Hi Pran* – though he knew she neither heard him nor was even aware of him watching as she picked up the cat to cuddle and whisper something in its ear, rubbing her nose against its wet nostrils, before it touched her cheek with its paw, just sometimes, which would make her laugh, close her eyes and tighten her embrace until it meowed and then she would release it back to the ground as it stretched and sniffed the air, rubbing its body against the trees or pouncing on some unfortunate creature crossing its path, and leaving Chareeya to sit in languor and listen to the wind rustling the foliage, thinking or dreaming about something; a movie she had just seen, a poem, or a melody.

In those instances, though he never told her, Pran saw her in a way he had never seen her before or would ever see her since. He saw her through the soundless movements as in a silent film, through the luminous angles of sunshine that shifted by tiny degrees with every passing day, through the opening petals and withering buds, through the seasons hidden in each of the leaves and the fragrant perfume, through dewdrops from the old days and the tranquil mornings that ended when she finished her coffee and walked barefoot to greet each of her plants until she disappeared into their midst. That was when Pran would get up, stretch and go to sleep. *See you Charee.*

Are you still sleepy? You only had a brief nap / No, but it's almost noon, do you have to go to work? / In the afternoon… I don't have much to do, just check the books. I have an assistant to look after the store / Are you making enough? / It's enough, I still have my cut from the rent and I work as a guide for French tourists sometimes, an easy job for easy money – I can always take them to Suthat temple. She smiles, *Do you remember? We used to go there when we were children.* Suddenly Pran felt the way people do when they realise they have lost something dear to them, a cold snap froze his heart when he remembered that he had once known happy days, happy days that were long past.

Let's go home, Pran. I miss Lika, and I miss the river. The limpid, slow-flowing river, the wild cane grass in wintry radiance, the transparent mist hanging above the water's surface, the raft of hyacinth and the pungent scent of its flowers, the smoke from an unseen fire mingling with the twilight aroma of the river – an aroma unlike any other he'd ever known. As if air bubbles were escaping his body, the memory of the river returned like a breath he had forgotten to take. Never before had Pran realised that he could miss the river this much.

But they didn't return to the house by the river, even after they had made the pledge before the fiery red flower called Desire. Instead, a couple days later, Pran and Chareeya visited Suthat temple to lie down in the sparsely frequented prayer hall and watch the whale crash onto the European junk. This time, the elusive deer, Marica, appeared in full splendour but the novice monks who had tried to appease the ravenous ghouls now roamed about freely, climbing the masts of the Chinese junks, riding on the back of the fire-breathing *naga* as it crossed the Great Ocean, mocking the pose of the reclining Buddha next to the monkeys smoking a bong, and even playing hide-and-seek behind the Great Bodhi Tree where the Lord Buddha attained enlightenment.

And, though they didn't catch sight of Jatayu fluttering across the hall, they still heard the thunderous roar of Singhakunchorn, only to discover that the noise actually came from an old monk who looked like Yoda from *Star Wars* and who, having mistaken them for foreign tourists tried to shoo them away: *Go, you! No sleep in temple, shoo! No sleep in temple!* Chareeya and Pran scrambled up and it dawned on them that the old days were indeed long gone and that they were no longer children.

The announcement of the lottery results had just been made and the city, which moments before had been wrapped in the silence of anticipation, returned to its usual energetic bustle. Chareeya led Pran against the flow of a crowd with huge amounts of adrenaline surging through its veins and they made their way to Khao San Road to buy a dry Chilean wine from a store hidden in a rundown alley. With a smile on her face, Chareeya marched forward and ignored Pran, who trailed behind and allowed himself to be lost, twice, by the distant memory of the most beautiful woman in the world.

Evening came and burnished the sky when Chareeya and Pran arrived at a small pier. Long abandoned, it was a rare peaceful spot in the busy river traffic of the Chao Phraya. *Do you remember the Kreutzer Sonata? / Whose? / Beethoven's.* Pran vaguely recalled a violin wrenching drama from its very first notes. *It was a popular piece of music – how could you forget it?* Chareeya protested and continued: *Eighty years later, Tolstoy heard it and it moved him so much that he wrote a story called "The Kreutzer Sonata", like the music.* She paused for a moment.

A man became jealous of his wife, a pianist, after seeing her play the Kreutzer Sonata with another violinist. The husband ended up killing her. Pran let out a sigh – he wasn't a man of emotional depth, but death always got to him. *It was a story about a game, the game of love. And about music… How shall I put it? Music so heart-rending that it can inspire any kind of action.* Pran nodded. He remembered Uncle Thanit's story about Beethoven's painful romance and the letter the composer addressed to the "Immortal Beloved", and that tumultuous music rang in his head.

The river traffic became calmer and flickers of light appeared along the banks. Chareeya handed Pran a white plastic cup. At that moment, as he looked down at the sad, slim fingers wound around the cup, his eyes caught a trace of lychee-coloured lipstick stamped on the cup's rim and he closed his eyes without knowing why. He felt like bubbles were bursting inside his body.

Thirty years later Janáček read the novel and was inspired to compose a string quartet. He called it "Kreutzer Sonata", like the book / Janáček? / Leoš Janáček, a Czech, early 20th century – we have his vinyl records at the river house, you must've heard some of them. Pran took the cup, seeing light reflected in her eyes. *Think about it, the agony had passed down from Beethoven to Tolstoy, from Tolstoy to Janáček – one hundred and twenty years between them / Right, now I want to hear it. Kreutzer, right?* Chareeya nodded. *So beautiful, both Janáček's and Beethoven's. I'll play them for you. You'll like them.* She turned and smiled, so bright and cheerful, just as he'd always remembered her.

Pran strained to recall the melody of the composition so iconic that it would have been impossible for him to have missed hearing it in the living room of that house. But as much as he tried, all that came to him was the first note: the raspy, dramatic sawing of a violin. *Don't you think music is like a diary? It records feelings that might have been lost in time.* The river wind ruffled her hair. *Schumann's Opus 47… A love letter.*

As if by reflex he looked down at the trace of lipstick on the cup. *The love letter Schumann wrote to his forbidden lover. Well, when he fell in love with Clara she was just nine years old.* She turned and smiled again. Pran raised his eyebrows slightly, surprised, as the shadow of a frizzy haired girl running through vegetable patches flashed through his mind and disappeared. *And Clara's father, who was Schumann's teacher, wanted his daughter to become a pianist so he stopped them from seeing each other.* The pier bobbed gently with the currents. *Back then a composer would publish his scores, like we have records today, and during the ten years they were forbidden from seeing each other Schumann wrote songs and published them. Clara read them at the store, like reading love letters – the notes were the alphabet.*

That explained why it was so poignant and bittersweet, its warmth laced with melancholia. *Did they live together in the end? / Yes, when*

Clara turned twenty and didn't need her parents' consent, she married Schumann. They lived together for a few years before he was sent to a mental asylum and died there. Pran couldn't suppress a sigh. *They say in his last days, Schumann went into a frenzy of composing. When he ran out of paper he tore down a curtain and scribbled on it until he had covered its entire surface. No one kept that music. It must be very special, don't you think?*

Pran didn't reply. The bubbles continued to burst inside his body as Schumann's Opus 47 wafted through his heart. This time it brought an overwhelming sadness as he turned the cup in his hands, deliberately, until the lipstick mark was facing him and, when he bent down and pressed his lips to the faded pink mark, he hardly knew what he was doing. He felt a longing so deep he didn't know he had it in him; it flooded over him, enveloping him tenderly and yet feverishly, and there was an ache somewhere deep inside his body as his lips closed around the rim of the cup and the clear liquid left a trail of heat from his mouth to his heart, which was still beating. Pran had to close his eyes again without understanding why.

When he opened them, he saw Chareeya staring absent-mindedly at the river. The lights were reflected in the water like stars and formed a backdrop for her hair, which was tussled and tangled by the wind, and appeared to be floating out onto the water. Pran looked at her profile without saying anything, and then he was reminded of another woman.

She was plain-looking, ordinary to a fault. Every morning, when he was still in college he saw her at the bus stop gazing up at the sky. He never thought to say hello, or to follow her onto the bus, because it never occurred to him to find out who she was, what she did, where she lived, where she came from, or where she was going. He was content to watch her, just like that; her back straight, one hand lightly touching the strap of the bag slung across her chest like someone taking an oath, her face slightly tilted as she looked up at the pale sky of the city where dreams are broken.

He had wanted her to be there every morning so that he could watch her; nothing more, nothing less. And then she had vanished.

He had waited, but she never returned. And Pran had no longer wanted to go to college or look up at the pale morning sky. He had felt like there was a rock weighing him down inside, but soon the rock disappeared, too, leaving only a hole where it had been; a hole inside a hole, inside a hole.

The Chilean wine kept him in a dreamy lull all night. When he was playing on stage, he felt the groovy sway of the pier that, a few hours earlier, had been rocking him gently by the Chao Phraya, bobbing playfully to the rhythm of the wind and waves against the shimmering, starry river. He felt it in the song of sorrow he played, in the irregular heartbeat of that moment in which he had swallowed the unintentional remnant of her kiss.

Flicking some bass notes from his fingers, he watched his own heart sink into a void as he thought back to Schumann's love letter and the empty abyss inside him; the abyss within the abyss, dug out from the core of his heart.

X

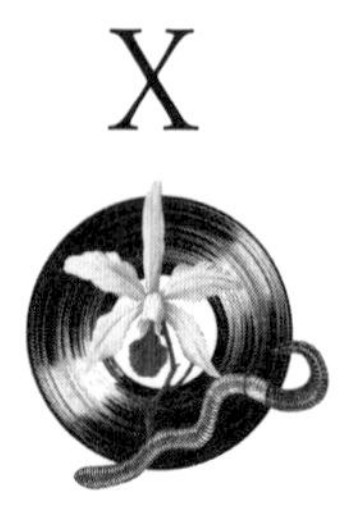

The Colony of Ants and the Laughing Crow

When he woke up that morning, Natee thought he smelled the distant scent of rain. Even when he sat down on the balcony with a cup of coffee, he still assumed it had been raining all night. It was only when he looked at the tin-coloured sky and the dry, smoggy city below that he remembered the monsoon was still a few months away. Yet, for quite some time afterwards, he couldn't locate the source of the mournful feeling that rose in him along with the illusory scent of rain.

Natee knew longing coloured by sadness and fear but he couldn't recall the last time he had felt it. He couldn't remember his other lives and could only remember the life he had now: waking up every day at six in the morning, making coffee and sitting down to look at a city he had never loved, seeing all those lives he would never know, then getting dressed and walking half a block to the video store he owned, and staying there until nightfall. In a way, he was happy. He had a wife, a job, a house, a simple life and no worries. When he wanted to feel something that would confirm his existence, he watched a movie; something he had already seen so that he could laugh at a joke he had already laughed at, cry at a scene that had already made him cry, or feel moved in a way that he rarely felt moved these days.

Suddenly, and without warning, his heart was seized by a rush of unfamiliar pain so excruciating that his body twisted and he doubled over his lap. It was a while before the pain eased up, and then he realized that it was actually spreading through his body, like a crack travelling across his chest inch by inch and gradually splitting his back apart. Natee drew a deep breath. He tried to sit upright but the pain returned, though this time he couldn't tell where it was located.

Pim, he called his wife, but no sound came out of him. Natee remembered she had just told him she was going downstairs to give alms to the monks. The pain stabbed through him again, a wave more intense than the last, as if something was grinding his heart to a pulp. Never before had he known the true feeling of chest pain; no wonder he was shedding so many tears. He mustered all his remaining strength and called his wife Pimpaka again, but the sound he made was just a croak. He tried to draw another deep breath only to find that the pain was so dense there was no space left in his body for air.

Smothered by agony, Natee struggled to sit up against the back of the chair and at that moment had an epiphany: he knew he was confronting the final moment of his life. With a trembling hand he brushed away the hair that had fallen over his forehead. He was going to make himself presentable in case Pimpaka returned so that she would find him at his usual spot, on the chair with a cup of coffee on the table, looking at the city as he did every morning, except that he would no longer be breathing. That would at least make his exit scene more impressive, much better than being found crumpled on the floor like a rag. Yes, the final moment: hadn't this always been his favourite scene?

Unlike Chalika and Pran, Natee had a solitary upbringing with parents who loved him and cared for him so much that they never let him out of their sight. When he was a child, his father would take him to the cinema he owned every Saturday and leave him with the projectionist while he went off to work. Natee would watch whatever movie was showing on the screen, over and over again throughout the entire day, until he could remember everything by heart; what the hero thought and said, when he said it, and how the leading lady responded.

Back at home, Natee would act out the scenes in front of a large mirror in his bedroom. Eyes squinting, legs spread, knees bent, he drew a gun from his hip with two fingers: *Bang! Bang*! Blowing smoke from the tips of his fingernails, he switched instantaneously to play the bad guy, one hand over his heart and the other twisted at an angle, slumped, slowly leaning back and staggering, eyes rolling, and, finally, dying. Then he would jump up and play the hero again, grim faced as his two fingers pocketed the gun into an invisible holster, clicked his tongue and sashayed, nonchalantly, out of the frame of the mirror.

Or, sometimes, he played a pensive, cooler-than-thou hero. His eyes would be blank, like a man with a tortured past, and he would suddenly leap up and fly through the air in accordance with the script in his head, wielding an invisible sword that sliced through empty space: *Whoosh!* He cut into the imaginary villain who let out a long cry, collapsed, and got up again. Another *Whoosh!* And the unwary hero had been stabbed in the back. He halted, lurched, and in full agony reached his hand around to yank the blade out of his flesh, then lurched again, wobbled, lost control, but, no, he couldn't die until he had finished off the bad guys. W*hoosh! Whoosh!* He closed his eyes and saw a picture of the corpse-strewn, blood-splattered floor. Then, in slow-motion, he staggered and fell. With his face resting against the handle of his invisible sword, eyes rolling, he died a courageous death.

As he moved into adolescence, Natee started playing the role of a star-crossed lover who wallowed in heartbreak but was still full of cocky charm as he was separated from the woman he loved. Sometimes he played a young man who had lost his lover to an incurable disease; he even played the dying woman himself by affecting a sentimental voice, tears streaming down his face as he confessed a secret, his whisper punctuated with dramatic pauses: *I… I… I love… you.* The actor gazed into his own eyes in the mirror as his character breathed her last breath.

He especially relished playing the scene from the hit film *Love Story* in which a woman was about to die of a terminal disease, and which popularised the quote "love means never having to say you're sorry" as the woman asked her lover to hold her for the last time before pushing him away so he wouldn't have to witness her final moment. It was a scene of overwhelming emotion that had crushed all hearts in the whole world in a single instant because there is no pain more moving than the pain of love – none.

When he became an adult, Natee didn't cut an especially striking figure but he did radiate the unruffled cool and charisma of an old-school movie actor. His voice was silky smooth, as if filtered through a microphone in a dubbing booth, yet still natural enough to the ear. His choice of words was measured and pleasant to those who heard him.

Instead of telling people the truth about being a political reporter, Natee liked to introduce himself as a war correspondent. For him, "war" sounded more dangerous and attractive: isn't it the ideal of journalists to sacrifice everything, including their own lives, to reveal the truth? He also thought they looked great in their clothes, mixing the desert trooper look with that of an archaeologist. They were chivalrous and reckless, and yet had a profound understanding of human conflict, like Zen monks. They were deep and romantic, sensitive and left-leaning, all the while maintaining an unwavering objectivity.

Natee never understood why he didn't just apply for a job as a war correspondent somewhere, except for the fact that he had had to take care of his elderly parents; though, by now, they had been dead many years. There was also the fact that he had been a pampered child who hardly had any adventurous episodes that might have trained him in the skills of survival. And, quite simply, he was scared.

One time, Natee accompanied a friend from abroad who was making a documentary about Karen soldiers at a camp on the Thai-Burmese border. Just looking at the hard-staring eyes of those soldiers, who were still kids, was enough to give him a chill. His rich imagination fanned the flames of terror in his heart convincing him that these kids might open fire on him with no pretext, without any qualms, and without even blinking. And, if they were starving, they might devour him for lunch, uncooked and half-alive, since it would take them too long to boil him. The sparse, unhygienic living conditions of the camp exhausted him further, with malaria and other jungle maladies lying in ambush; the thought of them prompting Natee to often hold his breath and later gasp for air. Not to mention the creepy crawlies, all the reptiles and blood-sucking creatures that constantly preyed on his body.

Still, Natee fashioned himself into that hybrid look between desert trooper and archaeologist: a thick-fabric shirt and loose khaki pants with lots of pockets, checkered scarves hanging loosely around his neck. He would sit solemnly while great adventures played out inside his head. Somewhere in a Middle-Eastern township he was scurrying around dodging bullets amidst a swirl of dust, or he had contracted a meningococcal disease and lay waiting in the jungle that buffered Thailand and Burma, or he had been captured and was imprisoned in an ancient well in an African oasis, held hostage along with the President of the United States.

When Natee wanted to impress a woman, he would say he was a "conflict reporter", and naturally they had no idea what that conflict was or if he was talking about a war or something else. The women in his life rarely differed from one another. In fact, it was as if they were all the same woman, with the same limited interests, speaking in the same tone. They were all lacking in ideas and imagination, just like the politicians they had no interest in. And they could provide wishy-washy comments on any topic, just like those cabinet members who got their jobs from the party quota: *Never mind*; *Whatever you say*; *Up to you*; or, most frequently, *That's good*. That's good, even in love and sex.

Once, he told a woman he was seeing that he had been assigned to cover a conflict in South Africa. After he described to her what sounded like the most barbaric situation in human history, stressing again and again that he would be at risk of physical harm and possibly fatal danger, she lowered her head and became silent for a while, before telling him softly that he mustn't worry about her, that she could take care of herself, and that she was happy he was doing something he loved.

She was beautiful and smart, and it was a tragedy that she really could take care of herself without him. Natee secretly followed her after she finished work and saw her visit a hairdresser, then go shopping and have dinner with a group of friends – she was living a carefree life as if nothing had happened. He liked her a lot and he knew she loved him, too, but what he wanted was a woman who wouldn't be able to eat or sleep when he was away. He wanted a woman who would be driven mad by the fear that he might get hurt or die. He wanted a woman who would cry her eyes out for fear of losing him forever. He didn't want someone who cheered him up or supported him. No, that wasn't what he wanted.

He almost fell in love with her and could have spent the rest of his life with her, had he gone back to see her again. Instead, he punished her imperturbability by vanishing from her life so that she would feel sad, assuming he had died in a bloody riot in South Africa, or been killed in action while covering mankind's largest massacre in Rwanda, or in some violent confrontation somewhere in the world – Baghdad, Tiananmen, Bosnia, Colombia, Gaza, Pakistan… Or anywhere, because the setting wouldn't have made any difference to either of them.

Natee smelled rain again. The scent of rain-soaked earth wafted through the air, blending with another scent, maybe of candy, no, it was detergent, the detergent his mother always used. At that instant, he saw himself running along a narrow alley in the neighbourhood where he had lived as a child; the rain had just stopped and the faint sunlight was like a sheet of glass, and he could smell the detergent mingled with the scent of rain and the moist perfume of moss covering a nearby wall. He didn't notice that his chest pain had gone. A crow flew past the balcony and laughed: *Caw, caw, caw…* Its black wings stretched out as if in slow motion, wider and wider until they threatened to block out the murky sky and cast a spell of blackness. Just half a second later Natee would have thought of Chareeya, but he didn't make it.

When Pimpaka found him, Natee had already stopped breathing. And he wasn't sitting on the chair pretending to look out on the city as he had intended. He had slipped from the chair and was lying face down, his eyes wide open, puzzled, gazing into the reflection of their own reflection of their own reflection in the coffee that had spilled on the white tiled floor. When she turned him over, she was shocked to see a pulsating swarm of ants gnawing at his body even though it was still warm, as if they had come to know the day of his death because it had been secretly foretold some fifteen years ago – though Pimpaka herself hadn't been aware of it – and had been stalking her husband's every move ever since, stalking him and waiting for this exact moment to come and devour him.

Suddenly, Pimpaka heard several loud gunshots and when she looked out over the balcony the tin-coloured sky had turned black, just as Natee had seen a few moments ago. This time it wasn't the black wings of a crow but the smoke from burning tyres on the streets that heralded one of the first signs of the political violence that broke out in 2010.* After the fire was doused and the terrible incidents ended days later, the city would still find itself cloaked in an impenetrable haze that prevented it from knowing the truth of what had actually happened. That darkness would remain in place for many years.

Pimpaka felt sorry for Natee when she realised how excited her husband would have been had he lived just a few days longer so that he could have witnessed with his own eyes the violent conflict; the very kind that he had plunged into with fervour when he was younger and still a war correspondent, risking his life in the most dangerous territories of the world to expose the truth.

* In May 2010, a long-standing anti-government protest staged in central Bangkok by the "Red Shirt" group was dispersed by the military, resulting in some 90 deaths.

XI

The Mollusk Without a Shell

After many years, the villagers who rowed past the house by the river still saw Chareeya's mother sitting under the *pikul* tree, though not with the same regularity as when she had just died and everyone, without exception, saw her at all times of the day – at dusk and dawn, even at noon. At least they hadn't forgotten her as completely and quickly as Chareeya had feared they might when she was still a child.

It was surprising that strangers could see her but the inhabitants of the house couldn't, both when she was dead but also when she was still alive; transparent, intangible, unaware of the eyes peering at her from the wall as she moved slowly behind Father, through the labyrinth of the furniture in the house that had been conquered by silence.

Only when she returned to the *pikul* tree after Thana had left her did Chareeya see Mother for the first time. She was sitting transfixed by memories that left no room for her children or anybody else to love her, and she was still following Father in his death as he slowly decomposed along with his favourite wicker chair moist with his desire for that other woman. Chareeya didn't understand how Father could have betrayed Mother, how he could have betrayed that woman, how he could have betrayed himself, or how one person could betray so many people in a single lifetime.

The bitter fragrance of *pikul* flowers drifted down the river and unsettled her. Chareeya was struck by a premonition that one day she would be like Mother, someone who couldn't quit loving a man even though he had dumped her as if she was a worthless object. Then she suddenly realised that she hadn't slept for ten days straight; except when she had dozed off momentarily, but when she opened her eyes tears flowed out until she had to close them again, without going to sleep, tormented by the wreckages of memory, disconnected bits and pieces of images, all overlaid on top of the despairing hope that one day Thana would change his mind and return to her.

Maybe that's how madness consumes someone, she thought. It's not because of love, not because of the unbearable pain of loss, but because of the inability to dream. Chareeya walked into the house and up to Uncle Thanit's bedroom. She picked up a bottle of sleeping pills that she had occasionally seen him take and returned to her own room. There were three pills left. Uncle Thanit probably wouldn't mind her taking one if he knew how long it had been since she'd had any sleep. Chareeya sat down on the edge of the bed, put the pill in her mouth, drank some water, lay down, and let herself sink.

But before sleep could free her she felt as if she had been jolted out of water and was gasping for air. And she saw Thana, so vivid in front of her, and heard the words he had often spoken to her when things were still rosy: *I have nothing for you, Charee, except the mountains, the rivers, the fields, the sky – I give them all to you, all the land is yours. Come with me, come Charee...* She sank again but couldn't reach the depths. Time was slow and sticky, and she felt so very sleepy but, still, sleep didn't come. *I give them all to you – the mountains, the sky, everything...* Chareeya sat up as Thana's voice reverberated in her head, repeating the same thing over and over. All she knew was that she had to get to sleep to shut him out of her mind.

Deliriously slumberous, Chareeya put the two remaining pills in her mouth and swallowed. She lay down again, her heart searing with pain, so heavy was the feeling that she had to flip her body face-down to suppress it. Then she started sinking again. When she had almost reached the bottom, she heard Thana calling her but this time his voice was coming from somewhere far away outside her.

Charee, Charee, Charee… It was Pran. He kept calling, but there was no answer.

It was almost noon. Uncle Thanit, who had left for Bangkok, was busy shopping for vegetable seeds at Koh Mon. Chalika was in a class learning to make a Thai dessert called Golden Teardrops with ninety-year-old Grandma Nu, whose sticky *kanom chan** tasted better than anyone else's in the whole world. Nual the nanny was dozing off even though her hands were soaking in the wash tub. And Pran was weeding pests from the stems of Chinese cabbage when a squadron of brown-yellow grasshoppers he had never seen before passed overhead and blocked out the sky. Pran got up and shielded his face with his hand to watch them until they disappeared. The wind stopped. Everything was quiet as it always was on a humid day by the river. Pran felt that something was happening, but he didn't know what it was.

He decided to go inside the house. He couldn't see Chareeya and, when he called to her, there was no answer. Going upstairs, Pran called her name again before knocking lightly on the door of her bedroom, and again, and again. He strained to hear anything but all was quiet, so quiet he could hear his own sweat streaming down his back as he opened the door. Chareeya lay face-down, one arm dangling over the side of the bed. *Charee, Charee,* Pran called her again as he shook her body. *Charee, Charee, Charee…* His Charee didn't stir, didn't even blink.

Grabbing the empty bottle, Pran launched himself down the stairs carrying Chareeya in his arms. From the stairs to the street he ran and ran, barefoot, stumbling a few times, not knowing if the water on his face was sweat or tears, not knowing why he was trembling in the scorching heat, not knowing where the fear that clawed his heart had come from. He didn't remember when or how he reached the hospital. And when a woman appeared before him and spoke to him, he couldn't hear her and only registered her mouth moving silently,

* Literally, "layered dessert", *kanom chan* is a famous Thai dessert made with rice flour, sugar and coconut milk.

until a security guard and two male nurses held him back and took her away.

You should've taken us to Japan with you then, like you promised Mother you would. Uncle Thanit nodded, took off his glasses and hid his tears behind cupped hands. Pran was deaf and mute, his body had no space left for any feeling other than the hot fury that threatened to shatter his chest. He kept seeing himself smacking Thana's face and hearing himself shout, *She's mine, you prick! I dragged her from that river, I snatched her from death, and I did all that so that an asshole like you could treat her like a toy?* Veins taut as rods, Pran clenched his fist and imagined himself repeatedly slamming it into Thana's face until Chalika got up from where she was and came to sit down beside him. She had stopped crying when she unclenched his fist and held it in hers. She put her arm around his shoulder and gently rocked his body in tender consolation. Then, she lowered her head and said something to him in a barely perceptible whisper, and the chaos that was raging inside Pran's head melted away. In that tiny moment, time stopped.

When she woke up, Chareeya didn't say anything about what had happened as she resurfaced from the torpor of a dream filled with Thana's image and voice. It took her some time to piece together what had transpired; that Uncle Thanit hadn't remembered there weren't enough pills in the bottle to kill her, and that Pran hadn't been able to rouse her from her thirst to dream. They had all been convinced that she had been defeated by the agony of love and were now sharing that pain with her. Guilt surged inside Chareeya but she was too damaged and weak to explain. It wouldn't have helped, after all that had happened. And no one said anything to her about it ever again.

Without having any reason to, Chareeya again got up before dawn. She lay down on the sofa with her right hand on her heart. This time she didn't play Brahms's heart-thumping fourth symphony; instead it was a gloomy tango by Piazzolla called *Oblivion*. And then, as if nothing had happened, she left the house again without saying goodbye. She left carrying a blue tin box with a rusty lid that was stuffed with love letters, yellowed and crisp with age.

She just didn't want to see the pain in Uncle Thanit's eyes, didn't want to feel guilty when she looked at Chalika, and didn't want to feel awkward with Pran who kept his vigilant eyes on her like a guard dog. She didn't want to see anyone or do anything, except listen to Piazzolla's *Oblivion* every day for the rest of her life.

But, no, Chareeya didn't listen to the sorrowful *Oblivion* every day for the rest of her life as she had intended when she was sixteen. Nor did the ache caused by that love diminish at all. But, as time went by, the shards of memories that had stabbed and tormented her with sleeplessness became indistinct to the extent that she wasn't sure whether she'd ever loved Thana and spent a brief part of her life with him. It was as if everything had been just a dream that left a deep wound on her soul.

She went back to work at the CD shop. The business was growing fast because the city had few other specialty stores dedicated to classical music and jazz. The store had grown four times bigger within two to three years, and had added two smaller branches. A year after she left home for the second time without telling anybody, Chareeya went back to visit the family once more. But everything had changed.

Uncle Thanit had quit farming pesticide-free vegetables and started trading antique fabrics. Pran had left home to study in Bangkok and gone incommunicado. Chalika had decided not to go to university and instead was looking for a spot to open a dessert store in the market. Once in a long while she would go with Uncle Thanit to Bangkok to look for second-hand novels and have a meal with her younger sister, but such visits were infrequent since Chalika disliked the traffic, the oppressive smoke, the ceaseless tumult of the crowds, the concrete slab of the expressway crouching over the city like a giant python.

That same year, Chareeya met Urai, a childhood friend who could laugh all the time, even when she was crying, and who had left the river-side town to study medicine in Bangkok. She also met Thanya, who worked at an advertising agency and who had decided to take a

French language course after seeing the film that featured the most beautiful song in the world, just like Chareeya had. She also struck up a friendship with Rawee, a young woman with drooping eyes who loved to write when she was sad, and who was so often sad that she became a writer of heartbreaking romance novels; she would stay up all night writing only to watch the first rays of sunlight seep around the edges of the buildings, waiting for Chareeya to open the store and choose a melancholy song for her, before going back to bed in tears. These four girls, who hardly had anything in common, founded a secret society that met every Friday night for many years. Calling themselves "The Witches", they assembled to worship the splendour of life in the shadows that radiated from tequila shots, laughing, weeping, whispering, getting wasted and devastated, and slowly growing together into women.

The following year, Chareeya was in love again – briefly – with Chanon, a university student who had been incorrectly educated to believe that love and sex were two separate things. Chanon was polite, serious and honest; a young man who chose to study history because he believed it would unlock the mysteries of the universe and not because he didn't know what else to study, as was the case with most of his friends enrolled in that major. He also loved cinema, music, philosophy, and was into difficult books by Nietzsche, Plato, Kant, Liao Fan and too many others for Chareeya to remember.

It was evening when he walked into her life. He stood at the counter and awkwardly flipped through a book he was holding in his hands: *Do you have... Brahms's Symphony No.3 Poco Allegretto? / We have the whole piece, not just the third movement.* She led him to the racks and ran her fingers along the CD covers. *Sorry, we're sold out*, she said while glancing at the book he was holding. It was French. *Aimez-vous Brahms?* she asked. *Does it mention this symphony?* Chanon handed her the book: *Yes*. Chareeya flipped through it earnestly: *Have you heard the piece before? / No, I haven't / His magnum opus – very beautiful. He wrote it for the only woman he loved – Clara, Schumann's widowed wife. I have a performance by Karajan that I can put on a disc for you in the meantime, until our new supply arrives. The book looks interesting – is it difficult?* Chareeya spoke without looking up at him.

Chanon didn't know Karajan, but the record store girl steeped in a repertoire of classical music who could also read French fascinated him. *No, it's not difficult. I've almost finished it – I'll lend it to you tomorrow when you give me the CD, okay?* Chareeya looked up at him, a smile lit up her face. The following night, Chanon found his life force drained from his body as he stood smothered by the melody of Brahms's sweetly tragic symphony and watched – through the thousand raindrops that covered the glass storefront – people chasing love in the rain on the footpath outside. When he turned around, he saw Chareeya standing nearby, her fingertips lightly touching the rain-splattered glass, her eyes closed. He, too, closed his eyes and drank in the music. From the moment he opened his eyes again, Chanon would never be able to free himself from the desire to have Chareeya just like that; her eyes closed, listening to music beside him.

He returned the following night and ended up spending that year's monsoon season in Chareeya's room. There, he listened to music and read and stole glances at her as she thumbed through a dictionary while reading that novel by Françoise Sagan. Chanon never touched her in all those months they were seeing each other, only to be roundly defeated by desire when loneliness ambushed him one night. But, despite that, the young man utterly failed to find a connection between his love and the repetitive cycles of world history, or between his feelings and Nietzsche's fabled saying, "God is dead", and the weight of guilt stopped him from seeing Chareeya ever again.

The following year, Chanon received a scholarship to study in the United States. There, he would complete a PhD, become a philosophy professor, and experience several episodes of emotional longing and physical love. Twenty years after the night he first heard Brahms's symphony, he would return to Thailand to scour CD shops with the hope that one of them would lead him to Chareeya, her eyes still closed behind a glass storefront covered in a thousand raindrops reflecting the upside-down world. Not only did he not find Chareeya, he could hardly find any CD shops, condemned as they were to their graves by data migration.

Chareeya, meanwhile, cried every day – for Thana, for Chanon, and for the woeful longing in Father's yellowed love letters, then again for Thana, in an endless cycle, without ever allowing herself to love anyone else. The closest she came was when she went to work as a part-time receptionist in a restaurant where she met a chef called Andre, who could bake cakes so majestic they looked like sculptures and who took her to watch films at the Alliance Française every Wednesday night during that cool season. For the rest of the night they would lean against each other under the sprawling branches of a giant frangipani tree and he would brush up her French by telling her stories of his childhood.

Chareeya could have fallen in love with him, got married and become a mother of four. She could have owned a small café in a small hamlet camouflaged by the grapevines of southern Burgundy. She could have spent her later years in the warmth of her twenty-two sons, grandsons and great-grandsons, and died at seventy-eight in Andre's embrace still as sweet and tender as his chiffon cakes. She could have had all that but, instead: she inherited an old, yellow, Mediterranean-style house large enough for her garden after Andre left Bangkok broken-hearted; adopted a tabby cat found, nearly dead, at a bus stop and called him "Uncle"; learned three-hundred-and-twenty-four recipes; planted two-thousand-six-hundred-and-ten trees; listened to three-hundred-and-sixty pieces of the world's most beautiful music; wandered aimlessly in her dreamless existence; and would have met Pran again, if Natee hadn't come into her life...

The circumstances of their meeting was the kind of serendipity only found in movies. *What time is it?* Natee asked a woman who was crossing his path, only to find that Chareeya had her eyes closed and was going to walk right past him, small earphones having blocked out any sound from the outside world. Natee was beside himself as he followed her through the mass of humanity that would never know what kind of sounds it wanted to hear, for half the length of the street, until she reached her store. He watched her from a distance and then finally approached her. He introduced himself, fell in love, and from that moment on loved her in a way no one had ever loved her before.

It was a torrent of love from a man whose only purpose in life was to love. Natee was extremely attentive and affectionate, and he even spoke in heartfelt and sugar-coated sentences that seemed to come straight out of American movie scripts. *You make me want to be a better man.* Or, *My life is nothing without the hope of seeing the reflection of the sun in your eyes.* He used simple unpretentious but unforgettable phrases like, *We were born for each other.* Or, *I never felt about anybody else the way I feel about you, Charee.*

More than that, he was caring and eager to please, and never once did he forget to bring her a small gift each time they met: a flower, sweets in an adorable box, and stories – little inspirational tales that he jotted down in a notebook after hearing them or reading about them in newspapers, so that he could read them aloud to her page by page.

A story about a sweet-natured man who had been born into the wrong body but who refused to surrender to his fate. He had been a cabaret dancer and had worked hard to save up for a sex-change operation to turn himself into a beautiful woman so that he could live life in the body that should have been his from the start; and, yet, she ended up being cheated for much of that life – conned and robbed by a series of real men with fake hearts before she finally found true love in a woman who hawked sweets outside the cabaret, and who became her true companion in times of pain and suffering.

A story about a man who grew up facing the world alone until, one day, he won the lottery jackpot. The next morning, he awoke to find himself mobbed by family and relatives he never even knew existed. They overran his house and celebrated, then took turns telling him the sad stories of their lives; tearful tales of unbearable misery followed by requests for loans. The tens of millions the man had won from the jackpot were gone within a few months, and so were the friends and relatives who disappeared as quickly as they had come. The poor man went back to living a hand-to-mouth existence, and yet he prayed that he would win the lottery once more, not because he wanted money and a lavish lifestyle but because he wanted his real and phony relatives to come visit him again, to make the house bustle with life again, even though he knew in his heart that none of those people were his real family.

And a short story about a mollusk that woke up to find its shell had gone missing while it was asleep. It spent the rest of its life creeping along, naked, in the cold loneliness of a beach shining with a million white shells, smuggling itself into each of those empty abodes, one by one, without ever being able to find a shell that fit quite like the battered old shell it had lost – not a single one.

XII

The Amethyst Tear

From a distance, Pran saw Chareeya talking to a female friend, but looking more carefully he realised it was actually a middle-aged man. They were sitting outside the house in a beam of sunlight. She looked animated and was chuckling, but a few minutes later he saw the man get up hurriedly and leave, his steps as swift as those of a young man. Only then did Pran realise that the man wasn't middle-aged, but in his thirties. Chareeya followed close behind him and they stood arguing at the door behind the *pheep* tree that was shedding its flowers into the wind. The man started walking again. Chareeya grabbed his arm to stop him. He stopped, his face tilted slightly in a mixture of pride and pain, before shaking off her grip and continuing on his way. Chareeya meekly wiped her tears with the back of her hand and returned to the house.

She didn't come to Bleeding Heart with her gang that Friday. Something troubled Pran but he didn't know quite what it was; something akin to worry, close to waiting, and reminiscent of loneliness. He didn't dare ask her three friends, and they didn't approach him to offer any information. Chareeya didn't show up the following Friday either, and this time the three Witches were also absent. He still watched her from his window every morning, and she was still there at her usual spot, sipping coffee, petting Uncle the cat, but she was also sadder. Something was troubling her, too;

something in the gusts of wind, in the tea-coloured sunlight, Pran wasn't sure what it was. Maybe the sadness was coming from him.

But, then, just a few minutes before his heart had been completely wrecked, on a quiet Sunday, she called the bar. Sounding as if nothing had happened: *Are you free tomorrow at noon? / Monday's my laundry day, I'm free after that / Come over, I'll cook something tasty for you / Such as…*? Pran raised his brows and smiled to himself. *Allure Curry / What? / Allure Curry / Is that real food? / Yes, a vintage recipe.* He thought of the pink lipstick mark on the plastic cup and the dry heat of Chilean wine surged in his chest. *Sounds delicious / It is. Come. Late morning is fine.*

Even before Pran reached the house the smell hit him – the perfumed, alluring top notes, just as the name promised. Chareeya had set a table in the garden, dishes and cutlery at the ready, food lined up with a bouquet of flowers in a glass in the middle, which reminded Pran of the time when he used to pick wild flowers along the road for the girls to arrange on the dinner table at the house by the river. Only when he was about to start eating did he realise the exotic flamboyance of this lunch.

There was Allure Curry with succulent meat and basil, Middle-Eastern saffron rice, a Greek-style grilled vegetable salad decked with sundried tomatoes and goat cheese, and some kind of fish, pan-fried with cumin and dill. *Cha Ca, you've never had it before I'm sure, it's Vietnamese.* The meal was rounded off with the seductively named subcontinental dessert *kulab jamun** – goat milk condensed and fried into lovely brown balls, dunked in rose-tinted syrup made from flowers in the garden, and so brain-numbingly sweet that when Pran took his first bite he had to force himself not to squeeze his eyes shut like he'd seen people do in TV adverts.

When the extravagant lunch in the garden was over and the sun caught up with them, Pran carried himself inside and flopped down on the peony-patterned cushion, so full he could hardly move.

* Seductively named because, in the Thai pronunciation, the word *kulab* means rose.

Chareeya left him with Philip Glass's desolate Violin Concerto and disappeared into the kitchen. Clanking noises, and Pran only hoped that there was no more food emerging from there; please, no more fried rice with sweet basil topped with eggs, *raad naa* noodles* or endless procession of dishes going on through eternity. Living by himself had made him skinny. Pran didn't just eat very little, he ate irregularly because when he was feeling too lazy he didn't make any attempt to find food. Chareeya's international lunch was tantamount to what he usually put into his mouth over three days combined, and he couldn't remember the last time he had eaten anything that tasted like real food.

What amazed and confounded him was Chareeya's endeavour in having mastered this disparate repertoire of various culinary origins, as well as her dedication to the art of cooking. But then it struck him that Chareeya's dedications had always bordered on the obsessive: she had spent years ambushing him in the house; she had watched the river for months on end, hoping to catch a glimpse of a mythical bug that had been extinct since the sixth reign**; she had stalked a lost earthworm for days without finding anything; she had conjured up this garden, so wonderful that he could hardly believe one woman could have pulled it off; and there was that time when she had followed love with such doggedness.

The violin screeched and Pran no longer wanted to think about anything sad. He got up and looked out at the garden gauzy in sunshine. Seeing the garden up close in the afternoon hours was different from when he looked at it through the window of his room each morning. It was full-bodied, teeming, lush with life, rambunctious with colour and activity. There were millipedes trudging here and there, light and shadow chasing each other in a strange waltz, fruit flies buzzing like a boiling fog, a parade of ants, leaves trembling in the wind.

It took him a long while to realise that these plants not only grew above, under and next to one another, they also grew *in* one another.

* *Raad naa* is a dish of rice noodles stir-fried in a thick gravy made from tapioca or corn starch.

** The reign of the sixth king of the Chakri dynasty, King Vajiravudh, lasted from 1910 until 1925.

The *pheep* tree in front of the house had a blue fern, the colour of an Andaman pearl, growing out of its trunk after the rains, while the *tabaek* tree mysteriously sprouted purple orchids. When Chareeya had taken him to see the flower named Desire, he had smelled frangipani despite there being no frangipani tree in the garden. He also registered the gentle aroma of pomelo flowers that he had once smelled in a different garden and that often drifted into his room in the middle of the night.

His thoughts involuntarily wandered to the room starlight didn't reach. Uncle Jang's windowless room on the second floor of his building was small and dark, having been partitioned from a large bedroom at the front. *I asked my family to let me stay here when I was a young man. By the time they died and there were spare rooms, I couldn't be bothered to move*, he said, smiling. Uncle Jang was in his seventies, a man who chose his words with care and whose eyes sparkled like those of a child. He spent an entire evening telling Pran stories from the past: about war, patriotism, Shanghai illuminated by a million lights, his years as a student in China, the Communist Party takeover, and love. In that dimly lit room the old man told Pran about the love that had held him captive for over half a century.

When the revolution took place, my mother sent me a letter telling me to come home because she was dying. I arrived to find her in her good health; I was her only son and she had just been afraid I would get stuck in China. When I saw she was alright, I wanted to return so that I could marry the woman I loved and bring her back with me. But China was in turmoil and my mother forbade me from leaving. While I waited, my friend sent me a letter telling me that her father had given her to another man because he was worried his daughter wouldn't have anyone to look after her. I told my mother that this was my woman and that I wanted her back. This time, my mother definitely didn't want me to go and wreck someone's home by stealing his wife. She wouldn't budge. I was a young man, hot-headed and implacable. I was furious that my mother lied to me about being sick and dying, I blamed her for losing the woman I loved. I gave her an ultimatum – if she refused to let me go to China, I would never work again in my life. If I couldn't have the woman I loved, I would become the most worthless man on earth.

And so Uncle Jang became a worthless man, just as he had promised he would. China became a hermit nation, closing its doors and dashing any hopes he had of returning for his lost love. From then on, he never worked to support himself. He lived a spartan existence in his windowless room, relying on his siblings and keeping only a single personal possession: a photograph of a young girl with a ponytail and Chinese eyes, tucked beneath a glass plate on his writing desk, next to a poem he had written to her a quarter of a century ago. *I still talk to her every day. I console her, telling her everything is all right. We have more than one life. We'll meet again in the next life. We'll try again.*

So much for trying not to think about something sad, Pran thought to himself. He turned and saw the woman with the bangs by Modigliani watching him forlornly from the wall. Pran smiled faintly at her. His gazed lower to a makeup tray with a turquoise ring next to it, along with those amethyst teardrops, a few cosmetics, a velvet red rose, a rusty blue tin box and a single tissue, folded in half, with a pale lychee-coloured lipstick mark stamped in the middle. He picked it up with a trembling hand and put it in his pocket. He would spend hours that night, and many other nights in his lonely life, gazing at the ever-fading kiss mark in dim light, feeling waves of heat and tenderness rising endlessly inside him.

She returned to the bar with her friends the following Friday. At the beginning of the long night, they were laughing and enjoying the party but, when the hour of shipwrecked hearts approached, Chareeya shed her first tear in her favourite corner, the teardrop falling at a perfect angle so as to cast a reflection like lightning into Pran's eyeline. He botched the bass line. He stammered when he should have been singing as he saw more teardrops fall. He felt as if he was standing on a river bank with the sun blazing above him.

Late that night, the Witches allowed him to take her home. As they walked, she dropped her tears like breadcrumbs in that fairytale – the one about the two children abandoned by their parents in a forest who marked their path in the hope of finding their way home, a home that no longer wanted them. The city was sleeping and the night was so quiet that he could hear starlight scraping her skin. The trees in the garden drooped in a state of gloom. The scent of *pheep*, usually so refreshing, was tainted by the acidic perfume of frangipani. On top of that was the phantom aroma of *ratree*, which hadn't been planted in the garden, floating in from some unknown place. The robin that usually sang at two a.m. was quiet. There wasn't even the hint of a breeze.

Thank you Pran, Chareeya mumbled when they reached the house. She lowered her head to hide her teary, swollen red eyes. He hesitated and the fear he had felt a long time ago returned when she didn't ask him to stay as he had been hoping she would. Looking inside, he saw a white butterfly circling a lamp, casting flickering shadows around the room. He knew she wanted him to leave so she could lie down and weep. Pran gave up hoping and set off but, just halfway along the path, he turned and retraced his steps. In the dim light, beneath a window just an arm's distance away, Pran saw Chareeya slumped on the peony-patterned cushion, crying over the sad story she hadn't told him.

Pran slowly sat down in the shadows as the journey of tears continued on the other side of the wall. Stung, exhausted, heavy hearted, he could smell the gentle fragrance of pomelo flowers emerging from the memory of those long-gone days before their separation, before the collapse of his dreams, before he had buried everything under the ruins and left. Now he couldn't stop the torrent of timeworn memories, the ones he had never allowed himself to register in his heart, which suddenly came back to him: the shimmering reflection of the city, wet and gleaming in the first light of day; its scent; its slow-moving inhabitants, so slow they could read each other's minds without speaking; the mute glow of cigarettes that appeared at twilight; a frisky wind blowing through a setting sun; and the memory of Lika, the ever-lovely Lika, and the little girl, wild-haired and running after a cloud until it disappeared. He wondered: what has happened?

What has happened to the girl whose smile revealed all of her teeth? What has happened to the explorer who indefatigably surveyed the santol orchards of her neighbourhood every day without fail? And the tears that fell to the rhythm of the flickering shadows made Pran wonder, too, what has happened to me? He wondered, ironically, what has life left me with? Waking up every day in a world full of strangers only to close his eyes again in the solitary night, forgetting and crushing his own dreams in order to replace them with cheap ready-made ones, and clinging onto endlessly forgettable minutes only to disintegrate slowly into numbness. Only this?

When dawn cast its vague outlines, Pran could no longer hear the weeping from the woman on the other side of the wall. There was no more white butterfly and no flickering shadows, just a glowing lamp that competed with the glaring sun and appeared like a white hole in the wall. Pran got up, saw that she was asleep, holding the cat, and then retraced his steps through the awakening garden. All the while he imagined his own room crawling with the spiderweb of solitude and the tangle of anxiety that would wrap him up inside its chilly cocoon.

Come Monday, Chareeya cooked him another epic lunch, as if that tearful episode had never happened. Again, it was a feast of international cuisines: Greek-style grilled mackerel with a splash of lemon, Kashmiri chicken korma with crushed cashew nuts, Catalan herbal rice, Afghan fattoush salad with pita bread sprinkled with a mysterious violet powder, and rounding off with panna cotta topped with a dusting of vanilla and masala tea brewed with young lemongrass.

She was completely cheerful, not mentioning a word about the night she had wept all the way home from the bar, or the previous incident when she had appeared to be tussling with a stranger – a man or a woman? – at the door of her house. And Pran didn't tell her about the imprint of her lips he had stolen as a souvenir, or how it had come flying into his grey-coloured dreams, the details of which he could no longer recall. He didn't tell her about the night he spent on the other side of the wall, beneath her window, when the flickering shadows had danced all night.

The afternoon passed pleasantly. They each read their books. They played with the cat. They lounged around in the placid sun. They talked of trivial things, closed their eyes, listened to music, then watched the day disappear. They said goodbye drinking sangria, tangy as the kind served at temple fairs. Twilight drew a blue curtain behind them as the Mon rose shed its petals and the *puttarn* flower folded its dark-red petals over itself.

A lazy, mundane afternoon, and many years later Pran would still wonder why he couldn't forget it. He couldn't forget the tender touch of the wind blowing through the garden, the wry aroma of *nang yaem* flowers, or her sad, slim fingers loosely wrapped around her knees when she played him "End of Love, End of Happiness" by Mantana Morakul, or the bright halo shining through the leaves that illuminated her face like a mirage of liquid as it struck her eyes.

Or when she turned to look at him and he noticed, for the first time, a fissure running across her left eye.

XIII

The Lightning Storm

Silence seized the house under its command once again. No one played music in the living room for the simple reason that every song reminded them of Chareeya. For similar reasons, the monthly excursion was discontinued. Though Uncle Thanit still went to Bangkok once or twice a month to buy vegetable seeds and antique fabric, Chalika always found an excuse not to go along. She was repelled by the idea that Charee was somewhere in that loud, mad city, and that her sister didn't want to see her again. Pran still worked the vegetable plots by the river, but also found excuses not to stay for dinner. Looking for Chareeya in her usual chair at the dining table only made him angry. Then, a young man around his age moved into the house next door.

It was a house that jutted out over the water like Pran's home, and the two houses were separated by a small alley. It had been so long since anyone had lived there that he couldn't remember the previous inhabitants. But, one night, he saw a red glow seeping through a half-opened window and it reminded him of the Pink Houses his father used to take him to. The glow kept luring his gaze towards the house. Several days passed, and the new tenant showed himself. The young man had long hair, dark skin, a beautiful face. He stood on the porch surrounded by water, his sad eyes looking at Pran. *Hey*. Short, curt, a foreign accent. He cocked his head by way of greeting, and a friendship began.

Paradorn lived alone in the house. He didn't go to school. And, like Pran, he was motherless. His father was a rock musician who played at bars in Berlin and sent him money for his expenses. At a time when Pran's heart was full of questions he had no answers to, the house devoid of adults came to feel like the warmest place in the world – a shabby world where people had all the answers and never asked any questions.

Paradorn's house didn't have much furniture. It was spacious, sparse, and contained only a collection of unusual objects that Pran had never seen before: a chair made from a car seat covered in flame-patterned red leather, a mug that looked like a woman's breast, a leopard-print rug, a skull-shaped ashtray, a century-old candelabra that doubled as a wine rack, an electric guitar that looked like a paper aeroplane, and some sort of percussion instrument that looked like a gourd and was filled with sand. *A bongo – there's an ocean inside it*, Paradorn said, slowly flipping the gourd up and down. Besides the blue-grey expanse of water that Pran had seen in the distance when he was a child on the train, the only other time he had seen the sea was when he went on a trip with Uncle Thanit, Chalika and Chareeya. He would later spend hours listening to the ocean trapped inside that little gourd.

In addition to the collection of odd items, Paradorn's house had an eccentric pet: a large Oscar fish called Susie, or Sexy Sue as she was more commonly known to the boys, with an orange stripe that resembled a sunset in winter, a morose face, lips perpetually puckered as if she was complaining while swimming back and forth in the wretchedness of that small tank barely large enough to contain her. She had to be fed with live creatures; crickets, geckos, little frogs, or cockroaches. And this sent Pran and Paradorn on daily hunting expeditions in the field behind the house. The boys would return with their catch and watch the horrifying spectacle of the poor prey being snapped up in those powerful jaws.

What attracted Pran most, however, was the vinyl. To be precise, it was a treasure trove of vinyl records, lined up against the walls and piled on the floor; the only items in Paradorn's house that were similar to those in Chareeya's. *Listen and you'll understand*, Paradorn said, as he put a set of headphones over Pran's head, cocking his head and smiling mischievously. Suddenly, Pran was bowled over by a heavy mass of sound and his inner being was never the same again. Something grafted itself inside him, an extension of the music Chareeya had left behind: the wailing guitar, the ferocious drumbeats, the thick, gruff bass lines, every sonic atom assaulting him simultaneously, preceding the primal scream of an unhappy young man – a scream that sounded the same as the one he had bottled up inside himself, a loud numbing anger trapped in a body with no way of escape, forsaken and nomadic, a scream that had found no outlet in Chareeya's classical soundwaves.

Pran taught himself to play the guitar and discovered another way to free the sounds trapped inside him. The instrument became an alternative to words, which for him had always been scarce, and though it sounded more like a madman's squeal than music, it eased the inexorable rage inside him and stopped it from exploding. He began to hang out at Paradorn's house late into the night, sometimes on into the following morning, walking his fingers along the taut strings while listening to that endless inventory of vinyl records, one by one, from classic rock to punk, from big-name guitarists to modern rockers unknown to most, from Rare Earth and Led Zeppelin to King Crimson and U2, the Cure and the Sex Pistols.

Every month or two, Patra, Paradorn's father, came home. He would only stay a few days. During that time, he would coach his son, and naturally Pran, on guitar technique. Patra was in his early thirties, good-looking, skinny, his hair hanging down his back, and he wore tight leather pants even on the hottest days. He came across as a cool gangster type and it was clear that he was the kind of guy who would never let anyone mess with him. Having been a father since he was fifteen meant that Patra was more like a brother to Paradorn, and he didn't treat Paradorn like a father would treat his son – they bantered, hung out, tussled and fake-fought like children all day long.

For Pran, Patra gradually replaced Uncle Thanit. There was a kind of warmth in his personality, almost like Uncle Thanit, but rawer and more thrilling; a rock version to the classical cool. He was also full of stories, but they were stories from a different world, an anarchic world characterised by extremes, obsessions, intoxication and music. A world in which no one bowed to anything, not even to God. A world summed up in that arrogant motto, "Live fast, die young."

People are assholes, remember. They pick and choose who they want to pretend to be good with, and they're too chicken to show how shitty they really are. We can't choose how we were born but, remember, we can always choose how to live our lives. Promise me, never let any prick treat you like shit – unless you wanna die like a mangy dog under their feet. In that heat and in that fury, Pran found a new family – Patra was his father, Paradorn his brother. And it was the first time he had the courage to dream, dreaming he would be like Patra when he grew up.

Dad is saving up to come back and open a bar. Bar Paradorn, wicked huh? / Very / He told me to tell you so you can get ready. He likes you a lot. He wants us to form a band, and he said you know classical music, that you have good ears, and you'll go far. Besides learning to play the guitar, Pran also learned to play truant, to smoke and drink, to get stoned. And yet he lurched through his final exams at high school. Once Uncle Thanit gave up on his pesticide-free vegetable farm, Pran spent all his time at Paradorn's place. There, the boys wrote songs and practiced late into the night. They started looking for a drummer, and maybe another guitarist. They even had the name ready: Broken Rainbow. "Broken Rainbow of Bar Paradorn" – what a sweet dream! At that point, Pran was certain that he wanted to study art but school had to wait because his grandmother's health was failing and she was always ill with one thing or another.

When Chareeya returned not long after breaking up with Thana, Pran nurtured a secret hope that things would go back to being the way they used to be, that they would again live together as a happy family; listening to music, biking around, rowing the boat out in the afternoons, hearing the tale of the king who fell into an eternal sleep in a sea of mercury, lying down in the back of a battered pick-up truck and gazing at the stars as they travelled imperceptibly across the sky; listening to her tell him, *Look, that's my star*, and falling asleep without crying, without dreaming a dream that would be forgotten when he opened his eyes.

Patra woke Paradorn and Pran at first light for a trip to Bangkok. They wandered around the Chattuchak weekend market all day, then headed to Khao San Road to find a guesthouse. After putting their things away, they went out for a dinner of hamburgers that tasted like wet newspaper topped with sweet ketchup and washed it down with coffee that tasted like bland, burnt tamarind seeds. They passed the time watching a large portion of the world's young population that had come from the four corners of the globe just to walk back and forth along this narrow street. At nightfall, they returned to their guest house, took a nap, woke up, showered, and went out again.

Pran couldn't help it: he swaggered. The effect of being with thc handsome father and son in their cool clothes was irresistible. Paradorn had lent him a David Bowie concert T-shirt and Doc Martens. Everywhere they walked, heads turned while girls giggled and pointed. They smiled at the trio, primarily at Patra and Paradorn but the spillover was enough for Pran. He was almost eighteen then but, having grown up in a small town with only a handful of female friends – Chalika, Chareeya and a few plain girls at school – meant that he had no experience in the flirting game. The honeyed looks and inviting smiles sent his way from female strangers made him duck in embarrassment, while Paradorn, who was only six months older, was adept at returning the smiles, with his teasing eyes and slightly raised eyebrows. But, still, this kind of thing was probably down to genetic inheritance, something Pran lacked in his DNA.

On the other hand, the men on the street didn't seem too pleased and kept glaring at them as if looking for a fight. But they looked away the moment Patra shot them back a look that said, "I'll bust your balls, asshole." On the way to Khao San Road, Patra had worn a simple T-shirt and jeans. Now, on their night-time prowl, he was decked out in full rocker regalia like those guys on the cover of a rock album. He had on a sleeveless, low-cut V-neck top, extremely tight black leather pants, silver accessories gleaming here and there, long, cross-shaped earrings, two or maybe three necklaces, large bangles, and fringed leather arm straps. His hair cascaded down his back and his eyes were painted with black shadows.

Below his T-shirt, on his exposed belly, Patra sported an emerald-green tattoo with three spirals coiling out of a central image, a heart. *It's a Celtic symbol, means wind*, Patra told Pran, who was staring at it. "*Pran" also means wind, free like the wind – that's what my heart is like*, Patra smiled and tapped his tattoo twice with his fist. *And your heart too, Pran, your heart is like the wind. Remember that.* At that point in his life, Pran had no idea how hard it could be for a person, or how far they would have to go to become free, or how many people there were who would never ever be free. But it wouldn't be long before he found out.

The bar called Soldier of Love was a brightly illuminated red box, packed with human beings, strobe lighting, cigarette smoke and loudspeakers. Everywhere he looked he saw only loudspeakers, row upon row, blocking every wall. It was a Sunday night jam session at which guest musicians jammed with a resident band. As soon as Patra's name was announced, the crowd roared. It was clear he had a strong following. Hair flying as he jumped on the fog-covered stage, Patra thrashed out U2's forceful anguish like a firebird in the midst of an electric storm: *I was broken, bent out of shape. I was naked in the clothes you made. Lips were dry, throat like rust. You gave me shelter from the heat and the dust. No more water in the well. No more water, water. Angel… Angel or devil. I was thirsty. And you wet my lips.* It was the first time Pran had seen Patra perform live. He sang hard and worked the guitar even harder, so passionately, so feverishly that Pran didn't dare blink for fear of missing something. Paradorn watched and smiled his crooked smile, one eyebrow raised, elbowing Pran every five seconds. *Look, man, look at my dad. He's the devil.*

The wall of loudspeakers thundered and roared. Deep bass lines rumbled every cell in Pran's body and he felt weightless as the crowd rocked their heads euphorically. Women screamed like lunatics when Patra's voice climbed to a velvety falsetto, as he howled and jumped and sliced the air with his arm in a circular movement – that Springsteen move. And they kept screaming at the top of their lungs, as if their lives had been drained out of their bodies, when they saw Patra standing still, panting, beads of sweat trickling over the tattoo on his chest, wet hair like a ragged curtain covering half his face in a staccato of bar-room lights.

Before that night of fire was over, Pran saw Patra exchanging glances with the most beautiful woman in the world during all that heavy breathing and that curtain of cigarette smoke and that final roar of the night's last song. They looked at each other without saying a word. She lifted her finger and touched his cheek lightly. Patra exploded in laughter, like a child. She stifled his laugh by pulling his head towards hers and kissing him, a tender and drawn-out kiss as if they were long lost lovers who had just been reunited. When the hour of heartache arrived and the lights came back on, Patra reluctantly detached himself from the most beautiful woman in the world and took her back with him. That night, in the next room, Pran and Paradorn lay listening to her endless purring.

My dad's the man. I don't need anything else, Pran, my dad is so fucking cool, Paradorn whispered over the moaning from the other side of the wall. *He said he'd work abroad for a while longer, a year and a half max, to save up enough to come back to Bangkok for good and open a bar… Bar Paradorn. And you'll be in my band. You'll come live with us. You'll be my brother.* Pran smiled in the dark, his mind wandering back to the time when a girl had wanted to take him home to be her brother but the memory was transient and the image vanished, leaving only a bitter aftertaste.

The rugged moaning continued all night long and, when morning finally came, Pran wasn't convinced she would really leave. She stared at Patra at length, as if wanting to register every detail of every thought inside his head. She lifted her hand to touch his face ever-so lightly, just like when she had invited him into her amorous sanctum. Then she broke into a smile, warm and bright, like something shining from the abyss of life, and walked away.

And she vanished into a crowd of heaving humanity, into a world full of strangers.

XIV

The Dancer in the Drizzle

No one remembered exactly when that café had been opened or when it had been closed down and left derelict but every day, as Chareeya walked past on the other side of the road on her way to work, she would glance over at the place. And each time she saw the doors shuttered and silent under the sign, which read in pinkish grey longhand lettering "Café Rosarin".

One day, a few alleys further down, when she was waiting for the rain to stop even though she had already been soaked, Chareeya saw the sign being blown off by the storm; it almost hit a boy who was playing with a yoyo under the same shelter as her. For several days it was left on the footpath, blocking the way of pedestrians, before someone finally decided they had had enough and pushed it up against an electricity pole. Once the sign was gone, Chareeya stopped looking at the shuttered café. When an optics store later replaced it, she forgot all about the former existence of Café Rosarin.

A few days after the sign was left by the electricity post, an old man dragged it away, scraping it along the hard surface of the road. When he got home, he carried it upstairs to his bedroom, moved it about until it fit the space, and used it as a screen to shield himself from the sound of his wife's snoring; his wife who had slept on the other side of the room and who had been dead for two years. But after a few days the old man removed the sign and dumped it on the rubbish tip because he couldn't bear the attacks of sorrow he felt as he was about to fall asleep without hearing the sound of his wife's breathing.

The sign was trashed, worthless, until a motorcycle taxi driver and his six friends hauled it off and spent an entire day turning it into a bench. First, they removed the lettering for "Café" and then they modified the remainder to create a back rest for the bench, with the word "Rosarin" in elegant longhand spanning the width of their ad hoc piece of furniture. Thus, their motorcycle taxi depot became known as the Rosarin depot and the nameless alley next to it was christened Rosarin Lane. Less than a year later, the depot moved to another spot not too far away that was closer to the network of sub-lanes and shortcuts leading to the main road teeming with traffic. Because the new depot lacked space, the Rosarin bench was left where it was, rusty and disintegrating into dust just days before the municipality installed an official sign – a solemn navy blue metal plaque with the words "Rosarin Lane" inside a gold frame, so stately that a rumour spread about Rosarin having been a member of the royal family who had once owned the land in that area.

But no sooner had the rumour started than others condemned it to oblivion. A woman who lived somewhere in the lane and who was eight-months pregnant slipped and fell down the stairs to her death at the same time as newspapers reported the death of another pregnant woman who had hanged herself from some kind of tree on some street somewhere as vengeance against her unfaithful husband. These deaths led to a rumour that spread far and wide about another pregnant woman called Rosarin who, heartbroken, had hanged herself from a tree in an abandoned lot in the alley to get back at her husband, inspiring the municipality to name the place Rosarin Lane as a morbid monument to her love.

And that urban legend would also have faded from memory had it not been for Aunt Linjee. She was a middle-aged woman who had been trying to sell a plot of land in that lane for years. When nobody showed any interest in the land, she decided to seek help from a shaman who advised her to make an offering of meat, sweets, red flowers and red incense to the area's guardian spirits in order to unlock the hindrances to her commercial enterprises. Another woman, walking past Aunt Linjee's red roses and vibrant offerings placed under a tamarind tree, assumed with great confidence that they were put there for the spirit of the woman called Rosarin – the source of that great romantic myth that had ended with a nylon rope. The following day, the woman put her own offerings and red roses under the tree while pleading with the ghost of Rosarin to help fulfill her romantic wishes, completely unaware of the irony that Rosarin herself had been helpless in her own endeavours and ended up in a noose. Soon passers-by saw the offerings and added their own, on and on until the spot became a shrine littered with roses and propitiatory objects.

When a woman who made an offering believed that her wishes had been granted, she repaid Rosarin by building a wooden spirit house at the spot without asking anyone's permission. And so, the holy aura of Rosarin bore physical proof – the spirit house was tangible evidence of her reputation and attracted an endless stream of worshippers. Aunt Linjee, still unable to sell her plot of land, saw the waves of believers arriving and decided to seek help from the shaman again. Consulting the oracular powers of the sun, the moon and Mars, the shaman came to the conclusion that it was impossible to chase away the believers and that, instead, Aunt Linjee should extend a warm welcome to the other lovesick spirits that had come to reside at the shrine along with its original inhabitant. That way, her lucky star might rise.

Aunt Linjee built a shack and recruited some homeless people in the area to work as cleaners at the shrine. But because she was stingy, she didn't want to pay them from her own pocket so she set up a donation box. Alas, she underestimated the sheer number of loveless women in the world and, as they kept coming to the shrine, the donation box filled up in no time prompting her to replace it with a bigger one, and then a bigger one, and, finally, the very biggest one she could find. And, still, she had to empty it every two days to put the money in the bank. From her original plan to live the rest of her life off money from the sale of her land, Aunt Linjee dreamt up a megalomaniac scheme to canvass for a large amount of donation money so that she could spend it on making merit as an investment in her afterlife.

As Chareeya was busy planting trees in her enchanted garden without any idea of what was going on elsewhere, Aunt Linjee hired workmen to build a permanent shrine in the style of modern Thai architecture. Then she hired an acquaintance to draw a picture of a woman – *Make her look sad and beautiful*, she instructed – and hung the drawing on the wall along with a one-page sob story about a pregnant woman defeated by love who had hanged herself from the tamarind tree. She dismantled the original shrine, which had become unstable from the weight of the desire to be loved that had been dumped upon it by worshippers. On the day Chareeya picked up a badly injured yellow cat from a bus stop and adopted him as her uncle, Aunt Linjee put up a red sign, twice as big as the one for the café, with which this story began. The sign read "Goddess Rosarin Shrine".

A few days after the official opening of the shrine, a van carrying a television crew punctured a tyre at the entrance to the lane. The crew had been on their way to film an episode about a singer's love scandal, but the accident made them miss their appointment and, as a substitute, they did an episode on Goddess Rosarin. Unexpectedly, it was an overnight sensation. The story of the lovelorn goddess became an instant hit. Every channel had to produce a scoop on the subject to draw ratings, and they milked it: there was the horror story about a pregnant woman seen dangling her legs from the branch of a tamarind tree on the night of a full moon; a drama series recounting the acrimonious love story of (Goddess) Rosarin; a testimony by a woman whose wishes had been granted nineteen consecutive times; tips on a technique for worshipping at the shrine with Valentine's Day flowers; the economical habits of Aunt Linjee, the charitable woman who owned the land on which the shrine stood; even a food programme recommending dishes from Somwang Grilled Chicken, which had opened a major branch across the road.

Even those who suffered from having too many lovers started coming to worship the Goddess. In barely a year, Aunt Linjee brought in ten million baht more than the original sale price she had put on her land. She also had mountains of cash coming in every day from donations. The motorcycle depot had to return to its original spot because the drivers could earn more from transporting lovesick passengers than from the busy traffic on the main road. They made more than enough to buy a new table made from rain-tree wood, freshly painted, with a chequerboard inlaid at its centre and a zinc roof overhead. Not one of the drivers dared tell a version of Goddess Rosarin's origin story that was different to the one posted on the wall.

One evening, when Chareeya happened to see "The Cursed Love of Goddess Rosarin" on television while at a roadside restaurant, her heart didn't skip a beat. She had no way of connecting the Goddess with the shuttered café that, for a time, she had walked past every day, or with the woman whose name appeared a thousand times in the bristling, yellowed letters that her father had written and that she had to cradle in her hands like babies when she read them – that name, which had unconsciously triggered something inside her and had made her turn to look at the sign above the café to begin with.

The Rosarin of the love letters never owned any land, neither was she ever pregnant nor was she a goddess. And she didn't hang herself. The only similarity she shared with the Rosarin in the made-up legend was that she had been roundly defeated by love. As a child, her family had called her Rose, short for Rosarin; a detail that echoed with the narrative of roses upheld by the worshippers. She came from a wealthy family and had been a graceful traditional dancer trained at a famous school. She had also been her mother's favourite daughter.

When she was nineteen, Rosarin was chosen by her school to dance at a reception for a conference of maths teachers. There, she met Tos, Chareeya's father. After a friendly conversation, Teacher Tos asked Rosarin to take him sightseeing around Bangkok the following day. By the end of that brief afternoon, they had become lovers. Chareeya's father returned home and wrote to her every day for a year and, when there was a vacancy at his school for the position of traditional dance teacher, he asked her to take the job and move to Nakhon Chai Si. He rented the small blue house and promised her with a single rose every day that he would divorce his wife and marry her.

It didn't take long for Rosarin's family to get wind of their favourite daughter living with a married man. Her mother vowed to denounce her if she didn't end the relationship and return home. Rosarin chose him. And when his wife caught him with his mistress on the day Chareeya was born and threatened to kill herself three years later, he asked Rosarin to wait. *I promise you, Rosarin, in life or in death, I'll come back to you.*

Rosarin didn't cry, not even once, and for six years she waited for him. She spent the prime of her life alone in that blue house, her sole consolation the letters he secretly wrote to her every few days. In the last year, his letters stopped without explanation. Nothing had arrived at her door for months until she had almost forgotten him when he showed up, old and skinny as if the longing in his heart had aged him thirty years. As they were together in the bed where he had once admired her beauty every afternoon over half a decade ago, Rosarin was assaulted by something unexpected: a smell.

The smell rose like a vapour from his body, so wrecked and weakened that it could no longer dispose of its own waste, of the dregs of medicine and the bitterness of life. It was a stench as miserable as that found in the communal wards of a state hospital; reeking, pungent, overpowering, and so alien that Rosarin couldn't bear it and had to get up in the middle of their lovemaking and rush over to the window to breathe. As she stood watching the distant river, she strove to recall what he had told her in those days gone-by, and what came to her mind were the melodramatic messages he had poured into his letters: *I miss you with every breath, Rosarin. It's so painful, it's like I am burning in hell. I don't understand how I could have dragged us into the abyss of this agony.*

You know, I always believed you'd come back… Rosarin left the sentence dangling, smiled a sad smile, and before she could carry on speaking – *but I thought it was over between us a long time ago, I just didn't realise it until this moment* – she turned around and found him dead. Naked, eyes rolling, hair over his forehead, mouth slightly gaping. There was a scar she had never seen before under his ribcage, from where the doctor had confiscated half his liver but left the cancer to spread. He lay there on the bed and for a long while

Rosarin couldn't believe what she was seeing. Then she realised she had no clothes on and it struck her that, if hadn't she got up, he would have died right there in the middle of their lovemaking.

Slumped beneath the window, Rosarin laughed and continued laughing without pause for an hour. And she still let out another long and irrepressible laugh as she carpeted his coffin with the many thousands of letters he had written her over the years. She hired a driver to help lift his body on top of them and drive the coffin to his house. After that, Rosarin packed a few belongings and caught the last bus to Bangkok, where she found that her status as a severed member of her family was irreparable. Her mother had died a few months earlier and the family blamed her for the death. They ganged up against her and forbade her from setting foot in the family home again. And her old friends had all scattered in different directions.

From then on, Rosarin lived alone and supported herself by dancing at birthday parties, weddings, house blessing ceremonies, shrines where worshippers wanted to please the deities, restaurants and even cremation rites. When she grew older she used her savings to open Café Rosarin on that street corner not far from the CD shop where Chareeya worked. Throughout her life she had been a quiet woman who hardly spoke or socialised but, when she turned thirty-eight, Rosarin suddenly started talking all the time – to herself. Her soliloquy was delivered in high volume and she blurted it out wherever she was, not caring about the way people looked at her.

At forty, she began talking to Chareeya's dead father as if he was standing before her, invisible. *What have I done to you for you to do this to me?* Or, *Well? You said you'd come back to me so why did you fucking die?* Shouting at the top of her lungs with eyes bulging and arms flailing in all directions, she scared off the customers and finally the café had to close down; that was about a year before Chareeya walked past it for the first time.

From that time on, Rosarin's isolation from the world became absolute. She never ventured out and kept talking loudly to herself about the past, like an undying echo in a sealed room, as if she wanted to make sure that Chareeya's father, hovering somewhere at the edges of her life, could hear her clearly. Even with the constant shouting no one took any notice when her voice stopped coming from the house, or when she disappeared from sight. One day, the neighbours were disturbed by a rotten smell and broke into the premises. They didn't find anything except for a large dead rat lying in the middle of a house in shambles with the several thousand letters that Chareeya's father had written and that Chareeya's mother had burned to ashes a dozen years ago – letters that Rosarin had memorised by heart and written out again for her own perusal.

A long time after that, Chareeya saw Rosarin with her own eyes when she was looking out from a bus window and noticed a strange woman dancing gracefully on a traffic island in the shimmering drizzle, shouting at a dead man as she moved along. Chareeya watched her in wonder and smiled at her for the brief second that their eyes met. And, still, many years later when she was irredeemably cast adrift amongst petals of Mon roses, when the image of Rosarin in the rain resurfaced in her mind amidst a million other images she had collected throughout her life, Chareeya was never able to see the tangled webs of connection between herself and the dancer in the drizzle.

XV

The Boy of the Night

Four forty-eight a.m., the entire neighbourhood was woken by a scream; the awful howling of a beast in anger, or great pain, belted out at intervals as if it was competing with the sound of the rain. Pran leapt up from his mattress and ran outside. The howling stopped, and then started again. Streetlights illuminated vertical raindrops like a million nails shooting down from the blood-red sky, and there was the hazy form of a figure dragging itself slowly along the road. Pran saw Patra, naked from the waist up, his legs about to give out, screaming that maddening scream. He was holding something in his arms: Paradorn.

Rain splashed on his face as Pran ran towards him and held out his arms to help support the body that was about slip from its father's embrace. But Patra jerked away and lost his balance. He fell to the ground but still held his son tightly as he wailed, *Pran, it's my fault – I did it.* Pran trembled though he didn't feel cold, not at all. *I did this to him!* Patra looked down at his son and sobbed.

I gave it to him. I gave it to him with my own hands, he said, looking up at Pran with eyes haunted by despair. His wailing was hoarse, croaky, hopeless. *Pran, I killed my son.* Lightning flashed and Pran started trembling again. *I gave him the powder – I injected the fucking stuff into him. I gave it to him and I lay down beside him, Pran. I lay down beside him all night…* Patra screamed that beastly scream again.

Paradorn's eyes were wide open, drifting, bleak, inundated by the rainwater pouring over his face. The moment Pran wiped his hand over his friend's eyes to close them, he started to cry. Pran had never expected this, never, and he wondered why it hadn't crossed his mind before. At that instant, as Pran burst out crying, his chest heaving, he closed his eyes and saw a father carefully pushing a syringe frothing with heroin into his son's vein, then covering him with a blanket, stroking his head and face lovingly, as he always did. After that, he administered the drug to himself and lay down beside the boy so they could plunge together into a dark wonderland, father following son, only to discover later that the boy hadn't come back out of the hole with him because he had become trapped, forever, somewhere in that fathomless neverland.

Devastated amid the ruins of the last family he would ever have, Pran could only sit there crying, rootless, demolished by fate in the piercing rain that kept stabbing him, over and over, one sharp drop after another, until he was completely wrecked, and, still, it continued penetrating inside him, devouring him, leaving only that unanswerable question: why…? When the hours of cold, hard rain that seemed to know no end finally ended, Pran stopped crying and, for the first time in his life, felt the curse of solitude that would remain with him until his final days.

The sky never brightened again. Patra didn't go back to Berlin; he wasn't there to witness the moment when the big wall was knocked down the following year, as he had thought he would be. He terminated his rental agreement on the house, gave all his possessions to Pran, cut his long flowing hair, which once fluttered in the light, and took his last journey to ordain as a monk in a small forest monastery in his hometown in the province of Phrae. *I have nothing left*, he said. That was all he said, and Pran was stunned. Something was still raining down hard inside him, even though he had felt only emptiness since the night Paradorn died.

Pran wanted to tell Patra that he still had him, that he shouldn't leave, that he should stay and let Pran console him as a friend, a brother, a son, someone who would be there for him – please stay, stay and be my friend, my brother, my father, don't leave me again because I don't have anyone else. But Pran didn't say anything. He gazed into eyes that were once full of beautiful dreams and that were now swollen and red, as if they had been crying all this time without emitting any tears. He saw a heart that had once been as free as the wind but was now crushed and imprisoned by unending misery. He looked at a man who was once so charming, an inspiration, a dream, but who was now shattered, destroyed. And all Pran could do was shout incomprehensibly in his own mind – don't go, don't go – as he let Patra hug him for the last time and then watched him walk away.

As soon as Patra was gone, Pran shook with anger and his fury reached a fever pitch when he found himself staggering towards the gazebo where he had once rescued Chareeya from the river. He was angry because everyone he loved had walked out on him. He was angry at every family he had ever had for breaking apart. He was angry at having to live a lonely life, over and over again. He was angry at everything for happening the way it had happened.

Then Chalika sat down beside him without saying a word. She slowly unclasped his rigid fists, hugged him lightly, rocked his body back and forth gently. Her words soothed him and he rested his face on her shoulder while stammering, babbling as if in a foreign tongue, until she leant down and whispered something into his ear, and the storm inside his chest calmed, grew faint, and time stopped again.

When Grandmother died just a few months later, Pran had no capacity left to feel anything. There was no goodbye, no last words, she just raised her hand – devoid of its little finger – over her head, slumped over a sweetly pink and exquisitely blooming lotus bouquet she had been arranging, and stopped breathing in the middle of an afternoon so beautiful Pran found it hard to believe anyone could die on such a glorious day. He couldn't understand why the birds still sang, why the wind still caressed his body, why the sun still basked the horizon with its splendid light. He couldn't understand how life could go on as if nothing had happened.

After Grandmother's funeral, Pran sold the house and moved to Bangkok. He enrolled in an art college and the following year he met a new friend who shared the same taste in music. When he found a drummer and a guitarist, he formed a band. Pran didn't call it Broken Rainbow, as he and Paradorn had once talked about, but Broken Soul, because that was how he felt. Inside him were threadbare ruins, a rancorous corpse that had taken over the best years of his life.

Later that year the band got a deal to do a studio recording with a small indie label. Though they hardly sold any albums, they at least got to play twice a week at a small bar in Patpong. They still managed to drag themselves up in the morning to attend classes and just barely passed their exams. They spent their energy writing songs and practicing, and released another record the following year. Again, it didn't sell. After that, they scored an on-going gig at the Bleeding Heart, playing at the bar six nights a week. And, in the end, they dropped out of college because it was just too much bother to get up in the mornings.

During those years, Pran wrote several songs for his family members: *Like a Grain of Sand* for Uncle Chit, *Light of the Day* for Uncle Thanit, a ballad called *The Moon and Stars are Melting* for Chareeya, *The Woman who Stopped Time* for Chalika, *Flame* for Patra, and *In the Dark* for Paradorn. But he hid them all in his heart, neither putting them down on paper nor playing them to anyone. And he never went back to the house by the river, as he had promised Chalika he would. If one thing changed, he was scared everything else would change so it was best to leave everything as it was when he had left it, leaving it somewhere in the unreachable depths of his heart and telling himself that it would remain there forever, unchanged.

Pran braced himself for the fact that nothing could stay the same forever, as he had been trying to fool himself it would, and when he finally returned to the house by the river with Chareeya, the scars inflicted by time made his heart quiver. The house was considerably worn. The walls and floors repaired by Uncle Thanit years ago were riddled with long cracks. The windows, once sealed shut during those days when Mother's moaning echoed through the house, had fallen from their frames. The paint was peeling off. The old pomelo tree was a skeleton of its former fulsome self. The long-faced swan deigned to turn and squint at him as he walked in, before flicking its head back and lowering its gaze again. The creature looked old, angry, sad, splotchy – its long face had grown longer and moodier, and Pran felt guilty.

When was the last time I saw you…? Chalika smiled. Pran put up his fingers to count. *Seven or eight years / You haven't changed, except the long hair, like a hippy.* Pran smiled a faint smile. *You're prettier / Don't sweet-talk me – you said you'd come back but you never did / I'm sorry / Forgiven, now that you're here / Uncle Thanit? / Travelling, as usual / When will he come back? / Months – I think his last telegram was from Ladakh, wherever that is.*

I've been coming home more often and I still never see him – we keep missing each other, said Chareeya, looking up from a stack of vinyl records. *He's gone to buy fabric?* Pran asked. *Yes / He's serious about it? / Yes, for many years now,* Chalika said. Pran thought about the last time he had seen Uncle Thanit, then still fit-looking, with the smile and glinting eyes of a young man. *You can always talk to me, you're like my nephew, you know that, right?* That was how Uncle Thanit had said goodbye to him, as if he would only be gone a few days, and Pran had never thought it would take this long for him to return.

Pran, stay the night. Sleep in Uncle Thanit's room and go back tomorrow. I'll row you out to a new restaurant, just beyond Grandpa Phum's vegetable garden / Near Grandpa Nong's haunted house? Chareeya asked in panic. Pran laughed. *Yup, it's the haunted house.* Pran laughed again. *But no one has seen Grandpa Nong for a while, not since the house became a fancy restaurant – where would his ghost find a place to sit down and cry? / I saw signs for several new restaurants on the way here / Yes, this isn't a backwater anymore / But I want to try the local dessert everyone in Bangkok is talking about – the dessert made by a chef pretty as an angel,* Pran teased. *Of course, tomorrow the angel will serve you sweets instead of breakfast.* Chalika laughed her delightful laugh. Right, Pran thought, when was the last time he had heard Chalika's laugh?

Chopin's Nocturne floated in, daintily, with a melody as delicate as when sound had first returned to the house. *Anyway, Lika, what dishes do you recommend at this restaurant? /* Hormok krok – *interested? Casseroles cooked in little pots / Fancy! My mouth is watering… / Their* *freshwater fish is good, home-made curries with okra leaves, boiled mackerel with* madan, *steamed horse fish, earthstar mushrooms in gravy*[*] */ Stop! I'm hungry now – what do you say, Pran?* Chareeya beseeched. *Sure, I don't have to play tonight, I can go back late morning tomorrow / Great, it's dinner with everyone / Yeah, I haven't had dinner with Lika for, what, seven years?*

In the middle of the sad Nocturne, Chareeya sat down beside Chalika, grabbed her sister's hand and implored her with a smile: *I want to have dinner with Lika, too, I misssss her...* They looked similar and had the same sparkle in their eyes, the same smile. Chalika was a sharp-featured beauty: shoulder-length hair, unpretentious, with a hint of internal strength like a woman from a small town. Chareeya had a fairer complexion with long wavy hair, not as pretty as her sister but more lively and fashionable. Images from the old days flashed across Pran's mind, images from when they were just two naughty girls playing in the mud – look how they had blossomed. Back then Pran could never have imagined them the way they were now.

Don't sweet talk me, Charee... Chalika feigned resentment at her sister. *Pran, you too. After dinner tonight, I'll have to wait another seven years to eat with you two again. Who made a promise to come back? If Charee hadn't run into you... / I'm sorry, Lika, I...* Pran faltered, a lump had made its way into his throat. He didn't know what to say to her. He didn't want to tell her how he had once mistaken a woman walking in the crowd for her, how his heart had sunk when the woman looked up and he had realised it wasn't her, and how, for a few seconds, his chest had pounded in delight when he thought he had run into her.

He didn't tell her that he had returned once but had only made it halfway, pacing around indecisively before getting back on the bus. He had been afraid that he wouldn't see her and Uncle Thanit the way they had been preserved in his memory. He didn't tell the two women that he used to lie down and look at the stars, thinking

* *Hormok krok* is a fish mousse made with coconut milk and steamed in little pots, *madan* is a Thai fruit used in savoury dishes, and "horse fish" refers to the boeseman croaker, native to Southeast Asian rivers.

back to a time when they had all lain in the back of a battered pick-up truck and watched the passage of the universe until it evaporated into morning. He didn't tell them how the world beyond his window was just a shithole of loneliness, or how he had been living his life, or how he had missed them every single day.

He didn't tell them how many times he had hoped beyond all hope that everything would come back to this living room in which they were sitting right now, with Chopin's saddest-music-in-the-world murmuring in the background as they talked and talked about nothing of importance, and an aroma of smoke wafted in from somewhere, blending with the evening fragrance of the river, on an ordinary evening that resembled no other evening on earth.

I'm sorry, Lika, I'm sorry I never amounted to anything more.

XVI

Shadow Play

When he was a young man, Natee believed he had been born to love – to love someone deeply, passionately, feverishly. When he met Chareeya, he was thirty-six, having lived half his life uneventfully without many adventures, having been with several women and almost marrying some, and having stopped hoping a long time ago that he would find a woman he could love deeply, passionately, feverishly.

After barely a month of dating, Natee told Chareeya he would be going to Sarajevo to cover the horrendous massacre taking place there. He related the barbaric conditions of the civil war in great detail as if he had witnessed them himself, and he kept warning her that he might not make it back alive. He only wanted to know how she felt about him, and how deep that feeling was. It was like he was testing her: *I don't want to go, it's dangerous. Before I met you, I didn't care what happened – my life had no meaning.* Natee looked out at the evening garden, watching the swaying treetops before turning his sad eyes back to Chareeya. *But now I have you, I don't want to risk my life anywhere again and I'm afraid something could happen to me. I want to live my life with you.* His last sentence trailed off tremulously.

Deep in the throes of love, Chareeya wept and sobbed heavily, and she kept crying until he had to promise he would call her every day to assure her that he was still breathing. But, of course, Natee never went anywhere. He waited for a week before calling her and Chareeya wept intensely over the phone, mumbling words that had no meaning. From then on, guilt gnawed at Natee's conscience, driving him to insomnia and long days of feeble will and inactivity; he was in agony because he was the reason for her suffering. On top of that was the debilitating torment of not seeing her, which drove him to indulge in nonsensical scenarios in which something terrible happened to her while he pretended to be away.

Plagued by these fears, Natee spied on her at the CD shop, positioning himself at a distance across the street. From that vantage point Chareeya looked wilted, abandoned, alone, and Natee was seized by a profundity of emotion that compelled him to write numerous poems dedicated to her. But, still, he didn't call her. He kept staring at the phone and several times almost succumbed to an irresistible urge in his hands to press the buttons. Come late afternoon, he would stalk her as she made her way home and as she stopped off at a noodle shop for a bite to eat. And he continued following her, standing like a zombie in the shadows and looking up at the illuminated window of her room. Then he would return home and toss about in his bed, half-asleep, half-wandering in fevered dreams. He endured this self-flagellation for three full weeks before dragging his sorry self back to Chareeya.

And he was nearly scorched to ashes by flames of desire he had never experienced. Never before in his thirty-six years had he loved someone with such passion – a maddening, smouldering love that brought pure joy when she was returned to his embrace. Weakened by longing, soggy with tears, in that fervour of desire, he kept saying he loved her, over and over again, covering her with kisses on the top of her head, on her forehead, her chin, her shoulder, her cheek. And when he thought back on the great misery of their separation he was so overwhelmed that even more tears streamed down his face.

The voluptuous longing, the head-over-heels magnificence... Natee's love was dizzying, obsessive. He had taken a page from *Romeo and Juliet* and peppered it with cutesy daily banter like the script of a Hollywood romcom, with classical music from the Romantic period as a private soundtrack in his head, complete with a stint of separation as a test of willpower, and with the city of lost angels as the backdrop. As a daughter unloved by her own mother, who had counted animals and trees as members of her family, been chronically sick with solitude, and lived most of her life in various forms of a fish tank, Chareeya had no choice but to plunge into the myth of love – the splendour of a passion that no one else would ever feel in their lives.

Even so, Natee couldn't suppress his need to fabricate tales of dangerous missions he was compelled to embark upon as part of his journalistic duty. He would disappear for a couple of weeks at a time and the lovers would repeat the longing, the I-miss-yous, the soul-crushing worries, and he listened to Chareeya cry as if she was about to die right there with her hand still clutching the phone. He imagined himself a young man, though he had lived long past that age, playing the role of an arrogant yet tortured lover. When the time was right, he returned to her restless embrace, an embrace that clambered to pull him into the epicentre of their obsessive love.

After a while, Chareeya began to adjust and get used to Natee's alleged near-death adventures in faraway war zones. She convinced herself that he would make it back unscathed, as he had done every single time. She would shed a few tears when he said goodbye and talk to him on the phone in her lonely little voice. Then she would wait for him, perfectly calm, and welcome him back with a warm embrace that increasingly came to resemble a motherly hug. For his part, Natee still yearned for that feeling of being loved so intensely, so inexorably, as if there was no tomorrow for either of them.

Once, during a camping trip in the mountains, while Chareeya was sleeping, Natee sneaked out of the tent for a stroll. On his return, he hid behind a bush and watched her seized with panic after waking up without him beside her. Only then did he reveal himself, playing it cool and collected: *C'mon, I was just taking a walk. Don't cry, dear, come to me.* Another time he stood Chareeya up, leaving her gripped by fear the entire night. Then he called her the next morning and told her he had contracted a meningococcal disease at the border outpost where he was staying. But, no, he wouldn't reveal the name of the town: *I don't want you to see me in this state, a half-dead wreck. If I don't make it back, you must remember, dear Charee, that I loved you.*

Chareeya didn't even know where he lived. He had told her only that he lived with his mother and that she didn't want to see her son in love with any woman. *It's all right, my mother is dying anyway – it's just a matter of time*, he assured her. Neither did he share his work address with Chareeya. *I'm a freelance journalist, I don't have an office. Freelance, you know what that means, right?* Deprived of information as to his whereabouts, Chareeya skipped work and blindly ran around to different hospitals. A week later, Natee returned, looking sunny. He had miraculously survived and was in great health after volunteering himself as a guinea pig for a newly discovered drug. *The person who developed this medicine will soon win the Nobel Prize, just wait and see.*

Not only did he keep fine-tuning the dramatic details of his daredevil assignments, Natee also played at being an emotional soul with unresolvable baggage, or sometimes a pensive introvert like the hero of a Japanese movie, or sometimes a complex, overly sensitive character like an arthouse filmmaker. One day he told her they were so different from each other, like oil and water, that there was no way their love could last. The next day he told her she was a hindrance, holding him back from becoming the intrepid correspondent he had always wanted to be. Then the day after that it was him who was dragging her down since he had no means of taking care of her like a good man should. *Leave me, Charee, you're too good for someone like me.* But out of the blue he switched again and become a jealous lover, imagining her unfaithful tendencies in great detail even though Chareeya never saw any other men.

Then he would disappear for days, weeks, sometimes months, and return a wretch; gaunt and weak from insomnia and starvation – poisoned by love. And that was who he really was, Natee wasn't acting. He believed with genuine conviction that he really was a war correspondent, that he had just been taking a stroll, that he had contracted a meningococcal disease, that he was an over-sensitive soul, and that he couldn't eat or sleep because he had been pummelled into near madness by a poisonous love.

The afternoon breeze brought with it a faint scent of *nang yaem* flowers, heralding a fine day. Natee had just reappeared after an absence of almost one month. The rekindling of love was soothing. They talked and came to an understanding, a promise that things would be different. Then, Natee opened a small book and read her a story about a lonely ten-year-old girl who tried to find herself a friend by writing a letter, putting it in a bottle, and floating it out to sea. The bottle circled the country three times and was picked up six years later by a boy of thirteen, who wrote back accepting the girl's offer of friendship. By then, however, the girl was sixteen and had outgrown the feelings she had in the past, and she was still too young to pay attention to a boy who was younger than her.

She didn't reply to him and forgot all about it. She grew up, got a boyfriend, got married, got divorced, and lived alone for much of her life. Then, when she was past middle age, she found a new love, the best man she had ever known. When she was arranging their belongings on the day he moved in with her, she found the letter she had written and cast adrift into the world decades ago. It was impossible to believe that the man she now loved was that boy who once wrote back, the boy she had rejected and erased from her memory. He, too, had forgotten the cruel girl who had spurned him and, yet, he had managed to find her again.

Touched by the tale, just as she had been by the stories of miracles told by Uncle Thanit, Chareeya was moved by the wonders of love and faith that had guided the two lovers through the labyrinth of time and the subterfuges of life and brought them together. Chareeya was still in Natee's embrace when he closed the book and told her in a calm voice that he had another woman.

This wasn't another episode in Natee's life that existed only his imagination. He had been taking Pimpaka out to dinners and movies even before he had met Chareeya. And he had kept seeing her during those absences when he told Chareeya he was risking his life in a conflict zone, or when he was sick with an imaginary meningococcal disease, or when he disappeared to relish the taste of longing, or when he calculated the balance sheet of love to decide if she loved him more than he loved her. For every second that his relationship with

Chareeya was rocked by time and familiarity, his feelings towards Pimpaka grew more intense. He wasn't the kind of man who juggled several women at once but, unwittingly, Natee's behavior was being indulged by his deep hunger to find scaffolding for the true worth of his love – something that could withstand the corrosion caused by familiarity, something painful and yet reaffirming.

There was a sentimental brevity to the moment that exploded into dust when Chareeya went ballistic: she became hysterical, refused to eat, threw things at the walls, got depressed, didn't go to sleep at night or in the day, and devised sixty-two ways to kill herself. She imagined running straight into a wall and collapsing backwards as he watched, or shouting until there was no sound left in her body. In the first week, she broke up with Natee eight hundred times. In the following week, four hundred. And since then, she did it fifty times a week even though she knew she couldn't live without him.

From there, her reaction was scaled down to sporadic moaning and occasional tantrums. Then she became completely quiet as if she had come to terms with the inevitable and concentrated her mind on putting the sixty-two suicide methods she had conceived of down on paper: these ranged from the classic trick, favoured by ancient Chinese dynasties, of swallowing opium; to the simple technique of hanging yourself from a doorknob and waiting for someone to open the door; to a no-brainer like starting to run and then to just keep running until you dropped dead; to an elaborate performance such as burying your head in the sand like an ostrich, or like all those people who are afraid of life. Chareeya stared at the piece of paper with the austere devotion of a worshipper performing rites. But the saddest part was, not only was Chareeya devoid of courage, she was, in fact, frightened – mortally afraid that she might accidentally kill herself using one of these methods.

When she took a break from these miserable activities, Chareeya cried in every possible manner. She cried audibly, inaudibly, in the privacy of her chest, loudly or softly depending on her energy that day, in public toilets, on buses, in crowded restaurants, and on the street. If she didn't have to go anywhere, she would stay in and cry at home, listening to sad music and sobbing against the peony-patterned cushion, or she would water the flowers with her profusion of tears until they radiated a heartbreaking aroma that floated out onto the street and caused babies to cry in their mothers' arms.

Time soon solidified the lovers' tragic romance into destiny. Natee continued to waver, unstable, neither staying nor leaving. And yet he was warm and affectionate, returning cheerful and sunny after his frequent disappearances, only to disappear again in tears and sorrow. Chareeya was fixated with this disastrous rollercoaster, grief-stricken and crying non-stop until a line of grey shadow etched itself across her left eye like a fissure. It didn't cause her any physical pain but it made that eye seem lonelier than the other, and it had the effect of discouraging the faint-hearted from looking straight at her. It also polluted her vision so that every image she saw had a grey crack slashed across it; through Chareeya's eyes, the entire world was about to break into pieces.

XVII

The Metropolis of Mice

Of all the women living along the riverbank, Chalika was hands-down the most beautiful. Not only had she inherited her mother's beauty and faith in love, but she also glowed with the magical aura of a literary heroine, complete with fortitude, virtue and patience. Still, she lived a quiet, uneventful life and spent her days making sweets, reading novels, daydreaming and crying for men who didn't exist in real life.

The day she learned that the military cadet, who was no longer a military cadet as she had always thought but now a military colonel, had gotten married, Chalika cried her eyes out and confessed her love to him eighty-seven thousand six hundred and fifty times; each time shedding one tear, each teardrop representing each hour since she had fallen in love with him when she was thirteen. Despite the magnitude of the drama, Chalika wasn't crying for any living, flesh-and-blood man, but for an illusory image of a man put together from a thousand images stored inside her head from romance novels, which had fed into her melancholic desire for someone about whom she knew nothing – not his name, his preferred colour, his hobbies, or his favourite curry.

She cried for herself: for the loss of a love she had never actually known, for the lonesome wandering in her own fantasy, and for the interminable wait for the hand of destiny. She was so obsessed with her own melancholy that she didn't register the presence of the municipal clerk who had been watching her secretly from the corner of the street since they were in primary school, and who had by now become a hopeless drunkard, drowning himself in whisky so that he could forget her and be able to sleep at night. She didn't notice the shy teacher who came to buy sweets from her every day and who left her shop with tears in his eyes. She didn't notice the car accidents that kept happening in front of her shop, or the bank employee who slipped and fell on the footpath and broke his arm, or the engineer whose mind wandered off while he was bicycling and who overshot a curve and landed in a ditch, or the western tourist who became a howling madman, prompting the locals to take him for sprinklings of holy water five times a day for ten days straight, or the postman who was fired because his heart kept skipping a beat and he kept delivering letters to the wrong addresses. Chalika didn't realise that all those men shared the same fate of having laid eyes on the beautiful woman who had blossomed from the inspiration of a million romance novels – the woman who couldn't understand why she wasn't able to stop sighing her sighs of regret.

Maybe it was down to the romance novels. Or maybe, just maybe, it was the irresistible sex appeal of Nual the nanny, who became the cook and later Chalika's helper at the dessert shop. Nual was also the mother of five children who shared three fathers – a mathematical riddle and parentage conundrum – and her touch had made Chalika's *thong yod* and *foi thong** sweeter than anyone else's and her *kanom chan* the most delicious in the world, as wonderful as those made by the late Grandma Nu who had passed down the recipe directly to the young woman herself.

Nakhon Chai Si by then had become a fully-fledged tourist town crawling with restless day-trippers from Bangkok. They came and bought everything and ate everything, as if cursed by an indefatigable hunger; even the children, who were usually always hungry, wondered

* Made from egg yolks and sugar, *thong yod* (literally, "golden drops") and *foi thong* ("golden threads") are auspicious Thai desserts.

why city people had such voracious appetites. As a result, Chalika's business prospered and her pastries sold out quicker and quicker; first by five p.m., and then by three p.m., and sometimes a client reserved everything she made and she had to close her shop at ten a.m.. But she never considered increasing production and continued to make the same amount of sweets because she wanted to have free time to read her novels in that dreary house whose members had scattered in different directions.

Uncle Thanit had become a stranger, his presence waning into shadow with each passing second as his fabric-hunting trips lengthened to months, or almost an entire year, and his sojourns at home became shorter and shorter until they lasted mere days. His fascination with antique textiles was something incomprehensible to most people, except to those who had the chance to marvel at them up close when they were illuminated by angled light – the only kind of light humankind had known before the invention of the light bulb moved the source of illumination to a spot above our heads, creating a wan, lifeless, pallid light that crushes and flattens everything beneath it, including humans.

A phantasmal shaft of afternoon sunshine pouring into a crepuscular room or the nocturnal flickering of candlelight was enough to flesh out the singular depth of each coloured thread in a piece of fabric: a mass of pink camouflaged amongst red threads rising up and spreading its brilliance; rustic orange glowing over an ebony-tree blackness, like the colours of the horizon at twilight; gold threads spiralling elegantly, catching fire and erupting in flames. This was how Uncle Thanit had first encountered textiles in the antique shop that day.

What cast a spell on him more powerfully than anything, however, was not the multi-dimensional majesty drawn out by the primordial angled light, but the complex melodies made by a million gossamer threads that wound around one another like a colossal symphony. And even more riveting than that was the story behind each piece of cloth, some just a few decades old and others woven before civilisation began.

Fabric with a tortuously baroque pattern that could be unspooled to reveal a spell, fabric dyed in curdled mud from a sacred riverbed where the water had dried up millennia ago, fabric woven to the chanting of ancient hymns, fabric so densely threaded that even a teardrop from a newborn baby could not seep through, fabric that the devil himself dare not look at, fabric that had been wrapped around a human arriving from the freezing cold into this world of solitude, and fabric that was wrapped around that person on their journey to the empire of souls.

Fabric woven by a mother who encoded within the threads a secret treasure map that only her favourite daughter could be taught to decode, fabric that could cover a woman's head thereby propelling her into the lost half of a man's soul, fabric that could transform an ordinary man into a celestial warrior if he draped it over his shoulders, and fabric that could bless every speck of dust in this faithless world and turn it into a vast holy realm – by just touching it to their foreheads all men, princely or lowborn, would appear before god as equals.

As the river kept changing its colour and fish continued to float like leaves, and as the pesticide-free vegetable garden could no longer fend off toxins, Uncle Thanit dedicated himself to the business of antique textiles. Without realising when it had happened or how, he found himself trapped in a sinuous quest and lurched endlessly from luminous cities to villages not recorded on any maps, from the Salween River to the Suriname, from a path drenched in blood in a time before Temüjin became the Great Khan to the ruins of a throne hall that had once been the domain of the Queen of Sheba.

He was lost for months in a nameless valley in Patagonia, and another time walked around in circles, dazed by the enchanting fragrance of an incense market secretly buried under Isfahan. He travelled for a year with a salt caravan of the Azure Warriors of the Sahara, into the desert where he drank water from the well of the Pink Gypsies of Thar – water that tasted like tears and that only made him thirstier with every drop.

Once, he trekked with a Bedouin sage searching the skies for the lost constellation over Rub'al Khali, then he walked on an opium cloud with Mujahidin in the honeycomb caves, untouched by sunlight, in the maze of the Great Hindu Kush. With a tribal chief in Shandong, he munched on the still-beating heart of a cow believed to have already been extinct for centuries. In Bethlehem, he dodged a hail of bullets in a messy holy war destined to last through eternity. He played football with an undiscovered tribe in Amazonia and witnessed the magical moment when the Shroud of Spirituality was unfurled over Shangri-la.

The sniffing out of clues became the pursuit of treasure and a peripatetic wind blew Uncle Thanit into a cycle of unfathomable solitude. He no longer had time in the afternoons to caress his prized collection of fabrics or to admire their dazzle in the flickering candlelight – a performance of light and colour that slipped back into the past – because he spent all his time, day and night, on his endless journey. He carried a small notebook in which he jotted down stories and legends almost forgotten by the world, and a small abacus that could calculate price but not value. He went in search of fabric to sell so that he could fund his next trip to search for more fabric to sell so that he could fund his next trip, ad infinitum.

Besides, every time he came home he had changed, bit by bit at first, then more and more until he had become someone else and was no longer the uncle the children used to know. A mesh of beard covered his face, he walked around the house in exotic costumes, alternating between a Sikkim-style vest, a Burmese sarong, a Middle-Eastern robe with a hem that grazed the floor, or tapered pantaloons like those worn by the genie rubbed out of Aladdin's lamp. He wore peculiar hats, even inside the house: a Japanese soldier's cap, a Mexican sombrero, the festooned cylindrical fez of Sufi dervishes, a wide-brimmed hat jingling with ornaments like those worn by Spanish court officials, a Tibetan felt hat.

Not to mention the accessories bedecking various parts of his body: a dragon-headed Celtic ring, bronze Khmer earrings, a Sumatran bracelet shaped like two snakes coiling around his wrist to eat their own tails, a bright blue eye-shaped locket from Turkey, the latticework on a Tuareg breastplate that resembled extraterrestrial hieroglyphics, a protective Mayan tattoo to ward off the golden scorpion, a hairpin from Xishuangbanna, a shrunken human head from Peru, a boar fang, a tiger claw, a moose antler, and so on.

And it went further than that. Everyone found it impossible to understand Uncle Thanit's speech because he would mix the vocabulary of nine different languages in a single sentence. He sometimes spoke to Chalika in a heavenly dialect understood exclusively by Zoroastrian priests which, at any rate, hadn't been used for three thousand and six hundred years. He also went around greeting the neighbours with unusual phrases: *ohaiyo*, *salam*, *namaste*, *aslamualaikum*, *ciao*, *ni hao*, *bonjour*… Only once in a while did it occur to him that all he wanted to say was just *sawasdee*[*].

Constantly traversing time zones also inflicted permanent damage to his biological clock. Uncle Thanit's sleep patterns were utterly chaotic. He went to sleep at eight in the morning and six in the evening. Sometimes he wouldn't sleep a wink for nine days. Other times he slept like a bear, not moving an inch for twenty-seven days straight. But the worst was his newly acquired habit of not taking a shower, possibly picked up from the desert warriors, as he filled the house with the pungent odour of months-old spices, rotten fruits and animal stink – a stench so suffocating that Chalika placed trays of charcoal in the corners of the house to absorb the smell, and had to keep them there for weeks after Uncle Thanit had left on a new quest.

It wasn't only Uncle Thanit who had become something of a missing person; Chareeya, too, had grown distant. Chalika hardly ever received any updates from her sister, and on the rare occasions when she did return home, she spoke in dark innuendoes that rattled her sister's conscience: *If I die, will you cry?* Or: *If there's really a next life, I want to be born as your sister again, Lika.* Or: *Which method of suicide do you think is the most foolproof?* These remarks unearthed old forebodings that had been stashed away in Chalika's mind, and she didn't dare inquire further. Instead, she sat there keeping watch over the telephone, fearfully awaiting news that something bad might have happened to Chareeya.

* *Sawasdee* is the common phrase of greeting in the Thai language.

The living room was abandoned. The fountain out front dried up, leaving only the moody plaster swan, its skin peeled off at random spots, amidst the thorns of pygmy roses long devoured by weeds. The banana grove metamorphosed into a forest teeming with one hundred and eighty identical frogs that all had round warts on the tips of their fingers and sentimental eyes; as indistinguishable from one another as if they had been produced under strict quality control in a factory. The vegetable patch once tended by Pran became a metropolis of field mice, while the lost Dvaravati city Chareeya once set out to discover was buried forever, even deeper, under a new concrete road.

XVIII

The Colour Blind Painter

The extravagant luncheons at Chareeya's house had become a permanent fixture every Monday. Pran would arrive late in the morning to help her clean vegetables or pound curry paste, stealing glances at her as she shed tears for the death of an onion and being entertained by the spectacle of her bare-knuckle wrestling match with a salad. Her complicated cooking regime was dictated by a rigid protocol; the precise measurement of ingredients, like a scientist in a laboratory, alternated with the casual simplicity of a painter's final touches. Then they would sit down and eat slowly and talk as time wore on and the afternoon turned into evening. *Like good Italians*, Chareeya said as she waved her hands in the air.

Despite the cosmopolitan exoticism of many of the dishes, there was also a homey, small-town sensibility manifested in Chareeya's meals: a *tom yam* soup* of various aromas and tastes that was unbound by any fixed routine, one bowl never the same as another, sometimes flavoured by tamarind leaves and other times by okra, bilimbi, *madan*, depending on what was flowering in the garden or available at the fresh market; wondrous chilli pastes concocted from an ever-changing list of ingredients, which made Pran wonder if there was

* *Tom yam* is a clear soup, usually seafood in a broth made from lemongrass, kaffir lime leaves, galangal or ginger, and chillies.

anything in the world that couldn't be ground into Thai chilli paste; and big plates piled with unidentified leaves that Chareeya would pick up and chew throughout the meal, like a giraffe.

After lunch, they would retire to the house and lounge on the peony-patterned cushion, listening to music, reading, or teasing the cat until he lost his temper so they could appease him by stroking his soft belly until he meowed. They would play board games or, if Chareeya happened to fall asleep, Pran would sneak into her bathroom and sniff each of the fragrant oils in coloured glass bottles lined up on the rim of the claw-footed bathtub, relishing feminine perfumes he hardly had a chance to smell these days. Come late evening, they would be out in the garden again, each with a glass of sangria or a mojito as refreshing as if they had just been drenched by a tropical monsoon, and they would watch the last light of the day slip away from the sky before saying goodbye with a promise – *See you soon* – made under the light of the first stars.

On Friday nights, Chareeya and the Witches would show up at the Bleeding Heart. The Witches still took turns crying, but Pran would never see Chareeya shed tears again. After the bar closed he would walk her home. They would pause at the crosswalk, watching the movement of emptiness that left no trace on the city, or laughing at a drunk repeatedly telling his own shadow to stop moaning. Once, they heard the stars blinking as starlight spilled down onto the damp streets.

On a free weekday, she might ask him to go out with her to a bookstore or a movie. Once she took him to a European film festival and Pran, who had come from a long night at the bar, kept dozing off in different cinemas as they watched three movies in a row. In his mind the plots bled and blurred into one long narrative that began with an orphaned boy who envisioned himself as Laika, the dog the Soviet scientists put in a spacecraft and launched into a perpetual orbit, then the boy grew up to become a legendary lover who could sate the desire of the entire female staff of the Italian court, before he became a colour blind artist who painted by reading the colour labels on his tubes of paint. In fact, his imaginary film wasn't bad, Pran thought, except for its length, and don't all the stories in our lives bleed and blur into one chaotic narrative anyway?

Or sometimes she would take him on a culinary expedition, leading him on foot around some fresh market on the city outskirts to look for dried red cotton tree flowers, or horseshoe crabs fermented in fish sauce, or southern *budu* sauce*, or salted baby shrimps. Or they would hang around a Pakistani rug shop trying to buy sumac powder, as violet as potassium permanganate and as delicately aromatic as rain carried on an Arabian wind. Once, she took him along a squalid alley in Chinatown so she could beg an old, hostile Chinese grandmother to sell them peanut oil, and then onwards to buy egg noodles from a shophouse factory hidden so impregnably within a maze of nameless alleys that they had to walk through three houses belonging to people they didn't know, then zigzag some more before reaching shuttered doors through which white clouds of steam billowed when opened and behind which a dozen muscular topless workers were violently flinging dough into long strips – an image that reminded Pran of Shaolin monks in a practice session.

But most of the time their weekday hangouts were no more thrilling than a trip to a café that smelled of loneliness, where they would plunge into heated conversations about nothing remotely world-changing, or an hour-long bus journey to some temple where they would spend a few precious minutes looking at a painting by Krua In Khong** from the late 19th century, or a sojourn in Lumpini Park, where they would lie on the grass as the sun took a break and watch clouds slowly materialise from nothingness into a variety of shapes – first in hygienic white, then a lovely cotton-candy pink – before drifting into the desolate twilight. Once, he saw two cranes flying across the sky: *Cranes, did you see them*? Chareeya whispered, *Like us, two cranes braving the world.* And sometimes, many times in fact, they would just wander aimlessly in the city of broken dreams amidst the heaving throng of strangers. Yes, two of us, braving the world.

* *Budu* is a southern style sauce made from fermented anchovies, also part of Malaysian cuisine.

** Krua In Khong was a Buddhist monk who introduced western painting techniques to Thai temple murals in the 19th century.

All of this meant that Pran began to have something to long for as he spent each night putting together the unfinishable jigsaw puzzle of the Andromeda Galaxy and waiting for the sun to rise – that moment when he could watch her from the safe distance of his window and mumble to himself before going to sleep, *What's up, Charee?* He began to dream of the next Friday and Monday and the occasional weekdays to come. Dreaming, yes: something he hadn't done since Paradorn's death.

That Monday was the turn of Hungarian mutton goulash with bay leaves and dried chilli, simmered so expertly that it nearly vapourised in their mouths. Plus sundried snapper, sliced and put out in the sun for a whole day before being soaked in olive oil and sprinkled with fragrant basil, and eaten with rice pilaf and Israeli tabbouleh salad. Then canned peaches topped with passion fruit juice and cream, washed down by Darjeeling tea seasoned with orange skin and kaffir lime leaves.

Chareeya set the table outside the house as usual. When they started eating, she turned on Bacalov's *Misa Tango*, which Pran considered it to be the most hot-blooded hymn to the glory of God he had ever heard. It made him feel as if he had been chosen to join the Last Supper with Jesus Christ in Argentina – a thought that left him wondering what would have happened had the world's three feuding religions been born in vivacious, love-soaked Latin America instead of the parched Middle East. This is what he was thinking about when Natee walked in.

I happened to be in the area... was his casual greeting as he flashed a smile. Chareeya smiled back but didn't say a word as she poured him a glass of water and disappeared into the kitchen. *I'm Pran*, he said first, and was suddenly put-off by the way Natee lifted his glass with his pinkie finger raised – though it was bent and not pointed Pran found the gesture affected and pretentious. *Finally. I'm Natee. Charee has talked about you.* The hint of some emotion appeared at the corner of his mouth as he spoke, a smile that threatened to become a scowl before quickly disappearing. Pran told himself it was all in his mind, and yet he couldn't resist the thought that Natee was being condescending toward him. There was something in his tone: in the way he gently tugged up his trousers as he lowered himself to sit and eased his way into a cross-legged position like a pampered gentleman; in the way he glanced sideways; in the buzzing of a goddamn fly that circled the air somewhere near him; in the heat; in the glare of the sunlight.

Chareeya returned with a plate of food for Natee. The godly tango still spilled out from the house. *This stew is fantastic, you should open a restaurant.* Natee complimented her, affectionately running his palm up and down her arm. *Where would I find the money? I spend all I've earned on what I want to eat myself.* Chareeya laughed, looking cheerful, shyly raising her hand to tuck a few loose strands of hair behind her ear. There was a gust of hot wind, that stupid fly still buzzing somewhere, and Pran thought he should just finish whatever he was eating and get out of there.

If it's only for what you want to eat and not to feed others, what you earn is more than enough. Pran stopped short, then resumed eating, slowly chewing his food and unconsciously clenching his jaw so tightly that his cheeks bulged. He hated Natee's melodramatic sarcasm – the kind you only heard in soap operas on TV – and his tone of playful disdain. *I made the fish myself, I had to put it out in the sun for…* Chareeya tried to change the subject but Natee wouldn't stop. *Not just you and me, sorry what's your name? Pran. Chareeya is such a charmer, today she's treating you, tomorrow it will be another man, and then another…* His tone again choking with sarcasm. Pran didn't look up, his eyes were fixed on his plate and he clenched his jaw until it creaked.

They all come to feast on the cook, not the food. Natee laughed a brash laugh. *She can expertly switch tracks like a busy train junction.* Asshole, shut the fuck up, Pran shouted in his head. When he looked up again Natee was already down on the ground next to the table; Pran wasn't sure when he had struck the man. Shut your filthy gob, prick. She's mine, get that into your head. I didn't snatch her from death so that an asshole like you could insult her. Waves of anger from the past consumed him, rolling in from distant days: from the empty chair in the dining room of the house by the river, from the bench outside the ER, from the loneliness that had ravaged him until his soul was frayed like a torn cloth, from all the times Pran thought had already been forgotten.

Without knowing what he was doing but knowing only that it would make him feel better, Pran closed in with the intent of striking one more time. But he didn't get the chance. Chareeya knocked him down and swung a punch at his mouth. *Stop, Pran,* she hissed and pressed her hand on his chest with all her weight until he couldn't breathe. She stared straight into his eyes like a cat. The image of her slowly getting up with her eyes fixed on him then moving to help Natee up was filtered by a mirage of tears that suddenly flooded Pran's own eyes.

Pran left, scrambling out in terror, through the hazy heat and shafts of sunlight piercing the foliage like the light of burning stars that dotted the shapeless stone path. But halfway through he stopped in his tracks when he looked up at the flowers of the red *praduu* tree interspersed among the blooms of *pu-jormpol* flowers, so magnificent he couldn't move his legs and was compelled to look at them through a curtain of tears, through the bitter taste of blood still salty and wet in his mouth, though the pangs of hurt that had spread throughout his throbbing heart. How is it possible, he thought, that something so breathtaking could appear before him at this very moment?

Hours later, the image of the red *praduu* tree against a blue sky was still etched in his mind when Pran found himself sitting mutely in front of Chalika. His blank eyes were fixed in the direction of the stacks of vinyls against the wall, though he couldn't really see anything. Pained and bewildered, he felt something weaken inside him. He had always faced the world alone; in solitude, incomplete, desiccated and abandoned, and, yet, he had survived. He no longer knew what hope he had ever had that it was possible for him to feel this hopeless now. On top of the anger, there was the feeling of being betrayed, the feeling of someone with no home to return to. What was it that kept churning madness and heat inside him?

Chalika sat down beside him and patted a warm towel over his cracked lips. She was silent, as usual, and didn't ask him anything. She unclasped his tightly balled fist and held his hand in hers, then put her other arm loosely around his shoulder and started to rock him gently, a tender consolation, before lowering her head to whisper something in his ear, a barely audible whisper. Once again, time stopped.

Sucked into a black hole that asserted itself from the-devil-knows-where, Pran lay his head upon the sanctuary of Chalika's shoulder, in silence and stillness, for a long time. He felt like crying when he thought of the solitude in her eyes that was the same solitude he saw in Chareeya's eyes, when his face touched the smooth complexion under which coursed the same blood that ran through Chareeya. And the urge to cry grew more powerful as he pulled her body closer and, clumsily but firmly, put his lips – still smarting with pain – on hers, on those lips that showered the same lonely smile as Chareeya's lips.

The desire to cry became irresistible when he realised the true devastation of his feelings, how the remains of his shipwrecked heart had led him on a desperate search to find Chareeya inside Chalika, and to make love to her.

XIX

The Eye of the Storm

One quiet afternoon, as he was walking down a winding village road somewhere in Xinghai, Uncle Thanit had no way of knowing that the next piece of cloth he was about to procure would be his last.

Of all the textiles he had set out to pursue, this millennium-old Khata scarf was not only the most special, it was also the most magical. No one knew who had made it or when. It was known only as a rare treasure passed down through generations of an ancient Tibetan dynasty before being entrusted to several lamas who had kept it safe for centuries. When China seized Tibet, the scarf was lost. Legend had it that it had wandered around the globe in a peripatetic odyssey before being smuggled back into the land of its origin.

The scarf was small and had been woven from a white Himalayan silk yarn writ with a prophecy of the apocalypse that was hidden beneath another layer of white thread originating in Peru, which had, in turn, been suffused with an occult substance believed to have been concocted by the great Persian alchemist Jabir ibn Hayyan. When exposed to sunlight, the scarf appeared completely white but, if immersed in a spiritual lake on a full-moon night, the apocalyptic divination would shimmer and rise above the black waters to reveal text in Devanagari script that appeared in reverse and could only be read using a mirror.

Uncle Thanit had first heard about the scarf many years ago in Andalusia. And in all the places he had been since then, he kept hearing bits and pieces of its legend – in Rome, Doha, Marrakesh, Jerusalem, the Tonle Sap, Petra, Nazca, Kalimantan, Paraiba, Ha Long, Samara, Rajasthan, Lhasa, Varanasi, Paris, Buriram, Champasak. It was as if the scarf was actually pursuing him, rather than the other way around.

When he reached the house of an antique merchant at the end of the village road, he saw a woman who had been watching him come down the path. Before he could say anything, the woman – whose eyes were kind, whose face was as beautiful as a goddess, and whose skin had the golden sheen of a twilight cloud – spoke first: *Please follow me inside.* Through the rarefied climate, through sunlight as white and cold as a sheet of ice, through the itinerant wind that blew in from thirteen lakes five times a day, through one layer after another, and another, her voice reached out to him, and it was as if she had been there waiting for him all along.

Uncle Thanit had never met this merchant before and hadn't shared his itinerary with anyone. He was just passing through this village on his way to another, where he hoped to meet a young monk who might have a clue as to the whereabouts of the Khata scarf. He happened to hear about this merchant, who was reputed to own an inventory of fine cloths, so Uncle Thanit had made a detour to visit him. *A storm is coming*, the woman said. Puzzled, Uncle Thanit looked up at a bright cloudless sky that showed no signs of an approaching tempest. Without knowing why, he followed the woman into the house.

Coming from glaring sunlight, Uncle Thanit was immediately blinded by the interior darkness and could hardly see a thing except for a faint glimmer reflecting off a few copper pots that hung from the ceiling, and, through a window, a lush green mountain upon which an arrangement of big and small rocks formed the wording of a mantra: *Ohm manee padme hum*. At that very moment, right before his eyes, a storm of dark-brown dust from god-knows-where tumbled across the mountainside. It was so violent and sudden that it didn't look like an avalanche of sand but like a malevolent implosion that was reducing everything to dust before crashing with thunderous fury onto the village.

Uncle Thanit rushed over to help the woman close the door and window. The room was plunged into absolute darkness. There was only the deafening echo of raining sand, furiously beating against the outside walls, and the sound of rustling silk. There was a delicate scent of tea and a sweet fragrance of incense that had been lit the previous night. Shortly, a speck of light burned in the dark and the woman appeared like a flickering shadow in the dim light, her hand cupping a lamp as she led him towards a raised platform at the centre of which was a burning stove.

Tonight, you'll have to take shelter here – my husband will return in the morning. Her voice floated above the roaring of the storm and the ceaseless pelting of sand on the roof and walls. Uncle Thanit had heard about the ruthless sandstorms in this part of the world, and knew he had no choice but to nod and murmur his thanks to the woman. She didn't say another word but got up and poured him some hot tea. Then she sat down across from him and started cooking.

The temperature dropped quickly. The wind was strong and seeped through the invisible gaps around the door and window, making the lamp flame flutter. Uncle Thanit sipped his tea silently. Without uttering a word, he stole glances at the woman's shadow dancing around the room in the light of the trembling wind-swept flame. The sweet aroma of the incense had gone and been replaced by the acrid smell of the spiced vegetable soup bubbling over the stove.

Without rhyme or reason, Uncle Thanit thought back to a lonely street in Kyoto basked in the pale blue evening light of summer. Back then, he would take out a chair, sit in front of his shop as night set in, and watch pedestrians amble along over his memory of a woman's back, a woman who had once walked away from him on that same street. And he had a sudden realisation: the longing that had tormented him in the depths of his heart – a longing for something he couldn't identify – was about to come to an end.

Night crept over the house in darkness and during the eye of the storm. As he lay next to the stove, listening to the wind and the sand continue to crash mercilessly against the house, he heard the door of the room slowly being pried open. Seconds later, he heard the jingling of the beads woven through her hair bumping lightly against each other. This was followed by the rustling of silk, ever-so gentle, as she came closer and closer, and stopped in front of him.

The moment he heard the sound of skin the colour of a twilight cloud softly unfurling over his body, Uncle Thanit became aware that this moment had existed since time immemorial, since before he was born, and that it would remain for all eternity. It was this very moment that had drawn him to this region in search of a small piece of cloth that no one knew for sure really existed, and to make a detour to this village to see a man he had never met, on an afternoon when a storm hit, and to be imprisoned within the perfume of tea leaves amidst a maddening maelstrom of sand, and, finally, inevitably, to succumb to the embrace of a woman who had come to him in the dark. After the moment passed, if he could turn back time and return to this place, in all certainty they would still be in each other's embrace.

Uncle Thanit slowly opened his eyes. He looked at her long black hair draped over his face, darkness descending upon darkness. And everything else that existed was shut out by that cool black curtain – the roar of the storm, the whole world, the life he had lived up to that point, even time itself. Uncle Thanit drew in air from her breath before relinquishing himself to the sovereignty of love – maybe it was love, if not something more – and he felt as if he had known the woman, whose name he didn't know, his entire life.

At the darkest hour of the night, before dawn broke, the storm subsided, leaving only the soft wailing of a placid wind billowing past alien grains of sand that had been blown from another planet. Uncle Thanit lay awake as she whispered through the darkness that blanketed his heart: *In one life…* She paused. *In another life, a man accidentally killed a boy in a war. The guilt bound him on a never-ending journey to find the boy in subsequent lives in order to repay the debt he owed. The boy who was killed also found himself stuck, waiting without end, for the killer to return and repay him with life.* The wind wailed and whistled. *This is our story.*

Uncle Thanit slowly closed his eyes and could see her shadow dance around the room in the flickering lamplight. He felt surprised that he didn't find any of this at all surprising – not the story she told, not its surreal simplicity, not even the sordid savagery she claimed was hidden beneath what he had been about to believe was love. He grew calm inside. Or, to be precise, he was made to feel calm yet couldn't understand how. *Tomorrow, when my husband returns, he will kill you.*

In that silence, as sand fell from the sky as slowly as sediment collecting at the bottom of a river, Uncle Thanit could saw everything with great clarity: the fragile love he had experienced so fleetingly; the woman who had run from the love she had for him and fled to the end of the world; the evening when *pikul* flowers had fallen down like rain; the golden flame of the *kanok** motif in the hazy light; the long, empty journey he had undertaken though he had no clue what he was really looking for; the crows flying home against the pale moon while he and his sister lay on their mother's lap, drifting out onto a river of uncertainty.

At that moment, there was a loud explosion and a flash of blinding light that left behind thick smoke hanging like a cloud in the still darkness. He couldn't hear a thing; his ears had stopped working and everything was quiet, black and motionless. Then someone ran out of that cloud. He pulled the trigger… No, he wasn't sure. He wasn't sure if he had fired the shot or if it had hit someone. He couldn't hear anything. The person stopped in their tracks, as if the bullet had pinned them down in the dark. Another flash of light in the distance. Yes, he wore a soldier's uniform, a gun in his hand, and then the dark, the cloud, and… Shit. He was just a boy, a young boy with the delicate face of a girl, pallid and puzzled and fragile, unable to comprehend where the blood spurting from his chest had come from. And he spoke… No, his ears weren't working.

* *Kanok* is a traditional Thai pattern that resembles a tapered flame and is used throughout Thai arts and crafts – in murals, lacquerware, architecture and fabric.

The boy didn't speak, didn't move, didn't fall. He was just standing there, staring straight at him, and he would keep staring at him for all eternity.

In that peculiar moment, without any warning, Uncle Thanit foresaw a day when the sky would be bright and an hour when all things would be basked in a balmy sun and his journey would finally come to an end. The boy with tender eyes would be born from him, from her, on a winter's day when this village would be abandoned, on a night when it would be buried beneath another sandstorm. Three children who loved each other would hurt each other at the inescapable hand of fate, and he foresaw the fading final moon cycle of his life. Everything had been predetermined. Everything. And he didn't feel bitter about it, not at all.

Grains of sand poured down from the roof like water and the last star was about to disappear from the sky when she put the necklace around Uncle Thanit's neck. It was made of silver threads entwined, one over the other, and resembled the sign of infinity, layer upon layer. *This is the eternal knot. It has no beginning and no end but twists around and around forever. It is a symbol of the cycle of life – samsara, the interwoven journey of life on this earth and in the world of spirits. The space in the middle is the void, the emptiness, the nothingness...*

The first light of day was brightly mirrored in those tender eyes as she softly ran her hands over his face, his eyelids, his lips, his cheeks, and then held his hands in hers and placed them on her heart. Uncle Thanit then cupped her hands and held them to his chest. He bowed his forehead until it touched hers and remained there for a long time. *Forgive me,* he whispered, eyes closed. *I forgive you,* she replied. Never before in his life and never again would Uncle Thanit feel the void of emptiness he felt in that moment.

Go, before my husband returns. Go as pure as when you came. For the last time, Uncle Thanit looked into those eyes, etching them onto the deepest part of his soul, and then walked away. *Anil...* she said softly behind him. Uncle Thanit paused. *I will call our son Anil.* That was her goodbye. Anil, he knew that word; it came from Sanskrit and meant wind. And he thought about another son he never had whose name also meant wind. Uncle Thanit smiled, nodded, and walked off without turning back.

Two days later, Uncle Thanit looked up at an ancient temple perched atop a precipitous cliff shrouded in mist. To reach it, he had to climb a rugged, steep and treacherous path for five more days. A soft wind caressed his body and warm sunlight fell upon him in that moment when he came into possession of the last piece of fabric he would acquire in his life. It was not the Khata scarf with its apocalyptic prophecy, the desire for which had enticed him to trek through the land of the thirteen lakes to begin with; it was the crimson robe of monkhood, which he wore on top of the symbol of nothingness that would hang over his heart for the rest of his life.

Uncle Thanit never came down from that mountain again, not until his death thirty-one years later, under the hazy shadow of the moon.

...The same moon he had seen on the night when he was caught in the eye of the storm.

XX

The Twins from the Land of Tears

Pran, I'm sorry.

The alley behind the Bleeding Heart bar on the night of the waning moon was damp and choked with a burnt smell. Pran's eyes were fixed on the ground. He said nothing. When he looked up, he averted his gaze. *I didn't mean to.* In the distance was the intersection where she had often paused to watch the lights change colour and several cars were waiting for the light to turn green. It would be hours before this night ended. *I'm sorry, Pran,* Chareeya said again. Without meaning to, he happened to glance in her direction and noticed the gleam in her eyes. It was the same gleam she had when her floating basket had capsized in the river, a gleam of irredeemable sorrow.

It's all right, Charee, he said, still not looking at her. *Does your mouth still hurt?* Her fingertips touched his lips. Pran turned his face away, his insides twisting into a coil. He didn't know how to tell her that it still hurt; not there, not on his lips, but somewhere deeper. He didn't tell her how much he hurt, or what he had done to soothe that hurt, or how, for a time, he had forgotten who he was, or how lonely he had been as he hacked through the rough thickets of his life, or what he had gone through before he had ended up so insane and so broken. Or who he had had beside him…

He didn't tell her that in that despair and unforgiving loneliness, he had set out to find her, staggering into the ruins of ragged memories and falling into sweet and warm embraces he knew he shouldn't have fallen into, and wandering into places he knew – with absolute certainty – he shouldn't have wandered into, only to find that she wasn't there. He didn't tell her that he always felt like crying, that he had nowhere to go. And he didn't tell her about what had happened between him and Chalika, that he hadn't meant for it to happen, that he hadn't meant for anything to happen the way it had.

Chareeya still came to the bar every Friday evening with her friends and Pran still walked her home late at night as he had always done. They walked together mostly in silence, exchanging barely a word. An air of loneliness trailed after her. She didn't tell him anything, and he didn't ask because he didn't want to know. Still, from his usual spot he would watch her scoop the cat into her arms, weed out the nut grass intruding on her garden, plant new flowers and trim old ones, and then whisper to them, one by one. He would watch her drink her coffee in the tea-coloured sunshine, watch her reading…

And he remembered small details from their afternoons together as he pieced together the unfinishable jigsaw of the Andromeda. He recalled mundane moments from their Mondays together, or the conversations they used to have late on Friday nights. He remembered the movies they had watched and the music they had listened to on weekdays. These stories and details gradually faded into the past, hobbling away at the end of the day, as he kept searching for a white smile that was as dazzling as a solar eclipse on the faces of the people he encountered. Some days he lay on the floor in his room with the tissue that had been touched by her kiss over his eye – placing it on the same side as Chareeya's permanently fissured eye – and gazed at the ceiling in the dark through his remaining eye. And sometimes he tried to deceive his own heart by telling it that the Monday when he had seen the red *praduu* tree against the sky had never happened.

When she asked him to have lunch with her again one Monday, Pran replied politely that he was busy. Chareeya didn't press him, as if surrendering to the distance that now separated them like a curtain of fog. He didn't tell her that he had already given his Mondays to Chalika.

Every Monday, Chalika hung a "We're Closed" sign outside her dessert shop and devoted her entire day to him. Pran would catch the first bus from Bangkok to the house by the river, spend the night there and leave in the late morning or afternoon of the following day. They would eat dishes cooked from simple recipes, nothing as sophisticated as Chareeya's international repertoire, and they would sit and talk about nothing in particular in that living room that Pran had hoped for much of his life to return to. In the afternoons, he would fall asleep without dreaming. In the evenings, they would go out on the rowing boat and drift into the familiar scent of the river he had longed for, where he would salvage fragments of memories scattered around its bends and reconstruct them in his dismal heart, and later in Chalika's embrace.

I talked to Charee on the phone about Uncle Thanit becoming a monk. I also told her about us, Chalika said. *She didn't seem surprised at all, Pran.* Pran lowered his head and went quiet. *But maybe she already knew,* she smiled. *Did you know we have a telepathic connection? Like twins. We've always known each other's thought without having to speak them, ever since we were kids. We used to pretend we were real twins. We stole Aunt Phong's skirt to wear. You remember Aunt Phong, don't you?* Pran nodded. *And we tied ourselves together with a belt, pretending to be Eng and Chan, and we hobbled together around the house like that.* Chalika laughed her crystal laugh. Pran pictured the two girls and couldn't help but chuckle.

Only Uncle Thanit doesn't know. He didn't say in his letter which temple he's staying at – there's no return address. I didn't know where to write back to. She paused. *Maybe he doesn't want to be bothered. He said he'll never leave the monkhood...* Chalika's eyes reddened. Pran ran his fingers along her arm in a consoling gesture. She pursed her lips and nodded. *Well, he's already given us so much. I just miss him. If he were here, he'd be so happy to see you back taking care of us... Just like the old days.*

In the same way as she had viewed the army cadet who hadn't been a cadet for a long time, Chalika saw Pran as a man from another world and not the flesh-and-blood Pran who lived in the here and now. Her Pran was a mongrel of heartthrobs bred from a million romance novels, though, in reality, he was nothing remotely like any one of those heroes in movies or books. He might be kind, but only to Chareeya and Chalika. He went along with other people's wishes, but he never sucked up to anyone. He acted in accordance with his feelings, but he didn't feel that much. He didn't assign any importance to his own feelings because that would have intensified his sense of bitterness in a world where nothing went the way he wanted it to. Pran wasn't sweet, neither was he sensitive, vulnerable, or obsessive, and nor did he have a head full of dreams. He didn't have inspiring life stories to share with others. And he never told her he loved her.

But Chalika never asked him either. She never demanded to hear anything from him. Not only was she a beauty who glowed with the hallowed aura of a heroine, over the years she had grown into the archetype of a leading lady. She was neither demanding, nor intrusive. She was reserved and she kept her feelings to herself. Whether he loved her or not, Pran nonetheless came to see her every Monday, and Chalika was happy to have him to herself for one whole day a week, to watch him sleep and dream through the night all the way until morning. Compared to the life she had spent all alone up until then, it was more than enough for her.

Though Pran wasn't trying to sort out his life or find any order in it at that time, she believed he would soon change. A hero in a novel was never the same person at the end of the story as he was at the beginning of the book, was he? Once Pran got older he would think about settling down, and then he might want to move back and find something to do there. Right now he was still young; still enjoying his work, wanting to make music, wanting to be the way he had always been.

Chalika's only older family member was Uncle Thanit, who had become a monk and abandoned all worldly demands. But, even if he had been present, he wouldn't have objected. And people in the neighbourhood weren't interested in gossiping about this household where unusual people had lived together – from masters to maids – for as long as they could remember. In this age of globalisation, as they called it, where the most private stories about celebrities became topics for public discussion on a daily basis, who would have any spare time to gossip about a dessert vendor like her? To live together without getting married might be a little too progressive, but it wasn't such a huge deal either in this day and age. She didn't see the necessity of a wedding, of wasting time and money on it. A marriage registration didn't guarantee an eternal union – just look at her parents as a prime example. And Chalika had known Pran since childhood. He wasn't a lady's man, and all heroes and heroines were bound together by a feeling in their hearts above all else. But…

Pran, I want a child. They were sitting on her mother's bench under the *pikul* tree. It was evening and Pran was looking out at the river. He didn't answer. *You don't have to live with me forever, but I want a child / I'll always be with you forever,* Pran finally said. *But I'm not sure about a child / I understand.* No, you don't, Lika; he knew she didn't understand. *I'm not sure I can take care of it – I can't even take care of you / I know, I can take care of myself, Pran, I can take care of a baby too – the shop is doing well and I get money from the rentals.*

Pran became silent. It wasn't that, it wasn't about the money. He had never had a proper parent before, and neither had Chalika and Chareeya. They had grown up, yes, but look at what they had become. They were eternal orphans: lost, isolated, estranged, different, living in the solitude of their own worlds, pursuing their own paths, and too desolate and lonely to be healed as they strayed into the black voids inside their hearts that could never be filled. *Soon, Lika, give me some time,* Pran pleaded. He had nothing to give anyone; he knew that for sure.

And Chareeya really didn't seem surprised, just like Chalika had said. *You should have told me yourself, Pran / Told you what? / About you and… Lika.* Pran didn't say anything. The city street was deserted and the blinking traffic light changed colours, presiding over emptiness and silence. *We grew up together, I'm not a stranger – Lika is my sister, you're like my brother.* He still didn't say a word. *You're treating me like a stranger.* There was rancour in her voice, yet Pran remained quiet. He didn't know how to respond.

Never mind, it wasn't necessary – she wasn't under any obligation to understand him and he wasn't under any obligation to explain the inexplicable or, indeed, to make any effort at all. It was just a Friday night that had caught him and Chareeya with too many unresolved feelings – he didn't know what they all were or where they had come rushing from. And so, it became just another Friday night, like any other Friday night before Chareeya had come back into his life.

And it was just another Friday night on which he imagined her standing before him, staring at him in the dark. There was a shimmer of light that grew bright and then faded into darkness, then grew bright again and faded again, like those traffic lights presiding over emptiness. Every time she reappeared in the bright light the distance between them grew wider and wider, and then she backed away from him one step at a time. Another step, and then another, until she disappeared forever into the dark void that had always been in his life.

XXI

Baby Seeds

Nual, can you tell which of your children belongs to which father? Chalika asked out of the blue. Nearby, Nual's five children from three fathers were cutting and wiping banana tree leaves to be used for wrapping desserts at the shop. Dissimilar in looks, shape, and complexion, they ranged in age from seventeen to six, and the only shared feature to indicate they were siblings was the wide, sincere smile inherited from their mother Nual.

Of course I can. Any mother can / Have you told the fathers which ones are theirs? / No, I haven't / Why not? / Because they never asked so why would I tell them? The kids all love all their fathers, and all the fathers love all their kids. What's the point of knowing who came from who? Nual said, looking straight ahead, eyes clear as a pond.

Listen, my grandma told me that children don't belong to their fathers. Seriously, they're like... Like seeds that have been in a woman's womb since she was born. Chalika listened, amused. *When we meet a man we love and he loves us, we'll dream / What kind of dream? / That we want to be with him, become his girlfriend, something like that. And if we keep dreaming for a while, the dream will make the seeds grow into babies in our bellies.*

Come on, Nual! You make it sound like babies are pomegranate seeds! Chalika let out a hearty laugh, her head tilted as she looked endearingly at Nual. To Chalika, Nual was a friend and sister, almost like the mother she and Chareeya had never had. Likewise, Chareeya and Chalika were the family Nual had never had. She had lived in the house since before Chalika was born, since she was still a girl herself, and after fate had taken her on a whirlwind journey across half the country.

Nual lived an ordinary childhood in the countryside until she turned twelve, at which point members of her family started to take turns dying. First, her uncle contracted a terminal disease caused by love. Then, another uncle fell sick with an outlandish malady that had no medical explanation and caused every bone in his body to rot and turn into a shapeless jelly, like old pillows, by the time his body was placed into a coffin. And that funeral was barely over when Nual's father died after he got lost in his own sleep and couldn't find his way back.

The council of elders in the village unanimously concluded that these deaths were the work of the ravenous *pob*[*] ghost, that demon that can possess a human without anyone knowing; once it descends upon a household it can take the lives of an entire family, starting with the men and rounding off with the remaining women. Frightened by the evil invasion, Nual's mother took her children and swam across the Mekong River to seek help from a Khmer witch doctor on the Cambodian side of the river. To ward off the *pob*, the shaman inked a blue tattoo of ancient Khmer hieroglyphics on Nual's arm. It was a lengthy scrawl that ran from the inside of her elbow down to her wrist, and years later the letters would fade and become unintelligible as Nual grew up and her limbs lengthened. Though the tattoo remained there in the shallows of her skin, it was useless and, actually, just a reminder of the pain she had endured when the needle pierced her body, and of her inescapable tragedy.

Worse, the tattoo didn't placate her mother's fears. And old Grandpa Sam next door fanned the flames of panic when he told her

* The ever-hungry *pob* is a kind of Thai ghost or demon that possesses humans and devours their entrails.

that the talismanic scribbling on her children's arms was in fact an archaic alphabet unused for three millennia. *The* pob *won't be able to read it – it won't be scared away,* he said wearily, shaking his head and walking off. Terrified that the *pob* couldn't read the ancient writing and would abduct her son in his sleep as it had done her husband, Nual's mother resorted to waking the boy every hour to make sure he couldn't wander so far off in his dreams that he wouldn't be able to find his way back. So, the boy could get neither a full dose of sleep nor a sufficient fix of dreams. After a few days, he couldn't bear it any longer and fell asleep while he was swimming, sinking sweetly and unfathomably into multiple layers of dreams in which he was asleep in each one. He woke up in the second layer of his reveries, couldn't surface to consciousness in time, and died in a river no deeper than the height of his own chest.

Late that night, both husband and son visited Nual's mother in her dream. They seemed to glow with health, and she couldn't believe that the two men who, when alive, had thought only about themselves would have the courtesy to drop by and bid farewell on their way to the next world. She interpreted their visit to mean that they had in fact come to take her with them to the afterlife. In panicked terror, Nual's mother woke her daughter up in the middle of a starless night intent on fleeing with her one remaining child to face an unknown destiny somewhere else, without waiting for dawn to break. In great haste, mother and daughter gathered their belongings beneath a dim light that flickered on and off, the electrical circuit having broken down when those who knew how to fix it were already dead. A gush of wind swept through the house and Nual's mother turned around to look but couldn't recognise her own shadow in the throng of shadows dancing around her. Jolted by fear, she sprang up and tripped over her own legs. The shadows swayed restlessly as Nual rushed to grab her mother's arm. In that critical second, the damned light went off completely and the mob of shadows leapt upon her mother as if they were yanking her back. The movement caused Nual to misjudge the distance between her and her mother so that her hand grasped nothing but air, leaving her mother to fall from their house-on-stilts and break her neck in the shadows' embrace.

The relatives were terrified and refused to take in the orphaned Nual for fear the girl would bring the *pob* to wreak havoc in their houses. Their solution, after all options had been exhausted, was to send Nual to live with a distant relative who knew nothing about the *pob*-induced calamity in the northeastern town of Mukdahan, hoping that the demon would leave the village to feast on the souls of those far-away people instead. From that day on, no one ever died in Nual's village again. Decades later, the village was populated by old men and women who staggered around, sick and undying. Rumours spread that it had become the lair of a new species of immortal *pob*, and strangers dared not pass through the village either by day or by night.

Not long after Nual moved to Mukdahan, the distant aunt she was with lost her job and sent her to work as a dishwasher with an acquaintance in Khorat. Soon, the patron in Khorat caught her husband making eyes at the girl and decided to nip it in the bud by sending Nual to a friend's vegetable farm in Ratchaburi. Shortly thereafter, the farmer in Ratchaburi grew sick of Nual's face for no apparent reason and shipped her off to work with a sister in an orange grove in Nakhon Chai Si. But, just as Nual arrived, the woman took off to Bangkok and she was entrusted with yet another acquaintance who promised to find her work. After being packed off to another acquaintance of another acquaintance no fewer than eighteen times, Nual met Aunt Phong the cook when Mother was pregnant with Chalika and looking for a nanny to help around the house. *Can a child look after a child?* Mother had wondered as she looked at Nual, all skin and bone, taking the girl into the house out of sympathy.

Her skin smooth and coffee-coloured, her voice as delicate as her name suggested*, her eyes as clear as a pond, Nual was barely fourteen on the day Chalika was born. She had traversed half the country, still horrified by her near homelessness and haunted by a premonition that she would die while fleeing her own shadows like her mother.

* In the Thai language, the name *Nual* conjures up feelings of softness, warmth and beauty.

At that point, she dug in and vowed that she would never run away again, that she would be ready to accept anything, including the three boys who came into her life concurrently.

Closer, baby, closer. Move closer, baby, move closer... The three boys busily sorting santol fruit looked up on hearing the silky voice singing a hit country tune by Pumpuang Duangchan*. They saw Nual with baby Chalika chuckling in her arms, gliding past them ever-so slowly in the shimmering sunlight that reflected off the river into the orchard, sparkling like an image from a dream. The three boys froze on the spot: love had struck them point blank and simultaneously.

The boys drew straws to decide the order in which they would take turns approaching her. They agreed that if the girl succumbed heart and body to one of them first, he would get to have her. After rebuffing him until she became too tired and soft-hearted, Nual allowed herself to fall into Pang's arms first. But she was such a sensitive and caring soul that she asked him to keep their relationship secret so as not to hurt Reow and Pan. Later, Nual fell for Reow and asked him to keep it a secret so as not to hurt Pan. Finally, she became sentimental over Pan since she didn't want him to feel humiliated after what had happened between her and his two friends.

As soon as everyone's turn was complete, as soon as the boys detected the heat coming off each other's bodies, as soon as the secrets were no longer secret, the three friends fell irredeemably for Nual. It was a clean sweep – such was her power. Even though their friendship had been formed in the orchard and their mutual feelings for the same women had compelled them to try and get out of each other's way, they still couldn't suppress their emotions, and none of them could resist Nual's genuine and unconditional love. After they finished sorting santol fruit each day, the three boys would go their separate ways but they still took turns visiting Nual.

Amidst that crowded love, Nual bound the three men together for life. *Reow's mother died yesterday, poor him – he doesn't earn enough to*

* Pumpuang Duangchan (1961-1992), daughter of a poverty-stricken farmer, became a legendary singer of *luk thung* (a style of Thai country music that chronicles the life and woes of the rural poor) and died tragically young.

organise a proper funeral, Nual pursed her lips, voice trembling, and Pang and Pan chipped in for the funeral costs. *Pang had a motorcycle accident and broke his arm. Now he can't work and he doesn't have enough to eat, I'm so worried,* Nual voiced her concerns, and Reow and Pan gave her rice and dried food so she could give them to Pang. *Pan's lost his job but he still has to send money home – he must be so stressed,* she said gloomily, and Reow and Pang gave her some money to give to him, then they went around looking for work for their unemployed friend. Time and again, just like that, they helped each other out to satisfy the woman they loved. The three friends were supposed to stop being friends and had no reason to look out for each other but before they even realised it they had become sworn brothers who would die for one another.

It was unfortunate that Nual had been terrorized by the *pob* as a child and didn't have a chance to get a proper education; she was illiterate, but the schooling she had received from the uncertainty of life had taught her not to expect anything. Not only did she satiate her lovers fairly and with the kind of all-encompassing degree of love that only family-less people can offer, she also saw and accepted each of them for what they were. Reow's compassion, Pang's intelligence, Pan's heated athleticism in bed – put them all together and it was a package that not even a fully educated and wealthy woman could hope to find in a husband.

And so it went on like that, without any kind of urgency. Nual and her three husbands and their five children would be joined by twelve more grandchildren in later years, and would pass their lives without any of them ever once feeling inadequate or lacking.

So, Nual, do you love all your children's fathers? / Yes / Equally? / Yes, extra-equally!

XXII

The Shipwrecked Heart

Pran never knew why he and Chareeya spent so much time watching emptiness move within the larger emptiness of that intersection. It was a small spot, barely visible on a map of the roads along the Chao Phraya River. When other parts of the city were still busy with traffic at that hour, the corner was deserted, hushed. A bend in the road was lined with three or four old shophouses with elaborate designs that evoked the elegance of the Victorian age. Besides that, there was nothing special about the place.

As they stood watching the traffic lights change colours, as was their habit every Friday night, a car stopped at the crossroads. In that instant, just before Pran could start walking, and at the precise moment when the light turned green, Chareeya rushed out in front of the car, which had just accelerated in haste. The driver had to yank the wheel violently to avoid her and the car scraped past Chareeya, who lost her balance and fell in the middle of the road.

Go die somewhere else, bitch. The car screeched to a halt and the enraged driver opened the car door to scold her. He was a young man, visibly drunk and unable to drag himself out of the vehicle. *Go fuck yourself bitch, don't get me into trouble.* He turned to glare at Pran, who was rushing over to help Chareeya. *Put a leash on your lady, mate, if she's upset with you don't let her mess with other people.* He babbled a catalogue of expletives to cap off his ranting. Pran waved him away and lowered his head in a gesture of apology. The driver, still angry, slammed the car door shut and floored the accelerator. The car sped away, leaving Chareeya sobbing on an invisible X-shape marked on the road.

Pran put his arms around her to help her up, supporting her weight until she was back on the pavement. He scanned her from head to toe for signs of injury. *Are you hurt? / I don't want to live, Pran.* Tears streamed down her face as she spoke. Before Pran could say another word, she shook him off and started running as fast as she could, as if she was running into empty space. But it wasn't empty space; she ran straight into a wall, hit the mass of bricks and collapsed backwards, slumping arse-first onto the ground. She carried on sobbing and Pran, confused by what had happened, stood transfixed, watching her. When he came around, he helped her back up again repeating, *Charee, Charee.*

Chareeya didn't reply. She just kept crying. A gust of wind from the river blew silently through the darkness, and then tranquility took over and all that remained was a trail of teardrops sparkling against the distant light of the stars. Pran grabbed her hand and held it tightly as they walked home, her tears falling all the way, and he didn't dare say a single word. He felt a simmering anger at himself for having been so self-absorbed with his own pain, his own despair, so much so that he never asked how she was doing, how she was getting along, what her problems were, or who had put her in such a state. One wave of fear after another swept over him – primal and oppressive and suffocating.

The garden radiated the familiar smell of burning leaves, an aroma of sorrow that wafted through the air all the way to the main road and caused a homeless man who had been sleeping at a bus stop to wake up and lose his mind, shouting and crying in such profusion that tears stained his soot-covered face like a meteor shower. And Pran found himself standing in front of Chareeya by the room with the yellow door, deaf and mute, as hesitant as he had been the last time. And she didn't ask him to stay and keep her company as he was hoping she would. Behind her, a grey shadow fell, shimmering, just like the last time, except there was no milky white butterfly in sight.

Thank you, Pran, was all she said. Though he knew, unequivocally, that she wanted him to leave so she could lie down and cry, he didn't budge. Chareeya stared at him for several seconds, then moved to close the door. Pran blocked it lightly with his hand. *Go home now, Pran,* she said weakly. The red bruise from her impact with the wall had become visible on her forehead. Pran was scared, his heart pounding too fast from the fear of having to leave her alone. Before she could protest any more, he took a step forward, occupying space just inches from the threshold so that she couldn't close the door again. The grey shadow behind her flickered with greater frequency.

Seeing him standing there, rooted to the spot and completely mute, Chareeya screamed with rage, *Go away!* She swung the door forcefully in his face and ran to the bedroom. Pran pushed the door with both hands and followed her. Chareeya slammed the door of her bedroom shut in his face. Pran growled as he kicked the door with all his strength. It sprung open and he stood, suddenly still, one leg propping the door up against the wall.

Panting, glaring at him with the eyes of a cat, like on the day of the red *praduu* tree, Chareeya's scream was fuelled by pure anger: *Life has betrayed me!* And with that she leapt at him, shoving him so aggressively that Pran staggered back as pain gripped his stomach. And yet, he ground his teeth and stepped forward to face her again. Chareeya howled like a madwoman and lunged at him again: *Life has betrayed me! Can't you hear me? It has betrayed me!* The third time she leapt at him he took her in his arms. *Life has betrayed me, don't you get it?*

Of course he got it, why wouldn't he? But not like this… *Don't do this, Charee, don't do this.* Chareeya struggled against his embrace; jerking, heaving, jumping, screeching the same phrase over and over again with untamed anger. And Pran just tightened his hold on her. She resisted, tensed, kicked, slapped, punched, shoved, and again: *Life has betrayed me! Life has betrayed me!* She kept yelling until her voice began to fade and her body grew limp in his arms as she sobbed. Slowly, Pran eased her down onto the mattress on the floor so she could keep crying as tragically as she wanted to, crying and crying upon his heart.

The bedroom was painted deep blue. It had no other furniture except for a mattress the same colour as the room. Spread over one of the walls was the outline of a black tree with branches that sprawled across the entire space and which shed one leaf for every teardrop that fell from Chareeya's eyes. The other walls were bare, dappled only by the faint grey shadows of the trees swaying outside, flickering in layers. A light blue curtain that hung from the ceiling and draped to the floor billowed languidly. The scent of ylang-ylang flowers drifting into the room was mixed with the misty scent of *pheep*. In the centre of the open doorway sat the amber-coloured cat with his head lowered and his body silhouetted against the glowing backdrop of the room that contained everything in the world. The invisible butterfly had stopped blinking its grey shadow, leaving only the shadow of a skinny black cat stretching out across the floor.

Pran let the long night creep past him, punctuated by the sound of tears dripping onto his heart and "Life has betrayed me!" echoing in his consciousness. Has life ever spared anyone from betrayal? Chareeya, why did you think I wouldn't understand how you feel? Don't you know what I've been through? To be born into someone else's wretched world, to wake up from one nightmare only to find myself in another, more nightmarish one, to hack my way through disenchantment day in day out without knowing why I'm doing it, to wander into the anonymous embrace of a stranger, to get lost in a wilderness I shouldn't have strayed into – and all of it just so I could forget myself for a short while. You have no idea what I've gone through, and what I've lost along the way.

He recalled the day three years ago when he experimented with that hellish powder – the day Kurt Cobain died – just because he wanted to know what it was exactly that had taken away his brothers. It gave him a feeling of profound sadness and desolation, plunged him down without him meaning it to. Then, it transported him to a plain of ecstasy more powerful than any he had ever experienced before, such ecstasy was frightening because something so damn good must be wrong, must be a lie. He had to take five sleeping pills to shield himself from that illusory happiness – illusory, at least, in the context of his own life. When he woke up two days later, he dragged his junkie friend to Tham Krabok, the temple where monks treat drug addicts by making them vomit their guts out, and he stayed there to take part in the vomit-fest with his friend, going slightly mad and pulling himself out of an addiction he didn't have, detoxifying veins that had no toxins but at least cleansing his memory and intimidating himself into never trying it again.

In this broken world, Charee, happiness wasn't meant for us. Everything that you've dreamt of, everything that you've done, that you are, that you see, understand, strive for, seek out, everything that we've been through, the price that we've paid, the death after death of our hearts, the dreams that keep falling apart, the loneliness that can't be cured, this maddening feeling... Everything. Why *wouldn't* I get it, Charee? Why wouldn't I understand how life could betray you?

At the darkest hour, just before dawn broke, and when not a single tear was left inside her body, Chareeya stopped crying. And the black tree stopped shedding its leaves, now that not a single one was left on its branches. Pran had a damp patch on his shirt around his chest, and his heart was leaden, lopsided, beating irregularly and slowly sinking, deeper and deeper, like a shipwreck descending into an ocean of tears, so black and lonely, so unbearable that Pran had to bite his own lips until they bled. He shut his eyes tightly and his voice was hoarse when he whispered, *I love you, Charee.*

The silence carried his words and passed them around the room, one following another, until the minute the last star disappeared from the sky and Chareeya slowly propped herself up and leaned over to kiss him. It was a sad kiss and it wiped away all the other kisses he had had during his entire life, releasing him from the cobweb of loneliness by taking him in her embrace, an embrace so cold it gave off heat. And she made love to him in the glimmer of the day's first light, achingly and tenderly, as the garden quivered to life, like an oasis in the desert.

Chareeya was woken by the gibbering cries of a flock of birds she had never seen before. She looked up and saw the silhouettes of small swallows lined up neatly on the branches of the black tree on the wall. Tiny young leaves had sprouted, replacing those that had fallen in droves the previous night alongside her tears. The sullen blue room turned ultramarine in the daylight as golden sunshine filtered through the curtain. Pran had woken up before her and was watching the birds on the wall in bewilderment. He wrapped Chareeya's naked body in his own nakedness, making her feel even more naked, like a sac of air – transparent, itinerant, floating ever onwards.

Swallows, she whispered. Pran blinked. *They've migrated from somewhere / From where? / I don't know, from someone's frozen dream, maybe...?* Pran smiled and pulled her closer to him. It was only now that he understood why, all his life, he had been unable to love anyone. *Maybe it's my frozen dream from the past, Pran.* He searched her eyes. They were forlorn as always but had no tears in them.

As if nothing had happened between them: *I'll cook something for you.* And it made Pran laugh. Chareeya kissed him lightly on his chin, wrapped a blanket around herself, got up, and pulled the curtain open before leaving the room. Pran sat up and followed her with his eyes, then turned to look out the window. A sea of blossoms rippled in the sun. He, too, felt weightless, floating. In his mind he saw a mirage of the melting sun hovering above a surface of mist, with a few pond skaters gliding across and a dragonfly flitting past. He didn't understand why that image came to him at that moment; couldn't recall if it was a scene he had recently witnessed or just a distant reflection from another moment in his life.

Chareeya returned with a dish of bruschetta, with tomatoes and cheese, and black coffee. Her hair was mussed up and she was still wrapped in the blue blanket, tucked in around her chest and dragging along behind her like those minimalist fashion models that were in vogue. Together, they lay down and ate breakfast on the mattress, exchanging playful glances as if they were having a telepathic conversation amidst the whistling wind and glistening sunlight before making love to each other again, and again.

When Pran woke up late in the afternoon, Uncle the cat, who had snuck in and was lying on a corner of the mattress, woke up too. He yawned and then crouched, looking up at the birds on the wall with great interest. They were still perched on the branches, their twittering had softened, and some had folded their heads beneath their wings. Chareeya cooked Persian-style fried rice with dill and boiled fish with tomatoes and basil leaves, Vietnamese-style, plus apple salad with celery, sprinkled with almonds. She played Opus 47 and told him she loved him eighteen times while he ate tiramisu and drank Irish coffee fragrant with a hint of whisky.

Pran had to muster all his willpower to stop himself from leading her back into the blue room and making love to her again, but he needed even more willpower than that to free himself from the bondage of her embrace in order to go to work. He lurched off into the blinding illumination, full of strangers, before running through the dark to fall back into her embrace a few hours later. Chareeya had prepared chicken samosas and raw mango with tamarind syrup; a three-a.m. meal that passed languidly on the mattress, in the same way as their breakfast had earlier. Putting the plates away, they chased each other around, wrestled, bear-hugged, teased and tickled and laughed until they were exhausted. Then, they pulled the curtain back and lay down together. Under the starlight, they made love again, and again.

Because they had grown up together, Chareeya and Pran kept playing and having fun like children who refused to mature. Even the physical act of making love was like a game to them, one without rules – uncomplicated, unceremonious, but tender, profound, passionate, and, occasionally, like lovers trapped in the middle of a war. In between their tight timetable of near-endless lovemaking, Chareeya squeezed in short slots of time to cook with the craving of a final-stage cancer patient. She was hungry all the time and she ate with the voracity of a fish that was about to spawn. At any given moment, there was bound to be a pot with something bubbling inside it or some kind of animal being grilled or roasted on a charcoal stove.

Outside, on tree branches that caught the sun, carcasses dangled: dried fish, beef, black pudding, fermented sausages, Yunnan-style sour pork. In the kitchen was a riot of fresh and dried food, or the half-fresh-half-dried kind, piled up in every corner until there was barely room to walk. When space became scarce, she colonised a corner of the living room – the room that contained everything in the world – and it came to resemble a scientific laboratory with its floor and shelves lined with biological specimens meticulously housed in glass jars of various sizes, preserved in oil, vinegar or lime mixed with salt containing: sun-dried tomatoes, mandrake roots, German pork trotters, horseshoe crab, pickled cucumbers, Chinese black olives, rugby beans, sea urchins, Asian spider flowers, kimchi, even anchovies she had travelled all the way to Samut Sakhon to buy and then salted herself. There were other flora and fauna but Pran decided to let their names and origins remain a mystery, and he refrained from asking her about them.

The garden was blooming more luxuriantly than it ever had. The flowers competed to blossom and barely left any room for new leaves to sprout. Chareeya had to prune the plants every morning so that the branches didn't take over the pathway and block them from getting out. The bedroom was chock-full of flowers to relieve the burden of a garden near breaking point from the phenomenal profusion of petals. There were flowers in vases and in glasses, floating in bowls, or, when there were no more vessels left, they carpeted the floor. Even the black tree on the wall, the branches of which had been full of leaves, began to flower; fragile flowers that were dark grey at the stem and faded away into the blue wall. Chareeya was waiting breathlessly for the black tree to bear fruit so she could plant its seeds on the room's three remaining walls.

When Pran told her about his rooftop room and how he had spied on her every morning as she made her rounds of the blossoming garden, Chareeya burst out laughing. She felt as naked as she had felt on their first night together. Some evenings, they would go out and look up at the rooftop room or at the black rectangle of the window, and Chareeya would picture him sitting all alone up there in a cocoon of shadow. But Pran never saw himself up in that room, on the contrary, he saw himself and Chareeya as tiny figures amid a sea of flowers in the blue twilight, sipping sangria as zesty as the kind served at temple fairs, with a ginger cat prowling around them. He saw them together, as if he was still up on the rooftop looking down.

Pran still played at the bar every night and the thought of making his own music again came back to him. He also planned to brush up his sculpting skills. Chareeya, too, still worked at the shop for a few hours every day, and as a tour guide for French tourists when she had time. He never saw her cry again; no more tears for Thana, Chanon, Natee, or for the grief-stricken longing in her father's love letters. Even so, Chareeya refused to let Pran terminate the lease on his rented room and move in with her. She also insisted that Pran go back to the house by the river every Monday.

Charee, I have to tell Lika… About us / No / I have to / No, Pran, you don't have to / Charee / Pran / I don't want to lie to Lika again / Then you don't have to be with me / It's not like that / It is like that / I want to be with you, not with Lika, you know that / No, I don't. Chareeya, no longer wanting to talk to him, turned around and disappeared behind the house where she was roasting a suckling pig.

Inside, the swallows fluttered and flew around the blue room.

XXIII

Black Flames

Charee, I need to talk to you. She was staring absent-mindedly at a Mon rose in a glass shedding its petals onto the floor. Slowly, she turned to look at him through the fissure in her eye. Natee looked gaunt, unhealthy, like an alcoholic, and older than his real age. His eyes were dim, sickly red and pained. *You have no idea how hard I tried. I never wanted it to be like this between us. I miss you, Charee, I miss you.*

How long had he been gone? One month, two, three, four? For how many months had Chareeya longed for his return? For how many months had she prayed for him *not* to return? She closed her eyes and pity swept into her heart; Natee, too, was broken. Both of us are broken, trespassing upon the lives of strangers. *We lived together like friends, me and Pimpaka – I told you to give me some time. When she's strong enough to be on her own without relying on me, I'll leave her. I never loved her. I love you. I love only you – you know that,* he murmured, head bowed.

And you don't love that man, Pran, or whatever he's called. Charee, you don't love him. You never loved him. His voice had begun to quiver. *You love me. Only we know what love is, real love – only we know how deep it is. We've been through so much together, how could you leave me just like this?* The birds on the branch shifted nervously. Seeing Chareeya's sad, slim hands glowing in the grey-black afternoon brought tears to Natee's eyes. *I can't live without you, Charee, it hurts. It hurts like a bullet ripping through my heart, all the time.*

She closed her eyes, thinking she had heard that sentence before somewhere – in a novel or maybe a movie – and thinking how it had made her laugh when she first heard it. Nobody could ever know what it feels like to have a bullet ripping through their heart; no one, not even the dead. But, though Natee was repeating a platitude he had borrowed from someone else, never before had he been so wounded, and never before had he felt so worthless and desperate as when he spoke those words to her. It completely eluded him how he had reached this point, or when it was that things had descended into a calamity he couldn't control.

I can't live like this – I can't, Charee, Natee mumbled against the rain that had begun to pour down around them. Chareeya still hadn't said a word. He had said things like this many times before, and not only had he told her how he might die, he had come back and then left her again a hundred times. How many times can a person stand the pain of being abandoned? The heavy scent of rain made her remember Chalika's "special days" from their childhood. Whenever Chalika had seen sunlight shining softly through a fine curtain of rain with a rainbow arching over the sky, she would tell Chareeya to open her mouth so she could catch the rainwater coming down through the rainbow. *It's rainbow syrup*, her sister had whispered, as if telling her one of the world's most wondrous secrets. And the rain was, in fact, strangely sweet and perfumed.

Dear Lika, there wasn't any way out. We were wandering in a blackness that kept stretching out into another blackness, on and on forever. No matter how hard we tried or how much we pushed, life still betrayed us. There were no special days, no syrup, no rainbows. There was only Madame Eng and Madame Chan, the Siamese Twins of Solitude. Don't you agree, Lika, this is the sole legacy we've inherited from Father? We were doubled over backwards inside ourselves, torn to pieces, and both of us were cast adrift along our own lonely paths. Lika, tell me, please, what should I do?

Why don't we just die together and end it all, Charee? You and me we love each other more than anyone else in this world ever could.

But we can't be together and we can't be apart from each other either. Why, Charee, why? She opened her eyes. Natee's devastating lament compelled her to lower her head and stare at her own sad, slim hands tangled together in a knot on her lap, as if they were afraid of being separated from each other. Can't be together, can't be apart. Suddenly, an achingly sad ode from Father's letters flashed through her mind:

...Rosarin, those afternoons are drifting further away from me, fading everyday. All that's left is me hanging on, trying to hold on to anything that will save me from going mad. Why didn't we just die together then, Rosarin? Wouldn't it have been better to die together than to endure this endless longing? Death can't be as excruciating as the torment of having to live without you.

The pale memory of rainbow syrup surged in her mouth, sour and sweetish. All that was left in her head was an echo chamber of Natee's words: *Can't be together, can't be apart, why don't we just die together and end it all.* Right, why don't we just die? Death can't be as excruciating as the torment of having to live... Without Pran.

As soon as Pran pushed open the door to the blue room, a gust of wind swept in from the window, hit him in the face, and blew past him. The first thing he saw was the blue curtain that hung floor-to-ceiling in six strands like the restless tentacles of an octopus, fluttering, agitated, and panicked. Next, he saw Chareeya sitting on the mattress, pale and blank, her hair chaotically tousled by the wind like burning black flames. Then, he saw Natee lying in a fetal position next to her, his hands tucked between his knees like a child, though his face had an expression of fatigue like that of an old woman, frowning, lips tightly pursed, and in so much pain that he looked as if a bullet was ripping through his heart.

Chareeya slowly turned to face him. Her eyes met his, and she raised her index and middle fingers to touch her lips, signaling him not to say a word, or imprinting the ghost of a kiss, or perhaps blowing him a kiss like she always used to do before he left for work. Her hair was still aflame beneath the trembling curtain. There was the sound of water dripping onto wood at hypnotic intervals, almost imperceptible, like on those many nights when her teardrops had fallen onto his heart. Pran realised, then, that he was still soaking wet from the relentless rain pouring outside. When he had left the river that morning, the sky had been bright blue and there was no sign of rain, none at all.

She got up and walked over slowly, stopping in front of him. The curtains fluttered, as if trying to reach out and hold her back. Pran moved like he was going to say something but he didn't know what to say and all he could do was stare into her eyes, frantically searching for Chareeya somewhere behind that fissure. Then she raised her index and middle fingers together and touched them lightly to his lips, again signalling him not to say a word, or transporting the ghost of a kiss from her lips to his. In that cold moment, which seemed to stretch out forever, she whispered – *Forget me* – through the unceasing wind, through the sound of water dripping from his body onto the floor, through the perfume of frangipani flowers rising faintly above the aroma of rain, through the thick, wet, dull air.

The flock of birds anxiously hopped up and down along the branches of the black tree, shaking off the fragile petals and stripping the tree bare. Then they flew around tumultuously, brushing against the walls like a storm of ashes and circling Natee, who lay with his knees still bent, amidst the bedlam. At that moment, Pran understood that he didn't really know anything. He didn't know who Natee was, where he had come from, how he had lived his life, and how desperate he must have been to have to come and lie down here curled up like this so that a bullet could rip through his heart in the middle of a storm. He also didn't know how Chareeya had fought through life, how far she had wandered in her solitude, what she did during those long, dark nights, who she had beside her to take care of her and pull her back. And he didn't know what had happened during all that time when he had yet to exist in her life – all those years when he hadn't even existed.

Slowly, Pran closed his eyes. Something was breaking inside him. In a flash it had shattered and the pieces fell into emptiness. But he was surprised not to feel anything, nothing at all. In that befuddling moment he thought back to the delicate smell of the *kanom chan* wrapped in banana leaf, and the other desserts Chalika had packed for him just a few hours earlier. He also thought back to her forlorn smile as she waved at him when his bus was leaving the terminal.

In his mind, he saw an image of pond skaters gliding over the reflection of the sun melting on the water's surface, but he couldn't tell if it was an image he had seen the evening of the day before when he had been sitting by the river with Chalika, or if it was a memory from some other time. In the next second, he saw the image of a thunderstorm crashing down upon the city as he was going along an elevated road and he thought about how Bangkok was so beautiful in the rain. Then came the image of the empty chair at the dining table where Chareeya usually sat, and this time he couldn't understand why it didn't make him angry like it had done before.

Cut to: the black rectangle of his window in the room cobwebbed by loneliness, with Uncle Jang's wistful poetry, the sea of flowers below, and many other things that had nothing to do whatsoever with the moment, or with Chareeya, or with either of them. Unimportant details that had never crossed his mind came flashing through his head: a scarecrow wiggling its fingers in a blaze of sunshine, the sugar-spun candies shaped like fish that his father had given him at some temple fair, a hamburger that tasted like old newspapers, diamond glitter shining from eyelashes and shimmering like a halo, the fiery petals of flame tree flowers falling like shards of glass in the twilight, a girl who made a promise in the morning light. These varied images passed through his mind, one after another.

When he opened his eyes again he saw a closed door before him. Pran put his hands on the plank of humid wood, feeling a violent stab of pain piercing him. He mumbled something but, no, maybe he didn't feel anything or say anything, or maybe he didn't remember feeling or saying anything. He couldn't remember how long he stood there, or when he walked away, or where he went, or what he did afterwards.

Not yet, though, it would be a long time before he walked out that door, a long time before he broke free from the spell of that last whisper, and a long time before he became aware with startling clarity that it was him, not her, who had not returned to the surface of the river that distant afternoon when they had met as children. He was the one who had sunk deeper and deeper, inescapably caught in an eddy of misery, lost and alone in that cold and soundless water, with only a glimmer of warm sunshine, somewhere farther away.

XXIV

Cats Don't Cry

The rain stopped and Chareeya remained seated on the mattress hugging her knees. She stared vacantly at the Mon rose petals among other flowers scattered across the floor and had been doing so without thinking, saying, or feeling anything for the past couple of hours – ever since Pran's footsteps had faded into the sound of the rain.

Natee was kneeling on the floor busily sorting dull-blue sleeping pills into two piles of equal quantity and muttering to himself. Chareeya wished he would stop repeating that sentimental mumbo jumbo before she changed her mind. *I never got how we had to end up like this. All my life, I've never loved anyone else, no one but you. The other women were just…* Just what? With a profound agony that cut through her like a knife, Chareeya stuffed a fistful of pills into her mouth before Natee could finish his sentence. Washing them down with water, she picked up stray pills that had fallen over the bed and put them into her mouth. Then she flopped down on the mattress, motionless.

Natee looked up at her, slack jawed and deeply confused. No, a life's final scene should have something more than this – pain, devastation, agony, rancour, passion, heartache, burning anguish, or whatever. But Chareeya was… It was too simple and death wasn't supposed to be so perfunctory. She had stuffed those pills into her mouth and lain down, stock-still, just like when she had run into a wall and fallen back in a perfectly straight line.

It did actually feel like running into a wall and falling back in a straight line – that's more like it. Chareeya let herself sink into the mattress, exhaled carefully and closed her eyes. She thought of the man who had stuck with her and walked beside her in the dark, someone as silent as a shadow, always watching her and always existing just at the edges of her peripheral vision, and all she had to do was turn her head a few degrees to find him there. Since their childhood, he had lain down beside her in the Himaphan Forest and taught her to see with her heart in a world where everyone sees with their eyes. He had waded into the thicket of night to cut down a banana stalk and make her a floating basket when hers had capsized in the river. He had taken her on a quest to find a fountain with a brooding swan, without ever complaining. He who had collected her tears on his heart, and whose life had been devastated alongside hers.

And she thought about her sister stuck inside a million cheap romance novels whose streams of stories had caught her in a whirlpool too rapid and byzantine to escape from. *I will be reborn as your sister again, Lika, my dearest Lika, my twin.* Then she thought about the Most Beautiful Suicide photograph; that black-and-white picture of a woman who had jumped from the Empire State building in the 1940s. The woman was exquisite, glamorously dressed, and must have turned the heads of many men as she glided down the street towards the building before she took that leap and flew down with her eyes closed, hitting a car and creating a dent in its shiny roof that filled with shards of glass reflecting the morning sunlight. And that made Chareeya realise that she was still in her old at-home clothes, looking unglamorous, with frazzled hair. And if someone took her photo it would have to be called the Ugliest Suicide. And yet her head was light, so light she couldn't muster the desire to get up and do anything more.

Then she thought about her blossoming garden, now blurry in her mind's eye, and she knew that it had bloomed just for her. Its fragrance would fade under the distressing aroma of sadness. Would the new owner take care to water and pamper the plants as she had done? And then she thought of her sister again: *Lika, I'm sorry...* Then the chubby face of Uncle Cat flashed before her. And then all the images fell apart. Eyes blurred by water, the Mon rose shedding its petals, *I'm sorry Lika, I want... A desolate rose...* Chareeya opened her eyes and looked at the wall. Natee was still muttering on about something. He had been talking incessantly all afternoon – talk, talk, talk until the birds on the black tree had become weary and had stuck their heads under their wings to shield themselves from the sound of his voice.

The birds... / What birds? / Those swallows, there / Where? Chareeya was perplexed. *There, those birds, the migratory birds on the tree...* Natee turned to look at the wall: *What birds?* He couldn't see anything. And she felt as if water had welled up and submerged her feet, cold as polar ice, surging over her in waves, drenching her, and creeping up inch by inch. She stretched out her hand to touch the face with which she had once been so deeply in love, but her hand grew crooked and stiff before her eyes, and Natee melted away into the background of her last memory of a star in the sky and the icy water overwhelmed her as she sank and sank into the darkness.

Natee still found it hard to believe it could be this sudden. He wanted to witness life's final scene in all its meaningfulness, with all its enduring sentimentalism and touching sensibilities – not something as abrupt and radical as this. But Chareeya had fallen asleep before he had even managed to do anything. He ran his hand over her hair, feeling as heartbroken as when Romeo saw Juliet dying: *I'm following you, Charee.* But, then, he changed his mind as he remembered a more lugubrious scene: *Please, hold me one last time...* Yes, that was the one. A sudden surge of sorrow flooded his heart until his cheeks were bathed in tears. He held her in his arms, tightened his embrace, and touched his face against her forehead.

Wait for me, Charee. Wait for me, dearest. Natee was sobbing faintly and no sooner had he opened his mouth to repeat that he loved her than he realised how cold she was, how death had crept in to occupy every inch of her body. It startled him and he almost pushed her back onto the mattress. But then he calmed himself and slowly laid her down. Her face was ashen, beads of sweat had formed at her hairline, the edges of her lips were starting to turn green, and her body was trembling. He lifted her cold arm and let it fall, lifted it and let it fall, lifted it and let it fall. He stared at her slender hands now horrifyingly stiffened and gnarled, before shaking her lightly. *Charee, Charee...* She didn't respond. Natee put his ear to her chest and heard mournful music, so soft it was almost inaudible. He straightened up and looked around to locate the source of the sound but saw nothing. When he lowered his ear to her heart again, the music was gone.

Suddenly, those scenes from Japanese horror movies came back to him. Fear gripped him, assaulting him so recklessly that he became panic-stricken. Thrashing his arms around, he knocked over the piles of sleeping pills as he scrambled back to his feet and lurched forward into the centre of the room. His body tensed and he regarded Chareeya with confusion. A million feelings rushed through his mind: a riot of sorrow, terror, anger, bafflement, despair, loneliness, worry, disorientation, repugnance, contempt, condescension, contradiction, fear, desire, yearning, love.

Love, that was it: love. Natee knew he loved her like he had never loved or would ever love anyone else, not in this life and for sure not in the next one either. *I love you, Charee, I love...* Natee murmured, tears welling up in his eyes. The thought of having to continue living without her was so painful that he almost changed his mind and took the pills; just a mouthful, then he would lie down and embrace her, go to sleep with her, be with her. He had wanted to live with her since the first day they met. And he still wanted to live with her now. He couldn't understand why it hadn't been possible, why there had been so many unsolvable problems, so many hassles, and such unnecessary ones at that.

Charee, we'll never be apart again, my dear. We'll be together forever, in the eternity of our deaths. At the mention of death, his body shivered involuntarily and it became worse when he glanced at her gnarled fingers, bent at a horrifying angle. Now it was those scary scenes from Korean films that flashed through his mind. *Charee, no, you shouldn't have... Charee...* He dithered. He looked at the pills scattered across the floor and then rallied his courage to turn and look at Chareeya again. Her body was quivering, and the spasms were more frequent and intense than before; her eyes pulsated frenetically beneath half-opened eyelids, her lips were purplish now, and a globule of foaming salvia had formed at the corner of her mouth.

Aaaaahhh... Natee let out a fearful moan and fled from the room. But he had hardly taken two steps when he had to stop in his tracks. Uncle Cat sat like a sentinel, blocking his escape route. The cat's tiny pink tongue stuck out of its ugly plump mouth; it was in the process of licking its front paw and the limb remained hanging mid-air as it turned to stare at Natee with its large green eyes, irises dilated to the widest possible aperture.

Natee was imagining a scene with the police when Chareeya's body was discovered the next day, or a few days later, and how they would trace it all back to him one way or another – how incredible the Thai police were! If they interrogated him, he would insist he knew nothing, that he and Chareeya had just been having a testy on-again-off-again relationship for years. No one saw what happened in that room anyway, except the stupid cat – the sole eyewitness to the case. Natee wasted no time. He lunged at Uncle Yellow, who let out a startled meow, scooped the cat up against his waist and left.

Once he was home he paced around in a panic, sitting down then standing up, nauseous, feverish, disconcerted, and when he couldn't bear it any longer, he called a taxi to take him back to Chareeya's house. Halfway there, he changed his mind and returned home again to sit out the rest of the night in hot-cold terror. The next day he bought every newspaper at the newsstand, and the day after that too. He poured through every column of newsprint looking for a report about a woman's mysterious death. But there was nothing, not even anything about a woman who had survived a suicide attempt. So does no one kill themselves over love these days?

Several weeks later, Natee gathered his courage and returned to Chareeya's yellow house. He arrived wearing dark glasses, a cap that covered half his face, and stood hesitantly trying to catch a glimpse of something but all he could see was a "For Sale" sign stuck on the door. A few months later, the yellow house and its blossoming garden were gone, replaced by a high-rise condominium. Natee went back to live with Pimpaka, the woman who had always lived only for him, and tried to forget Chareeya, the woman who had died for him. In those first few years, he still teared up and wept when he thought back to what had happened that day but, as time passed, his gifted imagination comforted him with a scenario: she hadn't died, at least not to his knowledge, and she now lived happily somewhere, perhaps with Pran, who had come to her rescue at the last minute, just like in the movies. Or, if not with Pran, then with some other lucky man who had entered her life after that episode.

Uncle Yellow continued to live with him and became old, tired, bored and soundless as both cat and man prowled the corners of the house, until one morning eight years later when he vanished in that way that all cats do as they refuse to let lowly humans watch them return to their true planets. So no one knew if Uncle Yellow ever missed his human niece, or if he had ever cried.

XXV

The Birds have Fled the Blackened Tree

Chareeya was jolted awake, gasping for air above the water. Then she sank back into sleep, before waking up and falling asleep again. She woke up one more time drifting on the blue, ice-cold currents that rolled furiously, wave upon wave, in a storm-tossed sea. The black tree on the wall was entirely submerged and, still, the water kept rising; the birds had already fled its branches. The waves sloshed Chareeya against the wall and dragged her back, then more waves rolled in from the other side of the room and hurled her against the wall, over and over again, until the bile-churning nausea in her stomach became unbearable. Right afterwards, the water reached the ceiling and the waves stopped rolling. Then, everything was tranquil as Chareeya slowly began to sink and sink…

She struggled, thrashed about and tried to reach the surface though she had no understanding of why she should even try. Unable to stop it, she vomited, like a goldfish spraying pellets of food from its tiny mouth. But it wasn't food that came out, it was letters. **Last nigh t I dre amt abou t yo u**. Chareeya looked in astonishment at the jumble of words stubbornly clinging to broken sentences, before they spread out and floated like a stream. **I ha v e to get b ack t o yo u, in li fe o r in de ath**.

She waved her hands around in front of her, looking to the left, right, and then left again before she threw up again: **Fo r s uch a l ong tim e all we c oul d do wa s th ink abo ut e ach o ther**. And again: **P lease do n't she d a ny te a rs fo r o ur l ove.** She found herself undulating in the beautiful handwriting, drifting and dissolving like an ink drop in water.

Eve ry da y wit h ev ery b rea th I m iss yo u Rosa rin I'm s o a n guis hed li k e I a m bu rn ing in hel l I d on't u n der st an d wh y we ha ve to p ut up w ith th is ag on y R os ar in f r th e ti i w us li k t bit t s ee Ri n on a

Chareeya looked around trying to comprehend words that were no longer words. She felt the water spiralling, counter-clockwise, faster and faster, until she couldn't steady herself and was thrown into the eye of the whirlpool spinning around the room. But then the water gradually condensed, thickening like dough that had been kneaded until it was gluey, and the stickier it became the more slowly it spun, slower and ever slower...

Like a slow-motion shot in a film, Chareeya spun in a corkscrew circle. The letters had melted away into nothingness. She heard a distant sound, perhaps a song, but it was indistinct, sluggish, and drawn out like the sound from an old cassette tape. Then a flower floated towards her, so bruised and drooping she couldn't tell what kind of flower it was. No, it wasn't a flower. It was two jellyfish squiggling forward inch by inch in the water that was churning ever-more slowly, slowing down until it had become like mucus, so thick it could no longer move. Jellyfish Lika and Jellyfish Charee disappeared. She looked around, trying to find them, and instead found herself trapped in a channel that was wet and icky like a blue-grey glue – opaque, greasy, vomitous.

The drawn-out sound also disappeared and all that remained was the noise of air whistling through a hollow spiral. A labyrinth, that is the labyrinth of the blind earthworm. So, *she* was Earthworm Charee, caught in a panic in the middle of her own labyrinth. Earthworm Charee, Earthworm Charee... She crept along the slimy channel, an inch at a time, mumbling, *Earthworm Charee, eating earth, shitting earth.*

The yucky, gooey feeling and the filthy blue colour brought back her nausea. She retched and stretched her neck, but before anything came out of her mouth the spiral she was in had vanished, and the next second she was sliding down a void, plunging into a bottomless pit at great speed, cold and dark. Chareeya woke up three more times, and each time she found that she was still plunging down that interminable void – down, down, down…

Four days after she swallowed the fistful of sleeping pills and a few other unidentifiable tablets, Chareeya woke up for the seventh time in that blue room, amid dried-up pools of her own blue-coloured vomit and the pills that Natee had scattered around the room. An evening light shone softly through the window but the black tree on the wall was a carcass, its branches drooping, blackened and charred as if it had been dead for a century. The migratory birds had migrated elsewhere and Natee wasn't lying dead beside her, as he had promised.

She got up and staggered around the house. In her heart, she was glad that Natee wasn't lying dead somewhere and that he had been strong enough to abandon her again. But Uncle Yellow was nowhere to be seen either. Chareeya looked for him in the garden and, when she couldn't find him there, she went to its deepest corner and sat down beneath the *kalapruek* tree that had been the cat's favourite siesta spot. There, she waited, still drowsy from her seemingly unending dream of drowning and plunging. And, there, she began to remember.

She remembered that the last thing she had told Pran was to forget her and, at once, a white emptiness appeared in front of her. It dazzled her for a second before a great wave of sorrow unlike anything she had ever felt before overcame her; so devastating was its power that she felt as if the earth was breaking into tiny pieces and that all of humanity would be wiped out entirely. Even the black universe that was turning the sky dark would no longer exist. Disoriented and shivering, she looked around and couldn't fathom why the leaves were still green, the flowers were still in bloom, the butterflies still chased each other around, the wind was still sweet, and why time still ticked forward in a mirage of evanescent sunshine.

And, still, even though she was weeping inside, Chareeya got up and went looking for Uncle Cat. She wandered ragged and brokenhearted, shouting every name she had ever used for him: *Phosphorescent Eyes, Palm Sugar Candy, My Marigold, Star Fruit, Jelly Belly, Uncle Yellow, Soda Lemon, Fat Face, Young Melon, Lazy Worm, Stale Coconut Milk, Ginger Bum, Magic Pumpkin…* But there was no sign of him. Along the way, she also looked for the alley that led to the building where Pran had his rooftop room. When she came upon it, an enormous man who had misjudged his own proportions while walking down the narrow lane had got stuck between the walls and blocked Chareeya's path to the building. She circled around several times only to find the man still wedged there trying to squeeze his way forward, inch by inch, and still blocking her way.

That evening, she went looking for Pran at the Bleeding Heart. His bandmates told her he had come in a few days ago and left a note saying he would never be back. He had also passed on his belongings to his friends: an art book of romantic sculptures by Camille Claudel, a pair of leather trousers, some concert T-shirts, a pair of boots, an electric guitar shaped like a paper plane, a jigsaw puzzle of some galaxy adrift in the lightless universe, a stack of vinyl records.

Those were all the treasures he owned and that he had taken from his rooftop room when he said goodbye to Uncle Jang, landlord and specialist in the toxicology of love, who could tell just by looking into the young man's eyes that his soul had been crushed. And yet the old man couldn't find the right words to resuscitate a heart that was about to give up. All he could do was hold Pran's hands in his own trembling hands for a long time before releasing him on his way. Uncle Jang died eleven months later, after lighting a charcoal stove next to his bed one chilly night and falling asleep in his lonely, windowless room. He died not because of the pain or bitterness caused by the solitude that had been with him all his life, but because he was done with the excruciatingly long wait for his present life to end so that a new one could begin.

Knowing that Pran would not return to the house by the river, Chareeya – channelling the same unrelenting mania as her mother – packed her things and went looking for him. Without saying goodbye to Chalika or the three Witches or anyone else, she left carrying a single record of the heart-pounding symphony that had once set her on a course to pursue endless love only to tear her away from him. *I will find you before you forget me*, she vowed with all the strength in her heart, confident that she *would* find him again just as she had so many times before.

And such is fate: there were many times when they would be on trains that were passing each other in the opposite direction, unable to see each other in the row of blank faces glimpsed through the train window; many times when she would inquire at a bar or a restaurant about a mysterious, silent musician only to be told that he had just quit a few days earlier; many times when she would sit down on the same bench he had just got up from at a train station; many times when he would sit down at the same table in a restaurant she had just left; many times when both of them would look up at the same star from the opposite side of a river, unable to see each other in the shadows; and many times when they would walk quietly as they used to do, only at the opposite ends of a street thronged with people, and miss each other in the heaving humanity and lost tribes of globetrotters.

In the drizzle, she lamented, *Where can I find you, Pran?* And he said, *Rantau Panjang,* as he purchased a ticket at a station. When Pran mumbled to himself on a starless night, *How are you doing, Charee?* She said, *I'm fine*, smiling at a porter who had helped carry her small bag as she walked away. When she mentioned in passing to a stranger in the next seat, *It's hot today*, Pran said, *Have some water*, to a worker who looked like he was going to faint from the heat. And when he asked the stars before going to sleep, *To forget – is that all you're asking of me?* Chareeya whispered to the wind, *Don't forget me, please, don't ever forget me.*

On the night when the whole world was celebrating the arrival of the third millennium, Chareeya checked into a room in a small guesthouse where Pran lay asleep in the next room dreaming of a woman with a fissure in one eye. Through the night, they listened to each other's footsteps hopelessly searching for something they would never find. Several months later, when Pran pushed open the door of a bookstore, he laid his hand on the invisible handprint Chareeya had left behind just a few minutes earlier. But such is fate: the lines on their palms ran in parallel and stretched out into eternity without ever overlapping.

Chareeya no longer cried the way she had cried since she was sixteen; whether it was for Thana, Chanon, Natee, for the lovelorn odes in her father's love letters, or even for Pran, or for herself once she had lost him. Her heart had become parched, desiccated, and she felt thirsty all the time. No matter how much she drank, her throat remained dry and she found herself unable to cry.

Having spent one thousand days wandering around looking for Pran, brushing past him without ever bumping into him, Chareeya felt Pran's presence the way she felt the freshness of laundry that has just been brought in from the sunshine. Unable to explain to herself why she couldn't find him, Chareeya became convinced that their separation had been predetermined by past sins she had committed as a child; that time she had fished a string of toads' eggs stuck together like black pearls from a ditch and pretended they were black jelly or when her impish impulses drove her to interrupt mating toads, disuniting them from their acts of love and sending them on their separate ways. Resigned to the consequences of her own karma and to the conviction that Pran would forget her before she could find him, Chareeya decided to return home.

Chalika had hardly eaten in the past few months and had become so small that Chareeya was confused as to whether or not her sister had reverted to a ten-year-old self. Like Mother, Chalika hardly said a word to anybody and spoke only silent words to the echoing whispers inside her head.

It was the third Monday that Pran hadn't show up when Chalika's desserts had started to lose their sweetness, becoming rough, coarse and devoid of fragrance. Even her legendary *kanom chan* became too gummy to chew. Her syrup tasted of tears and was sometimes even bitter, much to everyone's bemusement. The clairvoyance of a romantic heroine had told her that Pran had another woman in his heart. When he disappeared, and since Chareeya had also disappeared, Chalika was certain she knew who that woman was. When there was no news from either of them, the clairvoyance of that romantic heroine told her that neither her lover nor her sister would ever return.

Chalika closed her shop, stopped making desserts, abandoned the novels, never left the house, never spoke to anyone, never mentioned Pran or Chareeya, and did nothing during the day except sleep. At night, she paced around in the dark, her arms outstretched, groping and searching, clumsily wandering amidst the shadows that stood silently in the nooks and crannies of the house. One day she started telling everyone that she had a child, a lovely seven-year-old boy who came to play with her during the night.

When Chareeya returned home, she didn't tell her sister what had happened between her and Pran, or between her and Natee, on that storm-ravaged night, or about her nomadic wandering that had followed. And Chalika didn't ask her sister and didn't utter a single word about herself, or about the sweets that had become bitter, or the nights of blind groping, or all the things she knew – all the things she had deciphered through the sixth sense that belonged only to the heroine of a romance novel. The only thing she told Chareeya about was her child; the boy she had had without ever getting pregnant, the boy who would remain seven years old forever.

Silence continued to occupy the house, along with the profusion of weeds that had sprouted from the fountain and encroached upon the surroundings, from the gate to the metropolis of mice. The dining room was misted up with crystallised tears that kept appearing and that would reappear, shiny and sparkling, right after they had been swept away. The living room was littered with decaying vinyl records; done in by humidity and time, they sometimes emitted a shrill, unmusical noise, even though no one had touched them. A flock of shadows had migrated into the house, too, an unstoppable influx that eventually shrouded the place in perpetual gloom, as if it was always just about to rain.

Nual, along with the children and grandchildren in her ever-expanding family, had moved out to live in a house not far from the house where her three husbands now lived; the trio had moved in together some time ago, having put their combined efforts into renting a large plot of land and setting up an orchard to grow Vietnamese guava. They still took turns visiting Nual, who had left the house by the river after Chalika stopped making sweets so that she would have time to look after her enormous family. And yet Nual still came to clean, do the laundry and cook for Chalika every day or every couple of days, never asking to be paid.

XXVI

The Adopted Piglet and the Man who Murdered his Own Shadow

Forget me, forget me, forget me, she said repeatedly, her voice rising above images that moved backwards and were fading away: the verdant paddy fields that Pran had once found so enchanting, a black night sky in which a crescent moon dangled, luminous beads of rain clinging onto a window pane. *Forget you, just like that? Is that all you want me to do? It's a walk in the park, how hard could it be? I could forget everything, I could obliterate myself, or the whole world, whatever – I could do it for you, my dearest Chareeya, if that's what you want.*

And, so, once again, he found himself a perpetual passenger on a train, a wanderer always on the move. Hair cropped short to his skull, carrying as few belongings as possible, Pran travelled without purpose or destination, and only now was he able to understand why his father had never stopped moving all those years ago – not only did he want to go to places untouched by old memories, he also tried to avoid creating any new ones because he knew how some skeletons just couldn't be buried. If even a hint of warmth began to form, even if it was just a tiny bit, it might trigger the heat of the past and smother his heart once more.

When he started out on the road, Pran hardly had any savings and didn't think he would be able to sustain this vagabond lifestyle.

But, after a while, he learned that a person could live on much less than he had previously thought. He ate whatever he had and got by however he could. When there was nowhere to sleep he took shelter in a temple, when he ran out of money he found work, and when he had enough money he set out travelling again. Work, too, wasn't that hard to find if one wasn't choosy, and Pran wasn't interested in choosing anything anymore; he accepted whatever was on offer, from manual labour to singing gigs. Soon, he found that he was more content digging holes, picking fruit, doing farm labour or construction work, waiting tables or washing dishes, than playing music as he had done for most of his life.

Outside of Bangkok and some major provincial capitals, people weren't into rock music. They preferred country music, which he had nothing against and which in fact had a few numbers that were dear to his heart. Or they liked protest songs, which had a force-fed, anguished self-righteousness that irritated him, though he could at least tolerate them. What he despised most was folk music, with its instant job opportunities for any musician who showed up alone with a guitar and started crooning syrupy love songs basked in sunshine and cool breezes. Romantic songs laced with idealism disgusted him and made his stomach churn. Either you love me or you don't, it's as simple as the fact that the sun rises in the morning and sets in the evening, and there's nothing that should make your eyes well up with sentimentalism because we just feel what we feel. He didn't see the difference between idealism and prejudice – they were both just myths contained within myths.

Being constantly on the move unsettled Pran's temporal sensitivity, and sometimes he thought he had been on the road for a few days when he was actually circumnavigating the country for a third time – might as well, since time had lost its meaning anyway. Everything just came and went in passing, leaving no trace, leaving no cherished keepsakes and nothing to chase away from his heart. From one town to the next, he kept going. Sometimes he picked a popular destination he had known before: Pha Ngan Island, Chiang Mai, or Udon. Most of the time, he just got to a train station and picked out a nice-sounding place name: Songkhalia, Yotaka, Rantau Panjang, or exotic villages like Ban Amrit, Pa Sao, Prang Kali. Or he just closed his eyes and tossed a coin. Or he followed whatever whim was tugging at his heart in that moment. Anywhere but Bangkok or Nakhon Chai Si – anywhere else was all the same for him.

He stayed a few days in each place, maybe slightly longer, and whenever he began to feel a hint of familiarity – when he could tell north from south or knew who was doing what in the area or which restaurant was good and which was bad – he would set off again. The exceptions were those few times when he overheard a band playing cool music, Radiohead or Catherine Wheel, or one time when he got to jam with a band in Chiang Mai, which gave him a painful urge to make music again. Or another couple times when he met a woman who was so sweet and captivating that he almost abandoned his itinerant wandering and fantasised like a madman about settling down forever. He even hoped that he might be able to give himself another chance at learning how to love. But all of it only reminded him that what he was really looking for was that yellow house, and for Chareeya inside every woman that he met along the way. And, through all of it, he came to the realisation that, no, he hadn't forgotten her.

In a world with nothing worth remembering, he couldn't imagine how he would be able to forget her as he had intended to. Then he met a British man who had travelled the world and who had come to install an electric fence around a bear enclosure at a zoo. He explained to Pran that after a bear touches the fence and feels the shock several times, instinct warns it off the danger. Even when the fence is removed, the animal never wanders anywhere near the parameter again.

So Pran found himself a needle and every time he thought about Chareeya he pricked the tip of his finger repeatedly. In the beginning, his finger stung so much that he couldn't play the guitar. On some nights, when the unbearable longing waylaid him, he scratched his chest with the needle leaving long, blood-encrusted marks. And, before too long, whenever his mind drifted to Chareeya, he instinctively felt pain at the tip of his finger without having to prick it with the needle. Eventually, the pain was triggered preemptively even *before* he started thinking about her, and he would find something to do in order to distract himself and prevent the image of Chareeya flashing across his mind. As the intervals between his thoughts of her grew longer, so his memory of her became more nebulous and unclear.

Forgetting is hard but, in the end, anyone can forget, no matter how momentous, affectionate, or painful the memory. Pran once heard a story about a woman who let a piglet suckle her breast to compel the animal to forget its own mother and thus save it from starvation. He heard a story about a man who was plagued by implacable rancour and who eventually died of amnesia, having forgotten everything, including the wrath in his own heart. He heard a joke about a woman who had screamed the house down with the pain of giving birth, shouting that she would never let herself get pregnant ever again, only to forget her vow and her pain and her fear and bear five or six more children in breathless succession.

Forgetfulness is a wonderful defence mechanism. Humankind would have long become extinct were it not for our ability to forget: to forget how pathetic and contemptible we are to have been born alone and naked on this cruel earth, born without claws, tusks, or strength. We would have been long gone had it not been for our ability to disremember, to banish from our hearts the fact that to simply exist is agony and tribulation in itself, to erase from our heads who we are, what we've had to feel happy or sad about, or that we ever had anything to remember.

One thousand, nine hundred and sixty-three days into his journey, Pran finally forgot Chareeya. Though he would have to roam for another one thousand or so days in order to forget who he was, and to forget all that he had done, felt, laughed or cried about, and how much he had loved a woman whom he had already forgotten.

One morning, he woke up and all his memories from before the journey had vanished. What remained were only bits and pieces, torn fragments, like how he used to travel up and down the country when he was a child, which was what he was doing now. But, no matter how hard he tried to extract it from his receding well of remembering, he could never recall why a boy that age would have to travel so much. It was all a bit foggy; he vaguely recalled growing up in a large family with several aunts and uncles but sometimes he was confused as to whether he had actually been raised in a pink house full of women. That, and yet no other details came to him. He couldn't remember where he had come from, when he had started learning to play the guitar, who his friends were; only that he might have had an older or younger brother. When he forced himself to remember, sadness compelled him to stop. There was something painful there, a scar so deep that he was certain he had forced himself to forget it.

He could remember his father, the man who walked with his head down, back stooped, shoulders slightly curved, one hand always hidden in the pocket of his trousers. And his mother… She was, well, he wasn't sure, the woman he remembered was a little too old, too strict… No, not strict; indifferent and contemptuous. Then there was a sister, probably a younger sister, beautiful and radiating a sweet scent like some kind of dessert. It was strange that when her image flashed up, everything around her was frozen, motionless, and it was as if he was looking at a still photograph and she was the sole, animated object at its centre. The worst thing about his memory of this sister was the guilt he felt – it constricted his chest and stifled him, made it hard to breathe, and made him want to cry.

Many times, his memories bubbled up, triggered by familiar details. Once, he sat on the banks of the Ping River from noon till night, gazing at the meandering water that superimposed itself upon his ragged memory of another river. As hard as he tried to remember which river it was, he couldn't recall its name. He only saw a river that brimmed with limpid water flowing languidly in the balmy sunshine of the cool season; on its surface hovered a thin layer of mist and its bends were carpeted with blooming rafts of water hyacinth. And there was the pale scent of smoke mixed with an evening fragrance that smelled unlike any other place on earth, and Pran was assaulted by a deep longing though he couldn't quite place what it was that he was longing for.

And there were many times when he was ambushed by a succession of images that popped up in random order: a field basked in soft sunlight, a Mon rose squandering its petals, a pond skater gliding across the water's surface, fireflies flickering and flying away in a blue twilight. Sometimes the images came in unexpected sequences: a red *praduu* tree seemingly blurred by rain, an orange fish struggling to swim inside a tiny glass box, a log at the bottom of a river illuminated by shimmering sunlight, curtains curling and billowing like the tentacles of an octopus, traffic lights switching colours in the melancholic darkness of a deserted city street.

In the fog that obscured everything, in the overlapping layers of images, there was one thing that remained clear in Pran's mind, and it became clearer with each passing day: it was the feeling that he had to keep wandering in order to find someone whose identity he couldn't recall. He could feel the person's presence even though he couldn't quite picture their face. He knew only that the person lived in a yellow house, and that he could recall all the details of that house.

It was an old one-storey house painted yellow, like a sunflower. The rooms inside were also painted yellow and crammed with objects. There was a blue bedroom, sparse, with nothing in it except... Birds. He didn't know why but small black birds that had lost their way always seemed to end up in that room. At the back, there was a vintage bathtub with bottles of scented oils lined up along its edges. And then there was the smell. He could remember the mournful smell that permeated the rooms – a seductive, mellow, gentle fragrance. And it was a house that didn't have any mirrors.

At first Pran assumed it was the house by that river of longing, but he couldn't match anything between the two images. It was also strange that he felt the house belonged in a mythical forest teeming with blossoms, and with butterflies and birds fluttering through the air in rows. Then there was a chubby cat with short legs, though no matter how hard he tried he couldn't remember the colour of its fur. The house exuded a feeling unlike any other house he could remember: a feeling that nothing else in the whole world mattered and that everything else was insignificant, a feeling that once he was there he wouldn't have to go anywhere else, a feeling that he was home. Yet he knew it wasn't his home. Pran had tried to think about his own home before, several times, but he always emerged empty-handed from the void of his recollection; it was a clean slate, as if in the entirety of his life he had never had a home.

On some nights he dreamt about a partially obscured face and a woman's light-brown eye with a grey shadow slashed across its iris. That one eye was so lonely, so fathomless, that he would sob in his sleep and wake up in the mornings with a soaking wet pillow.

Pran had no way of knowing, while walking through a serene valley in Chiang Rai one morning, that the journey he was about to resume would be his last. It was cold in the vale, tucked within the shadow of the mountains, faint sunshine glittered over the slowly evaporating mist and orange blossoms exhaled a refreshing scent that wafted upon the wind. Pran thought that he wouldn't mind returning to this place one day. He was almost thirty-two years old and had covered nearly every inch of this small country, where one would hit a border after a day's travelling. It was only a matter of time before he found himself retracing his footsteps and coming back to where he had once been. Maybe... Maybe there were times when he might even have abandoned his search for that woman whose identity he couldn't recall, who must be living somewhere, perhaps with someone.

For a moment, he recalled the light-brown eyes of a Mon* woman he had met at the morning market. Her eyes, her smile... A smile he had never thought existed in the world, a smile that lit up her face the moment their eyes met, a smile that came from a deeper part of her. Maybe... Amused by his own fantasies, he quickly shook them out of his head.

Vaguely, he recalled that someone had once smiled at him just like that, once upon a time. The frayed memories still bubbled in his mind, like shadows of feelings – battered, blurred, beaten. Sometimes there were images so indistinct they seemed like splinters of memories within memories that flashed through him and vapourised like dewdrops exposed to the glow of the sun. They left behind a feeling

* The Mon civilisation was one of the earliest to exist in Southeast Asia; the Mon ethnic group has assimilated into Thai culture, but still exists in neighbouring Burma (Myanmar).

like the realisation of losing something precious; a feeling of vertigo, a void in the depth of his heart, followed by something that resembled pain, though he couldn't place where exactly it hurt.

A slope led him down a snaking narrow road with an expanse of orange orchards on one side and the world on the other. A large swathe of wild cane grass swayed and sparkled at a bend further along, and beyond there was a creek hidden in a hollow. Pran was slightly sad that he would never have another chance to stroll alongside that creek in the evening and, within his gloomy-blue memory of that creek, he heard the sound of a cello raining down gently.

He looked around trying to locate the source of the sound, only to find that it wasn't coming from anywhere. The notes were beseeching, pleading, but the aching melody was also warm, consoling yet somehow desolate and detached. Pran held his breath. He had heard that melody before, but from where? Then the sound of a piano rolled out like water, one drop at a time, dripping, dripping, dripping over the sound of someone whispering: *Close your eyes, Pran.*

He closed his eyes and continued walking slowly, letting the exquisite melody guide him as if in flight, weightless, floating, slaloming, just like... Like something he had once felt when he was with someone, once upon a time, someone he still couldn't remember; a memory so tenuous and delicate it was like holding the tip of a silk thread as it fluttered, twisted and threatened to slip away in a breeze and into oblivion.

When a grocery pick-up truck – a mobile supermarket carrying an assortment of vegetables, chillies, cucumbers, cabbages, oranges, string beans, dried fish, flip-flops, chequered scarves, lottery tickets, toothpaste, super glue, plastic buckets, clay jars, detergents, northern sausages, fermented beans, cough syrup, and everything in the entire world – came rumbling down the winding road, zigzagging past the bend with the cane grass, Pran didn't feel a thing as it hit him. The driver, distracted as he was reaching down and groping for the phone he had dropped but instead grabbing a toad that had hitched a ride and putting the slimy creature to his ear, had screamed in panic as his vehicle hit something though he wasn't sure what it was because Pran's body was so light, so weightless.

He flew into the air, suspended for a moment, before descending in featherweight slow-motion and landing gently on the field of cane grass by the road. His landing sent up a cloud of purple-grey pollen that shimmered in the air, then was dispersed, blown away, dissolving like a dream in the mellow breeze, at the same time as Pran's body sank slowly into the abyss of Schumann's Opus 47 and into Chareeya's whisper: *I miss you, Pran.*

Suddenly the charred ruins of the loneliness that had long disappeared from his heart returned like a bolt of lightning, filling up the void at the very core of his soul. Prone on his back, Pran watched in confusion as specks of cane grass pollen flew around his body into the sky, twinkling, glistening, iridescent like a nebula being born right before his eyes. In that fragile second, he saw her again, or for the first time, with such immaculate lucidity it was as if she had never been forgotten. He saw her standing in the middle of a blossoming garden, soaking wet in the bright sunshine, in front of a sunflower-yellow house, and she was watching him with her sad and profoundly lonely eyes.

Millions of memories returned in torrents and crashed inside him as if he was waking from a dream. Each minute he had lost now inundated his mind: a memory of the moon and the stars moving across the sky while she whispered, *That star, that's my star*; of her rolling on the floor with happy laughter when she told him she loved him for the first time under the last light of the stars; of her crying over the death of an onion; of her crying amethyst tears in her sleep in a room that contained everything in the world; of her seated on the ground weeding out nut grass next to a ginger cat, with a carpet of Mon rose petals spread out behind them; of a windowless room he had rented from an old man called Uncle Jang; of a boy with sad eyes who had gotten lost in the twilight. And at the precise moment when his heart finally collapsed, she turned towards him, so slowly, an aureole of sunlight dripping into her eyes, and he saw that fissure slashed across her eye.

Hi, Charee... Pran's whisper was raspy. So this is his sister, his family, his best friend, his woman, his home, the only beautiful thing he ever had in his life. By design or by fate he had finally met her again. Not since he swam in the womb of the mother he had never known had Pran felt such true tranquility, such unruffled, safe, still, and fulfilling peace. Pran smiled. It was his most tender smile; the same smile he had smiled at her under the flame tree years ago. Then he gently drew in his breath as the glistening particles of pollen that floated across the sky melted away, darkened, waned, and one by one were swallowed up by a darkness that came down like ash.

I miss you too, Charee.

XXVII

Swansong

Chareeya found herself walking along a narrow rust-coloured road that extended forever in either direction. On both sides, fields of grass rippled in the wind and stretched out to the horizons, like the road itself. The sky was overcast, painted the colour of plums. The clouds were in turmoil and rain drizzled down in a fine curtain. Cold and wet, Chareeya looked down and saw that she wasn't wearing any shoes. Still, she kept walking, not knowing where she was headed. Then she heard a child laugh. She stopped, looked around her, but saw no one. After that, she didn't hear anything else but the sound of the wind whistling through the grass.

Turning around again she found herself lying on the bed in her room, surrounded by a blanket of darkness. The whistling had gone, but the fragrance of rain coming off the wet dirt road in her dream lingered in the room. As she was about to doze off, she heard that laugh again. Chareeya got up and went to the window. Dawn was about to break in a gauzy blue glow. In that spectral fog she saw Chalika seated under Mother's old *pikul* tree, a child curled up on her lap.

As if knowing it was being watched, the child turned and serenely met Chareeya's gaze. Its mouth moved and it smiled at her tenderly. Chareeya left the window in such a hurry that she didn't return the smile, running through a mob of shadows that seemed to be waiting for Chalika. Under the *pikul* tree, in the twinkling of dewdrops that reflected the light of the metropolis, as the black shadows of mice shot past, Chareeya thought she could see Mother. But, as she got closer, it was indeed Chalika she had seen from the window. Lika, sitting by herself. *Lika*, Chareeya whispered and saw the last stars being blinked away from her sister's mournful eyes. *Lika, that boy… Is he your son?*

Chalika didn't answer and kept staring into the murky blankness in front of her as if she couldn't hear Chareeya. *Lika, my dear, please talk to me. Lika, I'm sorry, please talk to me.* Instead, Chalika shooed away the four people who had been shouting about the same thing over and over again in her head all night long; they had resumed their argument, even louder than before, now arguing over who should stop talking first. Seconds passed and they quietened down. Then, Chalika turned to her sister: *No, Charee, he's not my son.* She got up and smiled faintly, *He's your son.*

There was no starlight left in Chalika's eyes when Chareeya looked into them for the last time. Before she could say anything, Chalika whispered, *Let's go, Madame Chan, I'm sleepy.* And she placed her arm on Chareeya's shoulders, awkwardly. *Madame Eng*, Chareeya smiled a bright smile and wrapped her arm tightly around her sister's waist. Together, just like they did in the old days, the two sisters started walking, one step at a time, Madame Eng and Madame Chan, the conjoined twins, together again. And all of a sudden, time ceased to exist and in that febrile second everything that had been deposited at the depths of their streams of memory floated up as if none of it had ever been forgotten.

All of it, coming up from everywhere: from under the *pikul* tree that shed its flowers unceasingly; from the wafting scent of pomelo flowers that once tormented Pran during his lonely nights, a long time ago; from the dazzling starlight that had been burned onto the eyes of their parents, forever; from the broken music, a melody cracked and splintered, that echoed in the living room; from the valley of the fuchsia storks where the tiny laughter of two girls floated above the bends in the river; from *tabaybuya*, that abandoned melody and forgotten song. All of it, coming from everywhere right up until the moment Chalika lay down on her bed and… Slept.

Slept and dreamt that she was walking on the same rust-coloured dirt road that Chareeya had just been on, under the same overcast, plum-coloured sky, between the expanses of fields of grass rippling in the wind. Suddenly, she heard a child laugh. She stopped, turned around to look, but saw no one. Then, when she turned around again, Chalika saw a boy born from the solitary seed of a dream standing before her, on a road the colour of rust, between fields of grass rippling in the wind, under a plum-coloured sky, in a fine mist of rain, and she took his hand and they walked away together, barefoot, on that road that stretched towards eternity, without ever waking up again.

Chareeya resumed her horticultural mania. She soon buried the metropolis of mice along with the crystallised tears left behind by Mother and Chalika that had shone inexhaustibly from beneath the *pikul* tree. Within a few months, the house by the river was enveloped within the bloom of a magical garden just like the yellow house had been, and there were still trees on the waiting list since there was no longer enough space in that city of broken dreams. The bitter aroma of ylang-ylang flowers and frangipani sometimes wafted through the property even though neither tree was planted there. And Chareeya also had in store *pu-rahong* that she had grafted from the very first *pu-rahong* tree she had seen in her life; the one outside the school from which she hadn't graduated.

Then, she summoned someone to come and fix the dried-up fountain and plant pygmy roses around the sculpture of the moody swan, which she had spent nineteen days scrubbing into mint condition. She painted the entire house a pale sunflower yellow, hoping a dim hope that Pran might recognise it if he happened to pass by. She stopped listening to music and threw away those heart-pounding symphonies that had once driven her into a wild world, along with Uncle Thanit's other broken vinyls, because there wasn't any music in existence that could bring Pran back. And she never set foot in the kitchen again, because there was nothing that could quench the thirst she felt deep inside her heart.

The long journey in search of Pran, and Chalika's death, had wrecked the wondrous world Uncle Thanit had built to protect them from their wounded hearts. Once again, Chareeya became a daughter of the river, this time without the obsessive imaginings that had once swept her into a series of adventures in the neighbour's santol orchard, and that she had lost along the way wandering blindly through the land of tears. Each night, she lay down quietly, placing a slender hand that had stopped glowing long ago upon her heart and watching the stars move slowly past the window without knowing for sure which one of them was her star. And she waited. But the blue boy who had been lost along with Chalika in that infinitely narrow gap between dreaming and reality never returned because no matter how hard Pran tried, he couldn't find his way home.

One morning late in the cool season of that year, just days before the land of the Tigris and Euphrates, where Uncle Thanit had once dreamt of spending his final days, was bombed and the Iraqi war broke out a second time, Chareeya looked up from the last, tiny strip of earth in the garden where she had planted a Mon Rose and saw four or five little stars spiralling towards her. Suspended in the tranquil air between the tree branches, they flashed their opaque light at intervals before extinguishing themselves one by one on the ferns.

Chareeya looked around, her vision marred by the fissure in her eye. She saw leaves gradually separating themselves from branches. She saw treetops swaying, a flock of storks travelling across the sky, and everything seemed broken, like it had always been. But she couldn't hear anything; there was no cawing from the big crows, no rustling of leaves, not even the whistling of the wind that eddied non-stop over the river.

There was only a wintry breeze, a shivering chill. Chareeya slowly angled herself to fit the narrow path between the bushes and started walking sideways to the house. But upon passing a tangle of leaves, she found herself back at the same spot. Looking closely, or maybe not, because she couldn't find the last Mon rose she had planted just a moment ago. Chareeya scanned left and right, trying to locate the rose among the three hundred and fifteen she had already planted but she couldn't recognise it. *Madame Yeesoonsri*, she murmured. Madame *Yeesoonsri* withered and waned, her fragrance fading, as Chareeya retraced her footsteps in that maze of flowers.

And she kept circling like that until twilight descended like a diaphanous curtain. The light-blue colour masked all other colours, except for the vibrant pink of the Mon roses that hovered like random dots, or like phosphorescent jellyfish in the ocean. She was certain she could no longer pinpoint her own coordinates and the narrow exit had already been swallowed by the gloom of the trees, becoming non-existent. Chareeya decided to circle the garden one more time, beneath the shadow of the memory of the star under which she and Pran had said farewell and made a promise: *See you...* Such a long time ago.

Without a trace of bitterness, not in the slightest, Chareeya affectionately touched her fingertips to the leaves and flowers cloaked in the darkness. She leant over to touch them one by one with her face as she tenderly recited Frida's last words: *Viva la vida, viva la vida...*

When Nual the nanny – who later became the cook and Chalika's kitchen hand, mother of five children and grandmother of eight babies, whose once irresistible charm had begun to fade but who still had three men agreeing to share the roles of father and grandfather, who still dropped in on the house by the river every couple of days, and who refused payment for her services – arrived the following day and couldn't find Chareeya, she called her three sons to come and fell the big red *praduu* tree and clear an opening amid the impenetrably suffocating aroma of flowers.

Tumbling and groping about, spinning in all directions, hands stretched out to grasp empty space, Nual shouted, *Ms. Charee! Ms. Charee!* In a great panic she parted bushes and pushed aside shrubs, climbing haphazardly up to the highest branches and shaking them like a mother orangutan until fledgling flower buds spiralled down in a farewell dance, leaving the branches bare. Then she crawled about on the ground covered by thick ferns, knocking the earth and sending clouds of pollen up into the air like glittering confetti to be blown away by the wind.

Only when she realised that Chareeya wasn't there, wasn't anywhere, did Nual collapse on the ground and cry. She sobbed and wailed loudly, desperately clawing at the earth, and she kept wailing and digging until morning even though she knew she wouldn't find anything except for blind earthworms, one after another, lost in a labyrinth of their own making.

Play List

Chapter V

When Pran sees Chareeya again at the Bleeding Heart bar:
"Pictures of You" – The Cure

The wistful melody Chareeya plays for Pran: Piano Quartet in E flat major, Opus 47 (third movement) – Robert Schumann

Chapter VII

The beginning of Uncle Thanit's classical music syllabus: *Gymnopédies* No.1-3 – Erik Satie

Music to make the gardenias blossom: Violin Sonata in F major, Opus 24 ("Spring Sonata") – Ludwig van Beethoven + String Quartet No.2 in D major – Alexander Borodin

How overwhelming passion shakes the heart: Symphony No.4 in E minor, Opus 98 – Johannes Brahms

Lessons in desolation: Nocturnes No.1-21 – Fédéric Chopin

A funeral dirge for the heart: Symphony No.7 in A major, Opus 92 (second movement) – Ludwig van Beethoven

Melody for the brokenhearted: Piano Concerto No.2 in C minor, Opus 18 – Sergei Rachmaninoff

How to perceive the magic of moonlight: "Clair de Lune" (third movement of the Suite Bergamasque) – Claude Debussy

For the despair of war: Cello Concerto in E minor, Opus 85 – Edward Elgar

For the loss of a daughter: *In the Mists* – Leoš Janáček

Music to make you forget your homework: *The Tree of Dreams* (*L'arbre des songes*) – Henri Dutilleux

Proof of God's existence: Requiem in D minor, K. 626 – Wolfgang Amadeus Mozart

Chapter VIII

Thana's love song to Chareeya: "*Saengdao haeng sathaa*" (Starlight of Faith) – Jit Phumisak

The most beautiful song in the world, according to Chareeya: *La Wally*, Act 1 ("Ebben? Ne andrò lontana") – Alfredo Catalani

Chapter IX

Beethoven's agony: Violin Sonata No.9 in A major, Opus 47 (the "Kreutzer Sonata") – Ludwig van Beethoven

A story of Tolstoy's agony: String Quartet No.1 (the "Kreutzer Sonata") – Leoš Janáček

Chapter XI

Chareeya's sorrowful obsession: *Oblivion* – Astor Piazzolla

Music to drain the life force from Chanon's body: Symphony No.3 in F major, Opus 90 (third movement) – Johannes Brahms

Chapter XII

Music to hide from the sun: Violin Concerto – Philip Glass

The sad song Pran can't forget: "*Sin rak sin suk*" (End of Love, End of Happiness) – Mantana Morakul

Chapter XVIII

A hot-blooded hymn to the glory of God: *Misa Tango* – Luis Bacalov

Botanical List

Thai Names

asoke sapun - อโศกสปัน - scarlet flame bean or rose of Venezuela - *Brownea grandiceps*

bunnag - บุนนาค - Ceylon ironwood - *Mesua ferrea*

faikham - ฝ้ายคำ - buttercup or silk-cotton - *Cochlospermum religiosum*

huu-kwang - หูกวาง - Indian almond or sea almond - *Terminalia catappa*

intanin - อินทนิล - queen's crepe myrtle or pride of India - *Lagerstroemia speciosa*

jampi - จำปี - white champaca - *Michelia alba*

jik-nam - จิกน้ำ - red barringtonia or freshwater mangrove - *Barringtonia acutangula*

kalapruek - กาฬพฤกษ์ - pink shower - *Cassia grandis*

kankrao - กันเกรา - tembusu - *Fagraea fragrans*

kannikar - กรรณิการ์ - night-flowering jasmine or tree of sorrow - *Nyctanthes arbor-tristis*

krachao sidaa - กระเช้าสีดา - Indian birthwort or dutchman's pipe - *Aristolochia indica*

lamduan - ลำดวน - white cheesewood - *Melodorum fruticosum*

lampu - ลำพู - mangrove apple - *Sonneratia caseolaris*

mok - โมก - no common English name - *Wrightia religiosa*

montha - มณฑา - no common English name - *Talauma candollei*

nang yaem - นางแย้ม - glory bower or cashmere bouquet - *Clerodendron fragrans*

pheep - ปีบ - Indian cork - *Millingtonia hortensis*

pikul - พิกุล - bullet wood - *Mimusops elengi*

praduu daeng (red *praduu*) - ประดู่แดง - monkey-flower tree or fire of Pakistan - *Barnebydendron riedelii*

pu-jormpol - พู่จอมพล - red powder puff or blood-red tassel - *Calliandra haematocephala pu-rahong* - พู่ระหง - coral hibiscus or Japanese lantern - *Hibiscus schizopetalus*

puttarn - พุดตาน - Confederate rose or cotton rosemallow - *Hibiscus mutabilis*

ratree - night-blooming jasmine, or lady of the night - ราตรี - *Cestrum nocturnum*

saiyut - สายหยุด - Chinese desmos or dwarf ylang-ylang - *Desmos chinensis*

tabaek - ตะแบก - Bungor or myrtle - *Lagerstroemia calyculata*

yeesoon - ยี่สุ่น or กุหลาบมอญ - Mon rose or damask rose - *Rosa damascene*

English Names

bael - *matoom* - มะตูม - *Aegle marmelos*

butterfly-pea - *anchan* - อัญชัน - *Clitoria ternatea*

cane grass - *dok lao* - ดอกเลา - *Saccharum spontaneum*

chrysanthemum - *benjamart* - เบญจมาศ - *Dendranthema grandiflora*

dahlia - *rakrae* - รักเร่ - *Dahlia pinnata*

flame (tree) - *ton hang nok-yung* - ต้นหางนกยูง - *Delonix regia*

frangipani - *lantom* - ลั่นทม - - *Plumeria spp.*

gardenia, or cape jasmine - *pudsorn* - พุดซ้อน - *Gardenia jasminoides*

Indian rubber - *yang india* - ยางอินเดีย - *Ficus elastica*

Mon rose, or damask rose (also see *yeesoon* above) - ยี่สุ่น or กุหลาบมอญ - *Rosa damascene*

morning glory, or water spinach - *pak bung* - ผักบุ้ง - *Ipomea aquatica*

nut grass - *yaa haew moo* - หญ้าแห้วหมู - *Cyperus rotundus*

orchid - *kluay mai* - กล้วยไม้ - *Orchidaceae*

pomelo - *som-oh* - ส้มโอ - *Citrus maxima*

purple orchid - *chong-koh* - ชงโค - *Bauhinia purpurea*

santol - *krathorn* - กระท้อน - *Sandoricum koetjape*

ylang-ylang - *kradang-gna* - กระดังงา - *Cananga odorata*

zalacca - *rakham* - ระกำ - *Salacca zalacca*

©Kritdhakorn Suttikittibuth

VEERAPORN NITIPRAPHA started writing stories when she was a teenager. Born, raised and still residing in Bangkok, she used to work as an editor on a fashion magazine and as a copywriter for advertising agencies. These days, she is mother to a young man, owner of four moody cats, and a devoted cook and gardener. A full-time writer, she also runs a writing workshop. The title of her latest novel, published in Thai, roughly translates as "The Twilight Years and the Memory of a Memory of a Black Cat"- it won the S.E.A. Write Award in October 2018, making her the first female writer to win the award twice.

KONG RITHDEE has been writing about film, literature and culture for the *Bangkok Post* since 1996. He has also made documentary films (*The Convert, Baby Arabia*, and *Gaddhafi*) and collaborates with the Thai Film Archive, a public organisation dedicated to preserving Thailand's audiovisual heritage.